John Pomfret

The Poetical Works

With the Life of the Author

John Pomfret

The Poetical Works
With the Life of the Author

ISBN/EAN: 9783337415310

Printed in Europe, USA, Canada, Australia, Japan

Cover: Foto ©Andreas Hilbeck / pixelio.de

More available books at **www.hansebooks.com**

THE
POETICAL WORKS
OF
JOHN POMFRET.

WITH THE LIFE OF THE AUTHOR.

If Heav'n the grateful liberty would give,
That I might chufe my method how to live----
Near fome fair town I'd have a private feat,
Built uniform ; not little, nor too great----
I'd have a clear and competent eftate,
That I might live genteelly, but not great----
I'd have a little vault, but always ftor'd
With the beft wines each vintage could afford----
I'd chufe two friends, whofe company would be
A great advance to my felicity----
Would bounteous Heav'n once more indulge, I'd chufe
(For who would fo much fatisfaction lofe
As witty nymphs in converfation give?)
Near fome obliging modeft fair to live.----

> THE CHOICE.

EDINBURG:
AT THE Apollo Prefs, BY THE MARTINS.
Anno 1779.

THE

POETICAL WORKS

OF

JOHN POMFRET.

CONTAINING HIS

CHOICE,	LAST EPIPHANY,
PROSPECT OF DEATH,	DIVINE ATTRIBUTES,
REASON,	ELEAZAR'S LAMENTAT.

&c. &c. &c.

I'd be concern'd in no litigious jar ;
Belov'd by all, not vainly popular.
Whate'er affiftance I had pow'r to bring,
T'oblige my country, or to ferve my king,
Whene'er they call'd, I'd readily afford
My tongue, my pen, my counfel, or my fword——
If Heav'n a date of many years would give,
Thus I'd in pleafure, eafe, and plenty, live——
And when committed to the duft, I'd have
Few tears, but friendly, dropp'd into my grave :
Then would my exit fo propitious be,
All men would wifh to live and die like me.

THE CHOICE.

EDINBURG:

AT THE Apollo Prefs, BY THE MARTINS.

Anno 1779.

JOHN POMFRET.

F E w anecdotes concerning this poet have been tranf-
mitted to pofterity ; and therefore the reader cannot
expect a circumftantial detail either of the incidents
of his life, which probably were but few, and even
thefe not of much importance, nor an elaborate dif-
cuffion of the merit of his writings. That he was a
pious good man is a truth fufficiently eftablifhed from
his poems, and will further appear from the following
fhort narrative, dated in the 1724, which is all we have
been able to collect relative to this poet or his works.

The two pieces, Reafon, and *Dies Noviffima*, are
the only Poetical Remains of the Rev. Mr. Pomfret ;
and were lately found, among fome other of his pa-
pers of a private nature, in the cuftody of an intimate
friend.

The firft of them, entitled Reafon, was wrote by
him in the year 1700, when the debates concerning
the doctrine of the Trinity were carried on with fo
much heat by the clergy, one againft another, that
King William was obliged to interpofe his royal authority, by putting an end to that pernicious contro-
verfy, through an act of parliament, ftrictly forbid-
ding any perfons whatfoever to publifh their notions
on this fubject. It is, indeed, a fevere though very
juft fatire upon the antagonifts engaged in that dif-

pute, and was publifhed by Mr. Pomfret at the time it was wrote. The not inferting of it among his other poems, when he collected them into a volume, was on account of his having received very fignal favours from fome of the perfons therein mentioned; but they, as well as he, being now dead, it is hoped that the revival of it at this juncture will anfwer the fame good purpofes intended by the Author in its original compofition.

The other, entitled *Dies Noviffima;* or, The Laft Epiphany, a Pindaric ode, on Chrift's fecond appearance to judge the world, is now printed from a manufcript under his own hand. It muft be, indeed, confeffed, that many excellent pens have exercifed their talents upon this fubject; but yet, notwithftanding the different manner in which they have treated it, I dare fay there will be found fuch a holy warmth animating this piece throughout, that, as The Guardian has obferved of divine poetry, we fhall find a kind of refuge in our pleafure, and our diverfion will become our fafety.

Having thus given a faithful account of thefe valuable Remains, there is another natural piece of juftice ftill due to the memory of the Author. In the firft place, by giving fome account of his family, to clear him from the afperfions of fanaticifm, which have been generally caft on him through a notorious miftake; and, in the next place, to defend the genuinenefs of his writings from the injurious treatment of thofe who have, either through malice or ignorance, afcribed fome of them to other perfons.

The true account of his family is as follows, *viz.* Mr. Pomfret's father was Rector of Luton in Bedfordfhire, and himfelf was preferred to the living of Malden in the fame county. He was liberally educated at an eminent grammar-fchool in the country, from whence he was fent to the univerfity of Cambridge, but of what college he was entered I know not. There he wrote moft of his poetical compofitions, took the degree of Mafter of Arts, and very early accomplifhed himfelf in moft kinds of polite literature.

It was fhortly after his leaving the Univerfity that he was preferred to the living of Malden above mentioned; and fo far was he from being in the leaft tinctured with fanaticifm, that I have often heard him exprefs his abhorrence of the deftructive tenets maintained by thofe people, both againft our religious and civil rights.

This imputation, it feems, was caft on him by there having been one of his firname, though not any way related to him, a diffenting teacher, who died not long ago * : fo far diftant from the accufation were the principles of this excellent man.

* Mr. Samuel Pomfret, who publifhed fome rhymes upon fpiritual Subjects, as they are pleafed to call them.

About the year 1703 Mr. Pomfret came up to London, for inftitution and induction into a very confiderable living, but was retarded for fome time by a difguft taken by Dr. Henry Compton, then bifhop of London, at thefe four lines in the clofe of his poem, entitled The Choice.

> And as I near approach'd the verge of life,
> Some kind relation (for I'd have no wife)
> Should take upon him all my worldly care,
> While I did for a better ftate prepare.

The parenthefis in thefe verfes was fo malicioufly reprefented to the Bifhop, that his Lordfhip was given to underftand it could bear no other conftruction than that Mr. Pomfret preferred a miftrefs before a wife; though I think the contrary is felf-evident, the verfes implying no more than the preference of a fingle life to marriage, unlefs his brethren of the gown will affert that an unmarried clergyman cannot live without a miftrefs. But the worthy prelate was foon convinced of the propenfe malice of Mr. Pomfret's enemies towards him, he being at that time married: yet their bafe oppofition of his deferved merit had in fome meafure its effect; for by the obftructions he met with, and the fmall-pox being at that time very rife, he fickened of them, and died at London in the 36th year of his age.

The ungenerous treatment he has fince met with in regard to his poetical compofitions, is in a book entitled Poems by the Earl of Rofcommon and Mr.

Duke *; in the preface to which the publisher has peremptorily inserted the following paragraph : "In " this collection (says he) of my Lord Roscommon's " poems, care has been taken to insert all that I could " possibly procure that are truly genuine, there ha- " ving been several things published under his name " which were written by others, the authors of which " I could set down if it were material." Now, this arrogant editor would have been more just, both to the public and to the Earl of Roscommon's memory, in telling us what things had been published under his Lordship's name by others, than by concealing the authors of any such gross impositions : instead of which he is so much a stranger to impartiality, that he has been guilty of the very crime he exclaims a- gainst; for he has not only attributed The Prospect of Death to the Earl of Roscommon, which was wrote by Mr. Pomfret many years after his Lordship's de- cease, but likewise another piece, entitled The Prayer of Jeremy paraphrased, prophetically representing the passionate grief of the Jewish people for the loss of their town and sanctuary, written by Mr. South- cot, a worthy gentleman now living, who first pub- lished it himself in the year 1717 †: so that it is to be

* Printed for Jacob Tonson, 1717. Octavo.
† See Miscellaneous Poems and Translations. Printed for Bernard Lintot. Octavo.

hoped, in a future edition of the E. of Rofcommon's and Mr. Duke's poems, the fame care will be taken to do thefe gentlemen juftice, as to prevent any other perfon from hereafter injuring the memory of his Lordfhip.

1724.   PHILALETHES.

THE PREFACE.

IT will be to little purpose, the Author presumes, to offer any reasons why the following poems appear in public, for it is ten to one whether he gives the true, and if he does, it is much greater odds whether the gentle reader is so courteous as to believe him. He could tell the world, according to the laudable custom of Prefaces, that it was through the irresistible importunity of friends, or some other excuse of ancient renown, that he ventured them to the press; but he thought it much better to leave every man to guess for himself, and then he would be sure to satisfy himself; for, let what will be pretended, people are grown so very apt to fancy they are always in the right, that unless it hit their humour it is immediately condemned for a sham and hypocrisy.

In short, that which wants an excuse for being in print ought not to have been printed at all: but whether the ensuing Poems deserve to stand in that class the world must have leave to determine. What faults the true judgment of the gentleman may find out, it is to be hoped his candour and good humour will easily pardon; but those which the peevishness and ill nature of the critic may discover, must expect to be unmercifully used; though, methinks, it is a very preposterous pleasure to scratch other persons till the blood comes, and then laugh at and ridicule them.

Some persons, perhaps, may wonder how things of this nature dare come into the world without the protection of some great name, as they call it, and a fulsome epistle dedicatory to his Grace, or Right Honourable : for if a poem struts out under my Lord's patronage, the author imagines it is no less than *scandalum magnatum* to dislike it, especially if he thinks fit to tell the world that this same lord is a person of wonderful wit and understanding, a notable judge of poetry, and a very considerable poet himself. But if a poem have no intrinsic excellencies and real beauties, the greatest name in the world will never induce a man of sense to approve it; and if it has them, Tom Piper's is as good as my Lord Duke's; the only difference is, Tom claps half an ounce of snuff into the poet's hand, and his Grace twenty guineas : for, indeed, there lies the strength of a great name, and the greatest protection an author can receive from it.

. To please every one would be a new thing, and to write so as to please no body would be as new; for even Quarles and Wythers have their admirers. The Author is not so fond of fame to desire it from the injudicious many, nor of so mortified a temper not to wish it from the discerning few. It is not the multitude of applauses, but the good sense of the applauders, which establishes a valuable reputation; and if a Rymer or a Congreve say it is well, he will not be at all solicitous how great the majority may be to the contrary.

London, *anno* 1699.

4

MISCELLANIES.

THE CHOICE.

If Heav'n the grateful liberty would give,
That I might chufe my method how to live,
And all thofe hours propitious Fate fhould lend
In blifsful eafe and fatisfaction fpend :
   Near fome fair town I'd have a private feat,   *5*
Built uniform; not little, nor too great;
Better if on a rifing ground it ftood,
On this fide fields, on that a neighb'ring wood :
It fhould within no other things contain
But what are ufeful, neceffary, plain :   10
Methinks 'tis naufeous, and I'd ne'er endure
The needlefs pomp of gaudy furniture.
A little garden, grateful to the eye,
And a cool rivulet run murm'ring by,
On whofe delicious banks a ftately row   15
Of fhady limes or fycamores fhould grow;
At th' end of which a filent ftudy plac'd,
Should be with all the nobleft authors grac'd,
Horace and Virgil, in whofe mighty lines
Immortal wit and folid learning fhines;   20
Sharp Juvenal, and am'rous Ovid too,
Who all the turns of love's foft paffion knew;

B

He that with judgment reads his charming lines,
In which strong art with stronger nature joins,
Must grant his fancy does the best excel,   25
His thoughts so tender, and express'd so well;
With all those Moderns, men of steady sense,
Esteem'd for learning and for eloquence.
In some of these, as Fancy should advise,
I'd always take my morning exercise;   30
For sure no minutes bring us more content
Than those in pleasing useful studies spent.
I'd have a clear and competent estate,
That I might live genteelly, but not great;
As much as I could moderately spend;   35
A little more, sometimes t'oblige a friend:
Nor should the sons of Poverty repine
Too much at Fortune, they should taste of mine;
And all that objects of true pity were
Should be reliev'd with what my wants could spare:
For that our Maker has too largely giv'n   41
Should be return'd in gratitude to Heav'n.
A frugal plenty should my table spread,
With healthy, not luxurious, dishes fed;
Enough to satisfy, and something more,   45
To feed the stranger and the neighb'ring poor.
Strong meat indulges vice, and pamp'ring food
Creates diseases, and inflames the blood:
But what's sufficient to make nature strong,
And the bright lamp of life continue long,   50

I'd freely take; and, as I did poſſeſs,
The bounteous Author of my plenty bleſs,
I'd have a little vault, but always ſtor'd
With the beſt wines each vintage could afford.
Wine whets the wit, improves its native force, 55
And gives a pleaſant flavour to diſcourſe;
By making all our ſpirits debonair,
Throws off the lees, the ſediment of care:
But as the greateſt bleſſing Heaven lends
May be debauch'd, and ſerve ignoble ends, 60
So, but too oft', the grape's refreſhing juice
Does many miſchievous effects produce.
My houſe ſhould no ſuch rude diſorders know
As from high drinking conſequently flow,
Nor would I uſe what was ſo kindly giv'n 65
To the diſhonour of indulgent Heav'n.
If any neighbour came he ſhould be free,
Us'd with reſpect, and not uneaſy be
In my retreat, or to himſelf or me.
What freedom, prudence, and right reaſon, give, 70
All men may, with impunity, receive;
But the leaſt ſwerving from their rule's too much;
For what's forbidden us 'tis death to touch.
That life may be more comfortable yet,
And all my joys refin'd, ſincere, and great, 75
I'd chuſe two friends, whoſe company would be
A great advance to my felicity;

Well born, of humours fuited to my own,
Difcreet, and men as well as books have known;
Brave, gen'rous, witty, and exactly free   80
From loofe behaviour or formality;
Airy and prudent; merry, but not light;
Quick in difcerning, and in judging right;
Secret they fhould be, faithful to their truft,
In reas'ning cool, ftrong, temperate, and juft;   85
Obliging, open, without huffing brave,
Brifk in gay talking, and in fober grave;
Clofe in difpute, but not tenacious; try'd
By folid reafon, and let that decide;
Not prone to luft, revenge, or envious hate,   90
Nor bufy meddlers with intrigues of ftate;
Strangers to flander, and fworn foes to fpite;
Not quarrelfome, but ftout enough to fight;
Loyal and pious, friends to Cæfar; true,
As dying martyrs, to their Maker too: 95
In their fociety I could not mifs
A permanent, fincere, fubftantial, blifs.

   Would bounteous Heav'n once more indulge, I'd
(For who would fo much fatisfaction lofe   [chufe
As witty nymphs in converfation give?)   100
Near fome obliging modeft fair to live;
For there's that fweetnefs in a female mind
Which in a man's we cannot hope to find;
That, by a fecret but a pow'rful art,
Winds up the fpring of life, and does impart 105
Frefh vital heat to the tranfported heart.

I'd have her reason all her paſſion ſway;
Eaſy in company, in private gay;
Coy to a ſop, to the deſerving free;
Still conſtant to herſelf, and juſt to me :   110
A ſoul ſhe ſhould have for great actions fit,
Prudence and wiſdom to direct her wit;
Courage to look bold Danger in the face;
No fear, but only to be proud or baſe;
Quick to adviſe, by an emergence preſt,   115
To give good counſel, or to take the beſt :
I'd have th' expreſſion of her thoughts be ſuch,
She might not ſeem reſerv'd, nor talk too much;
That ſhews a want of judgment and of ſenſe ;
More than enough is but impertinence :   120
Her conduct regular, her mirth refin'd,
Civil to ſtrangers, to her neighbours kind ;
Averſe to vanity, revenge, and pride,
In all the methods of deceit untry'd;
So faithful to her friend, and good to all,   125
No cenſure might upon her actions fall :
Then would ev'n Envy be compell'd to ſay
She goes the leaſt of woman-kind aſtray.

'To this fair creature I'd ſometimes retire,
Her converſation would new joys inſpire,   130
Give life an edge ſo keen, no ſurly care
Would venture to aſſault my ſoul, or dare,
Near my retreat, to hide one ſecret ſnare.

B iij

But so divine, so noble, a repast
I'd seldom and with moderation taste;   135
For highest cordials all their virtue lose
By a too frequent and too bold a use;
And what would cheer the spirits in distress
Ruins our health when taken to excess.

   I'd be concern'd in no litigious jar;   140
Beloved by all, not vainly popular.
Whate'er assistance I had pow'r to bring,
T' oblige my country, or to serve my king,
Whene'er they call'd, I'd readily afford
My tongue, my pen, my counsel, or my sword. 145
Law-suits I'd shun with as much studious care
As I would dens where hungry lions are,
And rather put up injuries than be
A plague to him who'd be a plague to me.
I value quiet at a price too great   150
To give for my revenge so dear a rate;
For what do we by all our bustle gain
But counterfeit delight for real pain?

   If Heav'n a date of many years would give,
Thus I'd in pleasure, ease, and plenty, live;   155
And as I near approach'd the verge of life,
Some kind relation (for I'd have no wife)
Should take upon him all my worldly care,
Whilst I did for a better state prepare:
Then I'd not be with any trouble vex'd,   160
Nor have the ev'ning of my days perplex'd,

But, by a silent and a peaceful death,
Without a sigh resign my aged breath:
And when committed to the dust, I'd have
Few tears, but friendly, dropp'd into my grave : 165
Then would my exit so propitious be,
All men would wish to live and die like me.   167

A VISION.

Tho' gloomy thoughts difturb'd my anxious breaft
All the long night, and drove away my reft,
Juft as the dawning day began to rife
A grateful flumber clos'd my waking eyes;
But active Fancy to ftrange regions flew,   5
And brought furprifing objects to my view.
   Methought I walk'd in a delightful grove,
The foft retreat of gods, when gods make love;
Each beauteous object my charm'd foul amaz'd,
And I on each with equal wonder gaz'd,   10
Nor knew which moft delighted; all was fine,
The noble product of fome pow'r divine:
But as I travers'd the obliging fhade,
Which myrtle, jeffamine, and rofes, made,
I faw a perfon whofe celeftial face   15
At firft declar'd her goddefs of the place;
But I difcover'd, when approaching near,
An afpect full of beauty, but fevere:
Bold and majeftic, ev'ry awful look
Into my foul a fecret horror ftruck: 20
Advancing farther on fhe made a ftand,
And beckon'd me; I, kneeling, kifs'd her hand;
Then thus began——" Bright Deity! (for fo
" You are, no mortals fuch perfections know)
" I may intrude; but how I was convey'd   25
" To this ftrange place, or by what pow'rful aid,

" I'm wholly ignorant; nor know I more,
" Or where I am, or whom I do adore:
" Inftruct me, then, that I no longer may
" In darkpefs ferve the goddefs I obey."   30
    " Youth!" fhe reply'd, " this place belongs to one
" By whom you'll be, and thoufands are, undone.
" Thefe pleafant walks, and all thefe fhady bow'rs,
" Are in the government of dang'rous pow'rs.
" Love's the capricious mafter of this coaft,   35
" This fatal labyrinth, where fools are loft.
" I dwell not here amidft thefe gaudy things,
" Whofe fhort enjoyment no true pleafure brings,
" But have an empire of a nobler kind;
" My regal feat's in the celeftial mind,   40
" Where, with a godlike and a peaceful hand,
" I rule, and make thofe happy I command;
" For while I govern all within's at reft;
" No ftormy paffion revels in my breaft:
" But when my pow'r is defpicable grown,   45
" And rebel appetites ufurp the throne,
" The foul no longer quiet thoughts enjoys,
" But all is tumult and eternal noife.
" Know, Youth! I'm Reafon, which you've oft' de-
" I am that Reafon which you never priz'd; [fpis'd;
" And tho' my argument fuccefslefs prove,   51
" (For reafon feems impertinence in love)
" Yet I'll not fee my charge (for all mankind
" Are to my guardianfhip by Heav'n affign'd)

" Into the grafp of any ruin run   55
" That I can warm 'em of and they may fhun.
" Fly, Youth! thefe guilty fhades; retreat in time,
" Ere your miftake's converted to a crime;
" For ignorance no longer can atone
" When once the error and the fault is known.   60
" You thought, perhaps, as giddy youth inclines,
" Imprudently, to value all that fhines,
" In thefe retirements freely to poffefs
" True joy, and ftrong fubftantial happinefs:
" But here gay Folly keeps her court, and here,   65
" In crowds, her tributary fops appear,
" Who, blindly lavifh of their golden days,
" Confume them all in her fallacious ways.
" Pert Love with her, by joint commiffion, rules
" In this capacious realm of idle fools,   70
" Who, by falfe arts and popular deceits,
" The carelefs, fond, unthinking mortal cheats.
" 'Tis eafy to defcend into the fnare,
" By the pernicious conduct of the fair;
" But fafely to return from this abode   75
" Requires the wit, the prudence, of a god;
" Tho' you, who have not tafted that delight,
" Which only at a diftance charms your fight,
" May, with a little toil, retrieve your heart,
" Which loft, is fubject to eternal fmart.   80
" Bright Delia's beauty, I muft needs confefs,
" Is truly great, nor would I make it lefs;

" That were to wrong her where fhe merits moft;
" But dragons guard the fruit, and rocks the coaft:
" And who would run, that's moderately wife, 85
" A certain danger for a doubtful prize?
" If you mifcarry, you are loft fo far,
" (For there's no erring twice in love and war)
" You'll ne'er recover, but muft always wear
" Thofe chains you'll find it difficult to bear. 90
" Delia has charms, I own; fuch charms would move
" Old Age and frozen Impotence to love:
" But do not venture where fuch danger lies;
" Avoid the fight of thofe victorious eyes,
" Whofe pois'nous rays do to the foul impart 95
" Delicious ruin and a pleafing fmart.
" You draw, infenfibly, deftruction near,
" And love the danger which you ought to fear.
" If the light pains you labour under now
" Deftroy your eafe, and make your fpirits bow, 100
" You'll find 'em much more grievous to be borne,
" When heavier made by an imperious fcorn;
" Nor can you hope fhe will your paffion hear
" With fofter notions or a kinder ear
" Than thofe of other fwains, who always found 105
" She rather widen'd than clos'd up the wound.
" But grant fhe fhould indulge your flame, and give
" Whate'er you'd afk, nay, all you can receive;
" The fhort-liv'd pleafure would fo quickly cloy,
" Bring fuch a weak and fuch a feeble joy, 110

" You'd have but fmall encouragement to boaſt
" The tinfel rapture worth the pains it coſt.
" Confider, Strephon ! foberly of things,
" What ſtrange inquietudes love always brings;
" The foolifh fears, vain hopes, and jealoufies,   115
" Which ſtill attend upon this fond difeafe;
" How you muſt cringe and bow, fubmit and whine,
" Call ev'ry feature, ev'ry look, divine;
" Commend each fentence with an humble fmile;
" Tho' nonfenfe, fwear it is a heav'nly ſtyle;   120
" Servilely rail at all fhe difapproves,
" And as ignobly flatter all fhe loves;
" Renounce your very fenfe, and filent fit
" While fhe puts off impertinence for wit :
" Like fetting-dog, new whipp'd for fpringing game,
" You muſt be made, by due correction, tame.   126
" But if you can endure the naufeous rule
" Of woman, do; love on, and be a fool.
" You know the danger, your own methods ufe,
" The good or evil 's in your pow'r to chufe :   130
" But who 'd expect a fhort and dubious blifs
" On the declining of a precipice,
" Where, if he flips, not Fate itfelf can fave
" The falling wretch from an untimely grave ?"
    " Thou great Directrefs of our minds," faid I, 135
" We fafely on your dictates may rely,
" And that which you have now fo kindly preſt
" Is true, and, without contradiction, beſt;

" But with a fteady fentence to control
" The heat and vigour of a youthful foul,   140
" While gay temptations hover in our fight,
" And daily bring new objects of delight,
" Which on us with furprifing beauty fmile,
" Is difficult, but is a noble toil.
" The beft may flip, and the moft cautious fall; 145
" He 's more than mortal that ne'er err'd at all:
" And tho' fair Delia has my foul poffeft,
" I 'll chafe her bright idea from my breaft;
" At leaft I 'll make one effay : if I fail,
" And Delia's charms o'er Reafon do prevail,   150
" I may be, fure, from rigid cenfures free;
" Love was my foe, and Love's a deity."
   Then fhe rejoin'd; " May you fuccefsful prove
" In your attempt to curb imperious Love;
" Then will proud paffion own her rightful lord; 155
" You to yourfelf, I to my throne, reftor'd :
" But to confirm your courage, and infpire
" Your refolution with a bolder fire,
" Follow me, Youth! I 'll fhew you that fhall move
" Your foul to curfe the tyranny of Love."   160
   Then fhe convey'd me to a difmal fhade
Which melancholy yew and cyprefs made,
Where I beheld an antiquated pile
Of rugged building in a narrow aifle;
The water round it gave a naufeous fmell,   165
Like vapours fteeming from a fulph'rous cell;
                                                C

The ruin'd wall, compos'd of ftinking mud,
O'ergrown with hemlock, on fupporters ftood,
As did the roof, ungrateful to the view;
' Twas both an hofpital and bedlam too :   170
Before the ent'rance mould'ring bones were fpread,
Some fkeletons entire, fome lately dead;
A little rubbifh loofely fcatter'd o'er
Their bodies uninterr'd lay round the door :
No fun'ral rites to any here were paid,   175
But dead, like dogs, into the duft convey'd.
From hence, by Reafon's conduct, I was brought,
Thro' various turnings, to a fpacious vault,
Where I beheld, and 'twas a mournful fight,
Vaft crowds of wretches all debarr'd from light, 180
But what a few dim lamps, expiring, had,
Which made the profpect more amazing fad;
Some wept, fome rav'd, fome mufically mad;
Some fwearing loud, and others laughing ; fome
Were always talking, others always dumb :   185
Here one, a dagger in his breaft, expires,
And quenches with his blood his am'rous fires :
There hangs a fecond; and, not far remov'd,
A third lies poifon'd, who falfe Celia lov'd.
All forts of madnefs, ev'ry kind of death,   190
By which unhappy mortals lofe their breath,
Were here expos'd before my wond'ring eyes,
The fad effects of female treacheries.
Others I faw who were not quite bereft
Of fenfe, tho' very fmall remains were left,   195

Curfing the fatal folly of their youth
For trufting to perjurious woman's truth.
Thefe on the left—upon the right a view
Of equal horror, equal mis'ry, too;
Amazing, all employ'd my troubled thought,   200
And with new wonder new averfion brought.
There I beheld a wretched num'rous throng
Of pale lean mortals: fome lay ftretch'd along
On beds of ftraw, difconfolate and poor;
Others extended naked on the floor: 205
Exil'd from human pity here they lie,
And know no end of mis'ry till they die:
But death, which comes in gay and profp'rous days
Too foon, in time of mifery delays.

Thefe dreadful fpectacles had fo much pow'r,   210
I vow'd, and folemnly, to love no more;
For fure that flame is kindled from below
Which breeds fuch fad variety of woe.

Then we defcending by fome few degrees
From this ftupendous fcene of miferies,   215
Bold Reafon brought me to another cave,
Dark as the innmoft chambers of the grave:
" Here, Youth!" fhe cry'd, " in the acuteft pain
" Thofe villains lie who have their fathers flain,   219
" Stabb'd their own brothers, nay, their friends, to
" Ambitious, proud, revengeful, miftreffes,   [pleafe
" Who, after all their fervices, preferr'd
" Some rugged fellow of the brawny herd

C ij

" Before thofe wretches, who, defpairing, dwell
" In agonies no human tongue can tell.   225
" Darknefs prevents the too amazing fight,
" And you may blefs the happy want of light."
But my tormented ears were fill'd with fighs,
Expiring groans, and lamentable cries,
So very fad, I could endure no more;   230
Methought I felt the miferies they bore.
    Then to my guide faid I, " For pity, now
" Conduct me back; here I confirm my vow,
" Which if I dare infringe be this my fate,
" To die thus wretched, and repent too late.   235
" The charms of beauty I'll no more purfue;
" Delia! farewell; farewell for ever too."
    Then we return'd to the delightful grove,
Where Reafon ftill diffuaded me from love.
" You fee," fhe cry'd, " what mifery attends   240
" On love, and where too frequently it ends;
" And let not that unwieldy paffion fway
" Your foul, which none but whining fools obey.
" The mafculine brave fpirit fcorns to own
" The proud ufurper of my facred throne,   245
" Nor with idolatrous devotion pays
" To the falfe god or facrifice or praife.
" The Syren's mufic charms the failor's ear,
" But he is ruin'd if he ftops to hear;
" And if you liften, Love's harmonious voice   250
" As much delights as certainly deftroys.

" Ambrofia mix'd with aconite may have
" A pleafant tafte, but fends you to the grave;
" For tho' the latent poifon may be ftill
" A while, it very feldom fails to kill. 255
" But who'd partake the food of gods to die
" Within a day, or live in mifery?
" Who'd eat with emperors, if o'er his head
" A poniard hung but by a fingle thread * ?
" Love's banquets are extravagantly fweet, 260
" And either kill or furfeit all that eat,
" Who, when the fated appetite is tir'd,
" Ev'n loathe the thoughts of what they once admir'd.
" You 've promis'd, Strephon, to forfake the charms
" Of Delia, tho' fhe courts you to her arms; 265
" And fure I may your refolution truft;
" You 'll never want temptation, but be juft.
" Vows of this nature, Youth! muft not be broke;
" You 're always bound, tho' 'tis a gentle yoke.
" Would men be wife, and my advice purfue, 270
" Love's conquefts would be fmall, his triumphs few;
" For nothing can oppofe his tyranny
" With fuch a profpect of fuccefs as I.
" Me he detefts, and from my prefence flies,
" Who know his arts, and ftratagems defpife, 275
" By which he cancels mighty Wifdom's rules,
" To make himfelf the deity of fools :

* The feaft of Democles.

C iij

" Him dully they adore, him blindly ferve;
" Some while they're fots, and others while they
" For thofe who under his wild conduct go, [ftarve;
" Either come coxcombs, or he makes 'em fo :   281
" His charms deprive, by their ftrange influence,
" The brave of courage, and the wife of fenfe :
" In vain Philofophy would fet the mind
" At liberty, if once by him confin'd :   285
" The fcholar's learning and the poet's wit
" A while may ftruggle, but at laft fubmit :
" Well-weigh'd refults and wife conclufions feem
" But empty chat, impertinence, to him :
" His opiates feize fo ftrongly on the brain,   290
" They make all prudent application vain :
" If therefore you refolve to live at eafe,
" To tafte the fweetnefs of internal peace,
" Would not for fafety to a battle fly,
" Or chufe a fhipwreck, if afraid to die,   295
" Far from thefe pleafurable fhades remove,
" And leave the fond inglorious toil of Love."
   This faid, fhe vanifh'd; and methought I found
Myfelf tranfported to a rifing ground,
From whence I did a pleafant vale furvey;   300
Large was the profpect, beautiful and gay :
There I beheld th' apartments of delight,
Whofe curious forms oblig'd the wond'ring fight;
Some in full view upon the champaign plac'd,
With lofty walls and cooling ftreams embrac'd; 305

Others in fhady groves retir'd from noife,
The feat of private and exalted joys:
At a great diftance I perceiv'd there ftood
A ftately building in a fpacious wood,
Whofe gilded turrets rais'd their beauteous heads 310
High in the air, to view the neighb'ring meads,
Where vulgar lovers fpend their happy days
In ruftic dancing and delightful plays:
But while I gaz'd with admiration round,
I heard from far celeftial mufic found;   315
So foft, fo moving, fo harmonious, all
The artful charming notes did rife and fall,
My foul, tranfported with the graceful airs,
Shook off the preffures of its former fears;
I felt afrefh the little god begin   320
To ftir himfelf, and gently move within;
Then I repented I had vow'd no more
To love, or Delia's beauteous eyes adore.
" Why am I now condemn'd to banifhment,
" And made an exile by my own confent?"   325
I fighing cry'd. " Why fhould I live in pain
" Thofe fleeting hours which ne'er return again?
" O Delia! what can wretched Strephon do?
" Inhuman to himfelf, and falfe to you!
" 'Tis true, I've promis'd Reafon to remove   330
" From thefe retreats, and quit bright Delia's love:
" But is not Reafon partially unkind?
" Are all her votaries, like me, confin'd?

" Muſt none, that under her dominion live,
" To love and beauty veneration give?   335
" Why then did Nature youthful Delia grace
" With a majeſtic mien and charming face?
" Why did ſhe give her that ſurpriſing air,
" Make her ſo gay, ſo witty, and ſo fair,
" Miſtreſs of all that can affection move,   340
" If Reaſon will not ſuffer us to love?
" But ſince it muſt be ſo I'll haſte away;
" 'Tis fatal to return, and death to ſtay.
" From you, bleſs'd Shades! (if I may call you ſo
" Inculpable) with mighty pain I go: 345
" Compell'd from hence, I leave my quiet here;
" I may find ſafety, but I buy it dear."
ι Then, turning round, I ſaw a beauteous boy,
Such as of old were meſſengers of joy:
" Who art thou, or from whence? If ſent," ſaid I,
" To me, my haſte requires a quick reply."   351
    " I come," he cry'd, " from yon' celeſtial grove,
" Where ſtands the temple of the god of Love,
" With whoſe important favour you are grac'd,
" And juſtly in his high protection plac'd.   355
" Be grateful, Strephon, and obey that god
" Whoſe ſceptre ne'er is chang'd into a rod;
" That god to whom the haughty and the proud,
" The bold, the braveſt, nay, the beſt, have bow'd;
" That god whom all the leſſer gods adore,   360
" Firſt in exiſtence, and the firſt in pow'r:

" From him I come, on embaffy divine,
" To tell thee Delia, Delia may be thine,
" To whom all beauties rightful tribute pay;
" Delia ! the young, the lovely, and the gay !   365
" If you dare pufh your fortune, if you dare
" But be refolv'd, and prefs the yielding fair,
" Succefs and glory will your labours crown,
" For Fate does rarely on the valiant frown :
" But were you fure to be unkindly us'd,   370
" Coldly receiv'd, and fcornfully refus'd,
" He greater glory and more fame obtains
" Who lofes Delia than who Phyllis gains.
" But, to prevent all fears that may arife,
" (Tho' fears ne'er move the daring and the wife)375
" In the dark volumes of eternal doom,
" Where all things paft, and prefent, and to come,
" Are writ, I faw thefe words—" It is decreed
" That Strephon's love to Delia fhall fucceed."   379
" What would you more?—While youth and vigour
" Love, and be happy ; they decline too faft.   [laft
" In youth alone you 're capable to prove
" The mighty tranfports of a gen'rous love;
" For dull Old Age with fumbling labour cloys
" Before the blifs, or gives but wither'd joys.   385
" Youth's the beft time for action mortals have ;
" That paft, they touch the confines of the grave.
" Now, if you hope to lie in Delia's arms,
" To die in raptures, or diffolve in charms,

" Quick to the blifsful happy manfion fly,   390
" Where all is one continu'd ecftafy;
" Delia impatiently expects you there,
" And fure you will not difappoint the fair:
" None but the impotent or old would ftay
" When love invites, and beauty calls away."   395
     " Oh! you convey," faid I, " dear charming Boy!
" Into my foul a ftrange diforder'd joy.
" I would, but dare not, your advice purfue;
" I've promis'd Reafon, and I muft be true:
" Reafon 's the rightful emprefs of the foul,   400
" Does all exorbitant defires control,
" Checks ev'ry wild excurfion of the mind,
" By her wife dictates happily confin'd;
" And he that will not her commands obey
" Leaves a fafe convoy in a dang'rous fea.   405
" True, I love Delia to a vaft excefs,
" But I muft try to make my paffion lefs;
" Try if I can; if poffible I will;
" For I have vow'd, and muft that vow fulfil.
" Oh! had I not, with what a vig'rous flight   410
" Could I purfue the quarries of delight!
" How could I prefs fair Delia in thefe arms,
" Till I diffolv'd in love, and fhe in charms!
" But now no more muft I her beauties view,
" Yet tremble at the thoughts to leave her too.   415
" What would I give I might my flame allow!
" But 'tis forbid by Reafon and a vow,

" Two mighty obftacles; tho' love of old
" Has broke thro' greater, ftronger pow'rs controll'd.
" Should I offend, by high example taught,   420
" 'Twould not be an inexpiable fault:
" The crimes of malice have found grace above,
" And fure kind Heav'n will fpare the crimes of love.
" Couldft thou, my Angel! but inftruct me how
" I might be happy and not break my vow,   425
" Or by fome fubtle art diffolve the chain,
" You 'd foon revive my dying hopes again.
" Reafon and Love, I know, could ne'er agree;
" Both would command, and both fuperior be.
" Reafon 's fupported by the fin'wy force   430
" Of folid argument and wife difcourfe;
" But Love pretends to ufe no other arms
" Than foft impreffions and perfuafive charms.
" One muft be difobey'd; and fhall I prove
" A rebel to my reafon, or to love?   435
" But then, fuppofe I fhould my flame purfue,
" Delia may be unkind and faithlefs too,
" Reject my paffion with a proud difdain,
" And fcorn the love of fuch an humble fwain:
" Then fhould I labour under mighty grief,   440
" Beyond all hopes or profpect of relief;
" So that, methinks, 'tis fafer to obey
" Right Reafon, tho' fhe bears a rugged fway,
" Than Love's foft rule, whofe fubjects undergo,
" Early or late, too fad a fhare of woe.   445

" Can I so soon forget that wretched crew
" Reason just now expos'd before my view?
" If Delia should be cruel, I must be
" A sad partaker of their misery.
" But your encouragements so strongly move,   450
" I'm almost tempted to pursue my love;
" For sure no treacherous designs should dwell
" In one that argues and persuades so well;
" For what could Love by my destruction gain?
" Love's an immortal god and I a swain;   455
" And sure I may, without suspicion, trust
" A god, for gods can never be unjust."
    " Right you conclude," reply'd the smiling boy;
" Love ruins none; 'tis men themselves destroy;
" And those vile wretches which you lately saw 460
" Transgress'd his rules as well as Reason's law:
" They're not Love's subjects, but the slaves of lust;
" Nor is their punishment so great as just:
" For Love and Lust essentially divide,
" Like day and night, humility and pride: 465
" One darkness hides, t' other does always shine;
" This of infernal make, and that divine.
" Reason no gen'rous passion does oppose;
" 'Tis Lust (not Love) and Reason that are foes:
" She bids you scorn a base inglorious flame,   470
" Black as the gloomy shade from whence it came:
" In this her precepts should obedience find,
" But your's is not of that ignoble kind.

3

" You err in thinking she would disapprove
" The brave pursuit of honourable love,   475
" And therefore judge what's harmless an offence,
" Invert her meaning, and mistake her sense.
" She could not such insipid counsel give
" As not to love at all; 'tis not to live;
" But where bright virtue and true beauty lies, 480
" And that in Delia, charming Delia's eyes!
" Could you, contented, see th' angelic maid
" In old Alexis' dull embraces laid?
" Or rough-hewn Tityrus possess those charms
" Which are in heav'n, the heav'n of Delia's arms?
" Consider, Youth! what transport you forego,   486
" The most entire felicity below,
" Which is by Fate alone reserv'd for you;
" Monarchs have been deny'd, for monarchs sue.
" I own 'tis difficult to gain the prize,   490
" Or 't would be cheap and low in noble eyes;
" But there is one soft minute when the mind
" Is left unguarded, waiting to be kind,
" Which the wise lover understanding right,
" Steals in like day upon the wings of light.   495
" You urge your vow; but can those vows prevail
" Whose first foundation and whose reason fail?
" You vow'd to leave fair Delia, but you thought
" Your passion was a crime, your flame a fault:
" But since your judgment err'd, it has no force   500
" To bind at all, but is dissolv'd of course;

D

" And therefore hefitate no longer here,
" But banifh all the dull remains of fear.
" Dare you be happy, Youth! but dare, and be;
" I 'll be your convoy to the charming fhe.   505
" What! ftill irrefolute? debating ftill?
" View her, and then forfake her if you will."
     " I 'll go," faid I; " once more I 'll venture all;
" 'Tis brave to perifh by a noble fall.
" Beauty no mortal can refift, and Jove   510
" Laid by his grandeur to indulge his love.
" Reafon! if I do err, my crime forgive;
" Angels alone without offending live.
" I go aftray but as the wife have done,
" And act a folly which they did not fhun."   515
     Then we, defcending to a fpacious plain,
Were foon faluted by a num'rous train
Of happy lovers, who confum'd their hours
With conftant jollity in fhady bow'rs.
There I beheld the blefs'd variety   520
Of joy, from all corroding troubles free:
Each follow'd his own fancy to delight;
Tho' all went diff'rent ways, yet all went right.
None err'd, or mifs'd the happinefs he fought;
Love to one centre ev'ry twining brought.   525
We pafs'd thro' num'rous pleafant fields and glades,
By murm'ring fountains and by peaceful fhades,
Till we approach'd the confines of the wood,
Where mighty Love's immortal temple ftood.

Round the celeſtial fane, in goodly rows,   530
And beauteous order, am'rous myrtle grows,
Beneath whoſe ſhade expecting lovers wait
For the kind minute of indulgent Fate :
Each had his guardian Cupid, whoſe chief care,
By ſecret motions, was to warm the fair;   535
To kindle eager longings for the joy;
To move the ſlow, and to incline the coy.

   The glorious fabric charm'd my wond'ring ſight,
Of vaſt extent and of prodigious height :
The caſe was marble, but the poliſh'd ſtone   540
With ſuch an admirable luſtre ſhone,
As if ſome architect divine had ſtrove
T' outdo the palace of imperial Jove.
The pond'rous gates of maſſy gold were made,
With di'monds of a mighty ſize inlaid :   545
Here ſtood the winged guards, in order plac'd,
With ſhining darts and golden quivers grac'd :
As we approach'd they clapp'd their joyful wings,
And cry'd aloud, "Tune, tune your warbling ſtrings;
" The grateful youth is come to ſacrifice   550
" At Delia's altar to bright Delia's eyes :
" With harmony divine his ſoul inſpire,
" That he may boldly touch the ſacred fire :
" And ye that wait upon the bluſhing fair,
" Celeſtial incenſe and perfumes prepare,   555
" While our great god her panting boſom warms,
" Refines her beauties, and improves her charms."

Ent'ring the fpacious dome, my ravifh'd eyes
A wondrous fcene of glory did furprife;
The riches, fymmetry, and brightnefs, all   560
Did equally for admiration call;
But the defcription is a labour fit
For none beneath a laureat angel's wit.

Amidft the temple was an altar made
Of folid gold, where adoration 's paid: 565
Here I perform'd the ufual rites with fear,
Not daring boldly to approach too near,
Till from the god a fmiling Cupid came,
And bid me touch the confecrated flame;
Which done, my guide my eager fteps convey'd 570
To the apartment of the beauteous maid.

Before the entrance was her altar rais'd,
On pedeftals of polifh'd marble plac'd;
By it her guardian Cupid always ftands,
Who troops of miffionary Loves commands: 575
To him with foft addreffes all repair;
Each for his captive humbly begs the fair,
Tho' ftill in vain they importun'd; for he
Would give encouragement to none but me.   579
" There ftands the youth," he cry'd, " muft take the
" The lovely Delia can be none but his: [blifs,
" Fate has felected him; and mighty Love
" Confirms below what that decrees above.
" Then prefs no more; there 's not another fwain
" On earth but Strephon can bright Delia gain. 585

" Kneel, Youth! and with a grateful mind renew
" Your vows; fwear you 'll eternally be true :
" But if you dare be falfe, dare perjur'd prove,
" You 'll find, in fure revenge, affronted Love
" As hot, as fierce, as terrible, as Jove."   590
" Hear me, ye Gods!" faid I, " now hear me fwear,
" By all that's facred, and by all that's fair !
" If I prove falfe to Delia, let me fall   -
" The common obloquy, condemn'd by all;
" Let me the utmoft of your vengeance try,   595
" Forc'd to live wretched, and unpity'd die."
    Then he expos'd the lovely fleeping maid,
Upon a couch of new-blown rofes laid :
The blufhing colour in her cheeks expreft   599
What tender thoughts infpir'd her heaving breaft.
Sometimes a figh, half fmother'd, ftole away, [fay :
Then fhe would "Strephon, charming Strephon !"
Sometimes fhe, fmiling, cry'd, " You love, 'tis true ;
" But will you always, and be faithful too ?"
Ten thoufand Graces play'd about her face,   605
Ten thoufand charms attended ev'ry Grace :
Each admirable feature did impart
A fecret rapture to my throbbing heart.
The nymph * imprifon'd in the Brazen Tow'r,
When Jove defcended in a golden fhow'r,   610
Lefs beautiful appear'd, and yet her eyes
Brought down that god from the neglected fkies.

* Danae.

D iij

So moving, fo tranfporting, was the fight,
So much a goddefs Delia feem'd, fo bright,
My ravifh'd foul, with fecret wonder fraught,   615
Lay all diffolv'd in ecftafy of thought.

Long time I gaz'd; but as I, trembling, drew
Nearer, to take a more obliging view,
It thunder'd loud, and the ungrateful noife
Wak'd me, and put an end to all my joys.   620

THE FORTUNATE COMPLAINT.

As Strephon in a wither'd cyprefs fhade,
For anxious thought and fighing lovers made,
Revolving lay upon his wretched ftate,
And the hard ufage of too partial Fate,
Thus the fad youth complain'd : "Once happy fwain,
" Now the moft abject fhepherd of the plain !   . 6
" Where 's that harmonious concert of delights,
" Thofe peaceful days and pleafurable nights,
" That gen'rous mirth and noble jollity,
" Which gaily made the dancing minutes fly ?   10
" Difpers'd, and banifh'd from my troubled breaft,
" Nor leave me one fhort interval of reft.
      " Why do I profecute a hopelefs flame,
" And play in torment fuch a lofing game ?
" All things confpire to make my ruin fure ;   15
" When wounds are mortal they admit no cure :
" But Heav'n fometimes does a mirac'lous thing,
" When our laft hope is juft upon the wing,
" And in a moment drives thofe clouds away
" Whofe fullen darknefs hid a glorious day.   20
      " Why was I born ? or why do I furvive ?
" To be made wretched only kept alive ?
" Fate is too cruel in the harfh decree,
" That I muft live, yet live in mifery.
" Are all its pleafing happy moments gone ?   25
" Muft Strephon be unfortunate alone ?

" On other fwains it lavifhly beftows ;
" On them each nymph neglected favour throws;
" They meet compliance ftill in ev'ry face,
" And lodge their paffions in a kind embrace,   30
" Obtaining from the foft incurious maid
" True love for counterfeit, and gold for lead.
" Succefs on Mævius always does attend ;
" Inconftant Fortune is his conftant friend ;
" He levels blindly, yet the mark does hit,   35
" And owes the victory to chance, not wit :
" But let him conquer ere one blow be ftruck ;
" I 'd not be Mævius to have Mævius' luck :
" Proud of my fate, I would not change my chains
" For all the trophies purring Mævius gains,   40
" But rather ftill live Delia's flave, than be
" Like Mævius filly, and like Mævius free.
" But he is happy, loves the common road,
" And, pack-horfe like, jogs on beneath his load :
" If Phyllis peevifh or unkind does prove,   45
" It ne'er difturbs his grave mechanic love.
" A little joy his languid flame contents,
" And makes him eafy under all events :
" But when a paffion 's noble and fublime,
" And higher ftill would ev'ry moment climb,   50
" If 'tis accepted with a juft return,
" The fire's immortal, will for ever burn,
" And with fuch raptures fills the lover's breaft,
" That faints in Paradife are fcarce more bleft.

" But I lament my miferies in vain, 55
" For Delia hears me pitilefs complain.
" Suppofe fhe pities, and believes me true,
" What fatisfaction can from thence accrue,
" Unlefs her pity makes her love me too ?
" Perhaps fhe loves, ('tis but perhaps, I fear, 60
" For that's a blefling can't be bought too dear)
" If fhe has fcruples that oppofe her will,
" I muft, alas! be miferable ftill;
" Tho', if fhe loves, thofe fcruples foon will fly
" Before the reas'ning of the deity; 65
" For where Love enters he will rule alone,
" And fuffer no copartner in his throne ;
" And thofe falfe arguments that would repel
" His high injunctions teach us to rebel.
" What method can poor Strephon then propound
" To cure the bleeding of his fatal wound, 71
" If fhe who guided the vexatious dart
" Refolves to cherifh and increafe the fmart ?
" Go, youth, from thefe unhappy plains remove,
" Leave the purfuit of unfuccefsful love ; 75
" Go, and to foreign fwains thy griefs relate ;
" Tell 'em the cruelty of frowning Fate ;
" Tell 'em the noble charms of Delia's mind ;
" Tell 'em how fair, but tell 'em how unkind ;
" And when few years thou haft in forrow fpent, 80
" (For fure they cannot be of large extent)

" In pray'rs for her thou lov'ft refign thy breath,
" And blefs the minute gives thee eafe and death."
  Here paus'd the fwain——when Delia, driving by
Her bleating flock to fome frefh pafture nigh,   85
By Love directed, did her fteps convey
Where Strephon, wrapp'd in filent forrow, lay.
As foon as he perceiv'd the beauteous maid,
He rofe to meet her, and thus, trembling, faid:
  " When humble fuppliants would the gods appeafe,
" And in fevere afflictions beg for eafe,   91
" With conftant importunity they fue,
" And their petitions ev'ry day renew,
" Grow ftill more earneft as they are deny'd,
" Nor one well-weigh'd expedient leave untry'd, 95
" Till Heav'n thofe bleflings they enjoy'd before
" Not only does return, but gives 'em more.
  " O! do not blame me, Delia, if I prefs
" So much, and with impatience, for redrefs:
" My pond'rous griefs no eafe my foul allow,   100
" For they are next t' intolerable now:
" How fhall I then fupport 'em when they grow
" To an excefs, to a diftracting woe?
" Since you're endow'd with a celeftial mind,
" Relieve like Heav'n, and, like the gods, be kind.
" Did you perceive the torments I endure,   106
" Which you firft caus'd, and you alone can cure,
" They would your virgin foul to pity move,
" And pity may at laft be chang'd to love.

" Some fwains, I own, impofe upon the fair,   110
" And lead th' incautious maid into a fnare;
" But let them fuffer for their perjury,
" And do not punifh others' crimes in me.
" If there's fo many of our fex untruc,
" Your's fhould more kindly ufe the faithful few; 115
" Tho' innocence too oft' incurs the fate
" Of guilt, and clears itfelf fometimes too late.
  " Your nature is to tendernefs inclin'd;
" And why to me, to me alone, unkind?
" A common love, by other perfons fhown,   120
" Meets with a full return, but mine has none;
" Nay, fcarce believ'd, tho' from deceit as free
" As angels' flames can for archangels be.
" A paffion feign'd at no repulfe is griev'd,
" And values little if it ben't receiv'd;   125
" But love fincere refents the fmalleft fcorn,
" And the unkindnefs does in fecret mourn.
  " Sometimes I pleafe myfelf, and think you are
" Too good to make me wretched by defpair;
" That tendernefs which in your foul is plac'd   130
" Will move you to compaffion fure at laft:
" But when I come to take a fecond view
" Of my own merits, I defpond of you;
" For what can Delia, beauteous Delia! fee
" To raife in her the leaft efteem for me?   135
" I've nought that can encourage my addrefs;
" My fortune's little, and my worth is lefs:

" But if a love of the fublimeft kind
" Can make impreffion on a gen'rous mind;
" If all has real value that's divine,   140
" There cannot be a nobler flame than mine.
    " Perhaps you pity me; I know you muft,
" And my affection can no more diftruft:
" But what, alas! will helplefs pity do?
" You pity, but you may defpife me too.   145
" Still I am wretched if no more you give;
" The ftarving orphan can't on pity live;
" He muft receive the food for which he cries,
" Or he confumes, and, tho' much pity'd, dies.
    " My torments ftill do with my paffion grow; 150
" The more I love the more I undergo:
" But fuffer me no longer to remain
" Beneath the preffure of fo vaft a pain:
" My wound requires fome fpeedy remedy;
" Delays are fatal when defpair is nigh.   155
" Much I've endur'd, much more than I can tell;
" Too much, indeed, for one that loves fo well.
" When will the end of all my forrows be?
" Can you not love? I'm fure you pity me:
" But if I muft new miferies fuftain,   160
" And be condemn'd to more and ftronger pain,
" I'll not accufe you, fince my fate is fuch;
" I pleafe too little, and I love too much."
    " Strephon, no more," the blufhing Delia faid;
" Excufe the conduct of a tim'rous maid: · 165

2

" Now I 'm convinc'd your love 's fublime and true,
" Such as I always wifh'd to find in you :
" Each kind expreffion, ev'ry tender thought,
" A mighty tranfport in my bofom wrought ;
" And tho' in fecret I your flame approv'd,   170
" I figh'd and griev'd, but durft not own I lov'd :
" Tho' now——O Strephon ! be fo kind to guefs
" What fhame will not allow me to confefs."
 The youth, encompafs'd with a joy fo bright,
Had hardly ftrength to bear the vaft delight :   175
By too fublime an ecftafy poffeft,
He trembled, gaz'd, and clafp'd her to his breaft ;
Ador'd the nymph that did his pain remove,
Vow'd endlefs truth and everlafting love.   179

E

A PASTORAL ESSAY

ON THE DEATH OF

QUEEN MARY.

ANNO MDCXCIV.

As gentle Strephon to his fold convey'd
A wand'ring lamb, which from the flocks had ftray'd,
Beneath a mournful cyprefs fhade he found
Cofmelia weeping on the dewy ground:
Amaz'd, with eager hafte he ran to know   5
The fatal caufe of her intemp'rate woe,
And clafping her to his impatient breaft,
In thefe foft words his tender care expreft.

  STREPH. Why mourns my dear Cofmelia? why ap-
My life, my foul, diffolv'd in briny tears?   [pears
Has fome fierce tiger thy lov'd heifer flain,   11
While I was wand'ring on the neighb'ring plain?
Or has fome greedy wolf devour'd thy fheep?
What fad misfortune makes Cofmelia weep?
Speak, that I may prevent thy grief's increafe,   15
Partake thy forrows, or reftore thy peace.

  COS. Do you not hear from far that mournful bell?
'Tis for---I cannot the fad tidings tell.
Oh! whither are my fainting fpirits fled!
'Tis for Celeftia---Strephon, oh!---fhe's dead!   20
The brighteft nymph, the princefs of the plain,
By an untimely dart untimely flain!

STREPH. Dead! 'tis impoffible! fhe cannot die!
She's too divine, too much a deity:
'Tis a falfe rumour fome ill fwains have fpread,   25
Who wifh, perhaps, the good Celeftia dead.

Cos. Ah! no; the truth in ev'ry face appears,
For ev'ry face you meet's o'erflow'd with tears.
Trembling and pale I ran thro' all the plain,
From flock to flock, and afk'd of ev'ry fwain,   30
But each, fcarce lifting his dejected head,
Cry'd, "Oh! Cofmelia; oh! Celeftia's dead."

STREPH. Something was meant by that ill-bo- ⎤
Of the prophetic raven from the oak, [ding croak ⎬
Which ftraight by lightning was in fhivers broke; ⎦
But we our mifchief feel before we fee,   36
Seiz'd and o'erwhelm'd at once with mifery.

Cos. Since then we have no trophies to beftow,
No pompous things to make a glorious fhow,
(For all the tribute a poor fwain can bring,   40
In rural numbers is to mourn and fing)
Let us beneath the gloomy fhade rehearfe
Celeftia's facred name in no lefs facred verfe.

STREPH. Celeftia dead! then 'tis in vain to live;
What's all the comfort that the plains can give,   45
Since fhe, by whofe bright influence alone
Our flocks increas'd, and we rejoic'd, is gone?
Since fhe, who round fuch beams of goodnefs fpread
As gave new life to ev'ry fwain, is dead?

Cos. In vain we wifh for the delightful fpring;   50
What joys can flow'ry May or April bring,

When she, for whom the spacious plains were spread
With early flow'rs and cheerful greens, is dead?
In vain did courtly Damon warm the earth,
To give to summer fruits a winter birth;   55
In vain we autumn wait, which crowns the fields
With wealthy crops, and various plenty yields;
Since that fair nymph, for whom the boundless store
Of Nature was preserv'd, is now no more.

STREPH. Farewell for ever then to all that's gay;
You will forget to sing and I to play :   61
No more with cheerful songs, in cooling bow'rs,
Shall we consume the pleasurable hours :
All joys are banish'd, all delights are fled,
Ne'er to return, now fair Celestia's dead!   65

Cos. If e'er I sing, they shall be mournful lays
Of great Celestia's name, Celestia's praise;
How good she was, how generous, how wise!
How beautiful her shape, how bright her eyes!
How charming all! how much she was ador'd,   70
Alive; when dead, how much her loss deplor'd!
A noble theme, and able to inspire
The humblest Muse with the sublimest fire.
And since we do of such a princess sing,
Let ours ascend upon a stronger wing,   75
And while we do the lofty numbers join,
Her name will make the harmony divine.
Raise, then, thy tuneful voice, and be the song
Sweet as her temper, as her virtue strong.   79

STREPH. When her great Lord to foreign wars was
And left Celeſtia here to rule alone,   [gone,
With how ſerene a brow, how void of fear,
When ſtorms aroſe, did ſhe the veſſel ſteer!
And when the raging of the waves did ceaſe,
How gentle was her ſway in times of peace!   85
Juſtice and Mercy did their beams unite,
And round her temples ſpread a glorious light:
So quick ſhe eas'd the wrongs of ev'ry ſwain,
She hardly gave them leiſure to complain:
Impatient to reward, but ſlow to draw   90
Th' avenging ſword of neceſſary law;
Like Heav'n, ſhe took no pleaſure to deſtroy;
With grief ſhe puniſh'd, and ſhe ſav'd with joy.

Cos. When godlike Belliger from war's alarms
Return'd in triumph to Celeſtia's arms,   95
She met her hero with a full deſire,
But chaſte as light, and vigorous as fire:
Such mutual flames, ſo equally divine,
Did in each breaſt with ſuch a luſtre ſhine,
His could not ſeem the greater, her's the leſs;   100
Both were immenſe, for both were in exceſs.

STREPH. Oh! godlike princeſs! oh! thrice happy
While ſhe preſided o'er the fruitful plains!   [ſwains!
While ſhe, for ever raviſh'd from our eyes,
To mingle with her kindred of the ſkies,   105
Did for your peace her conſtant thoughts employ,
The nymph's good angel, and the ſhepherd's joy!

E iij

Cos. All that was noble beautify'd her mind;
There Wifdom fat, with folid Reafon join'd;
There, too, did Piety and Greatnefs wait,   110
Meeknefs on Grandeur, Modefty on State:
Humble amidft the fplendours of a throne,
Plac'd above all, and yet defpifing none;
And when a crown was forc'd on her by Fate,
She with fome pain fubmitted to be great.   115

STREPH. Her pious foul with emulation ftrove
To gain the mighty Pan's important love,
To whofe myfterious rites fhe always came
With fuch an active fo intenfe a flame,
The duties of religion feem'd to be   120
No more her care than her felicity.

Cos. Virtue unmix'd, without the leaft allay,
Pure as the light of a celeftial ray,
Commanded all the motions of the foul
With fuch a foft but abfolute control,   125
That as fhe knew what beft great Pan would pleafe,
She ftill perform'd it with the greateft eafe;
Him for her high exemplar fhe defign'd,
Like him benevolent to all mankind.
Her foes fhe pity'd, not defir'd their blood,   130
And, to revenge their crimes, fhe did them good;
Nay, all affronts fo unconcern'd fhe bore,
(Maugre that violent temptation pow'r)
As if fhe thought it vulgar to refent,
Or wifh'd forgivenefs their worft punifhment.   135

· Streph. Next mighty Pan was her illustrious lord,
His high vicegerent, sacredly ador'd;
Him with such piety and zeal she lov'd,
The noble passion ev'ry hour improv'd,
Till it ascended to that glorious height   140
'Twas next (if only next) to infinite :
This made her so entire a duty pay,
She grew at last impatient to obey,
And met his wishes with as prompt a zeal
As an archangel his Creator's will.   145

   Cos. Mature for heav'n, the fatal mandate came,
With it a chariot of ethereal flame,
In which, Elijah-like, she pass'd the spheres,
Brought joy to heav'n, but left the world in tears.

   Streph. Methinks I see her on the plains of light
All glorious, all incomparably bright !   151
While the immortal minds around her gaze
On the excessive splendour of her rays,
And scarce believe a human soul could be
Endow'd with such stupendous majesty.   155

   Cos. Who can lament too much ? O! who can mourn
Enough o'er beautiful Celestia's urn ?
So great a loss as this deserves excess
Of sorrow ; all 's too little that is less.
But to supply the universal woe,   160
Tears from all eyes, without cessation, flow :
All that have pow'r to weep, or voice to groan,
With throbbing breasts Celestia's fate bemoan ;

While marble rocks the common griefs partake, 164
And echo back thofe cries they cannot make.

   Streph. Weep then, (once fruitful) Vales! and
        fpring with yew,
Ye thirfty barren Mountains! weep with dew;
Let ev'ry flow'r on this extended plain
Not droop, but fhrink into its womb again,
Ne'er to receive anew its yearly birth;   170
Let ev'ry thing that's grateful leave the earth;
Let mournful cyprefs, with each noxious weed,
And baneful venoms in their place fucceed.
Ye purling quer'llous Brooks! o'ercharg'd with grief,
Hafte fwiftly to the fea for more relief;   175
Then tiding back, each to his facred head,
Tell your aftonifh'd fprings Celeftia's dead!

   Cos. Well have you fung, in an exalted ftrain,
The faireft nymph e'er grac'd the Britifh plain.
Who knows but fome officious angel may   180
Your grateful numbers to her ears convey,
That fhe may fmile upon us from above,
And blefs our mournful plains with peace and love?

   Streph. But fee! our flocks do to their fold repair,
For night with fable clouds obfcures the air;   185
Cold damps defcend from the unwholefome fky,
And fafety bids us to our cottage fly.
'Tho' with each morn our forrows will return,
Each ev'n, like nightingales, we'll fing and mourn,
'Till death conveys us to the peaceful urn.   190

THE EARL OF A——

WITH THE COUNTESS OF S——.

Triumphant beauty never looks so gay
As on the morning of a nuptial day;
Love then within a larger circle moves,
New graces adds, and ev'ry charm improves.
While Hymen does his sacred rites prepare,   5
The busy nymphs attend the trembling fair,
Whose veins are swell'd with an unusual heat,
And eager pulses with strange motions beat;
Alternate passions various thoughts impart,
And painful joys distend her throbbing heart;   10
Her fears are great, and her desires are strong;
The minutes fly too fast——yet stay too long:
Now she is ready——the next moment not;
All things are done——then something is forgot:·
She fears——yet wishes the strange work were done;
Delays——yet is impatient to be gone.   16
Disorders thus from ev'ry thought arise;
What Love persuades I know not what denies.

    Achates' choice does his firm judgment prove,
And shews at once he can be wife and love,   20
Because it from no spurious passion came,
But was the product of a noble flame;

C..

Bold without rudenefs, without blazing bright,
Pure as fix'd ftars, and uncorrupt as light,
By juft degrees it to perfection grew, 25
An early ripenefs, and a lafting too.
So the bright fun afcending to his noon
Moves not too flowly, nor is there too foon.

But tho' Achates was unkindly driv'n
From his own land, he's banifh'd into heav'n; 30
For fure the raptures of Cofmelia's love
Are next, if only next, to thofe above.
Thus pow'r divine does with his foes engage,
Rewards his virtues, and defeats their rage;
For firft it did to fair Cofmelia give 35
All that a human creature could receive;
Whate'er can raife our wonder or delight,
Tranfport the foul, or gratify the fight,
Then, in the full perfection of her charms,
Lodg'd the bright virgin in Achates' arms. 40

What angels are is in Cofmelia feen,
Their awful glories, and their godlike mien;
For in her afpect all the Graces meet,
All that is noble, beautiful, or fweet;
There ev'ry charm in lofty triumph fits, 45
Scorns poor defect, and to no fault fubmits;
There fymmetry, complexion, air, unite,
Sublimely noble, and amazing bright.
So, newly finifh'd, by the hand divine,
Before her fall, did the firft woman fhine: 50

But Eve in one great point she does excel;
Cosmelia never err'd at all; she fell:
From her temptation, in despair, withdrew,
Nor more assaults whom it could ne'er subdue.

    Virtue confirm'd, and regularly brought   55
To full maturity by serious thought, ·
Her actions with a watchful eye surveys,
Each passion guides, and every moment sways:
Not the least failure in her conduct lies,
So gaily modest, and so freely wise.   60

    Her judgment sure, impartial, and refin'd,
With wit that 's clear and penetrating join'd,
O'er all the efforts of her mind presides,
And to the noblest end her labours guides:
She knows the best, and does the best pursue,   65
And treads the maze of life without a clue;
That the weak only and the wav'ring lack,
When they 're mistaken, to conduct 'em back:
She does, amidst ten thousand ways, prefer
The right, as if not capable to err.   70

    Her fancy, strong, vivacious, and sublime,
Seldom betrays her converse to a crime,
And tho' it moves with a luxuriant heat,
'Tis ne'er precipitous, but always great;
For each expression, ev'ry teeming thought,   75
Is to the scanning of her judgment brought,
Which wisely separates the finest gold,
And casts the image in a beauteous mould.

No trifling words debase her eloquence,
But all's pathetic, all is sterling sense,   80
Refin'd from drossy chat and idle noise,
With which the female conversation cloys:
So well she knows, what's understood by few,
To time her thoughts, and to express 'em too,
That what she speaks does to the soul transmit   85
The fair ideas of delightful wit.

    Illustrious born, and as illustrious bred,
By great example to wise actions led,
Much to the fame her lineal heroes bore
She owes, but to her own high genius more;   90
And by a noble emulation mov'd,
Excell'd their virtues, and her own improv'd,
Till they arriv'd to that celestial height,
Scarce angels greater be, or saints so bright.

    But if Cosmelia could yet lovelier be,   95
Of nobler birth, or more a deity,
Achates merits her, tho' none but he,
Whose gen'rous soul abhors a base disguise,
Resolv'd in action, and in council wise;
Too well confirm'd and fortify'd within   100
For threats to force, or flattery to win;
Unmov'd amidst the hurricane he stood;
He dare be guiltless, and he will be good.

    Since the first pair in Paradise were join'd,
Two hearts were ne'er so happily combin'd.   105

Achates life to fair Cofmelia gives;
In fair Cofmelia great Achates lives :
Each is to other the divineſt blifs;
He is her heav'n, and ſhe is more than his.
Oh! may the kindeſt influence above
Protect their perfons, and indulge their love!   111

An Inſcription for the monument of

DIANA

COUNTESS OF OXFORD AND ELGIN.

DIANA OXONII ET ELGINI COMITISSA,
Quæ
Illuſtri orta ſanguine, ſanguinem illuſtravit :
Ceciliorum meritis, clara, ſuis clariſſima;
Ut quæ neſciret minor eſſe maximis.
Vitam ineuntem innocentia;
Procedentem ampla virtutum cohors :   5
Exeuntem mors beatiſſima decoravit;
(Volente Numine)
Ut nuſpiam deeſſet aut virtus aut felicitas.
Duobus conjuncta maritis,
Utrique chariſſima :   10
Primum
(Quem ad annum habuit)
Impenſe dilexit :

F

Secundum

(Quem ad annos viginti quatuor)   15

Tanta pietate et amore coluit;

Ut qui, vivens,

Obfequium tanquam patri præftitit;

Moriens,

Patrimonium, tanquam filio, reliquit.   20

Noverca cum effet,

Maternam pietatem facile fuperavit.

Famulitii adeo mitem prudentemque curam geffit,

Ut non tam Domina familiæ præeffe,

Quam anima corpori ineffe videretur.   25

Denique,

Cum pudico, humili, forti, fancto animo,

Virginibus, conjugibus, viduis, omnibus,

Exemplum confecraffet integerrimum,

Terris anima major, ad fimiles evolavit fuperos.   30

THE FOREGOING INSCRIPTION

ATTEMPTED IN ENGLISH.

DIANA COUNTESS OF OXFORD AND ELGIN,
Who from a race of noble heroes came,
And added luftre to its ancient fame;
Round her the virtues of the Cecils fhone,
But with inferior brightnefs to her own,
Which fhe refin'd to that fublime degree,   5
The greateft mortal could not greater be.

Each stage of life peculiar splendour had;
Her tender years with innocence were clad;
Maturer grown, whate'er was brave and good
In the retinue of her virtues stood;   10
And at the final period of her breath
She crown'd her life with a propitious death.
That no occasion might be wanting here
To make her virtues fam'd or joys sincere,
Two noble lords her genial bed possest,   15
A wife to both the deareft and the best:
Oxford submitted in one year to Fate,
For whom her passion was exceeding great;
To Elgin full fix *lustra* were assign'd,
And him she lov'd with fo intense a mind,   20
That, living, like a father she obey'd,
Dying, as to a son, left all she had.
When a stepmother, she foon foar'd above
The common height ev'n of maternal love.
She did her num'rous family command   25
With such a tender care, fo wife a hand,
She feem'd no otherwise a miftrefs there,
Than godlike fouls in human bodies are:
But when to all she had example shew'd,
How to be great and humble, chafte and good,   30
Her foul, for earth too excellent, too high,
Flew to its peers, the princes of the sky.   32

F ij

ELEAZAR'S LAMENTATION
OVER JERUSALEM.

PARAPHRASED OUT OF JOSEPHUS.

I.

Alas! Jerusalem! alas! where's now
Thy priſtine glory, thy unmatch'd renown,
To which the Heathen monarchies did bow?
Ah! haplefs, miferable town!
Where's all thy majeſty, thy beauty, gone? 5
Thou once moſt noble, celebrated place,
The joy and the delight of all the earth,
Who gav'ſt to godlike princes birth,
And bred up heroes, an immortal race,
Where's now the vaſt magnificence which made 10
The fouls of foreigners adore
Thy wondrous brightnefs, which no more
Shall fhine, but lie in an eternal fhade?
Oh! mifery! where's all her mighty ſtate,
Her fplendid train of num'rous kings, · 15
Her noble edifices, noble things,
Which made her feem fo eminently great,
That barb'rous princes in her gates appear'd,
And wealthy prefents, as their tribute, brought
To court her friendſhip? for her ſtrength they fear'd, 20
And all her wide protection fought.
But now, ah! now they laugh and cry,
" See how her lofty buildings lie!
" See how her flaming turrets gild the fky!"

II.

Where's all the young, the valiant, and the gay,   25
That on her festivals were us'd to play
Harmonious tunes, and beautify the day?
The glitt'ring troops which did from far
Bring home the trophies and the spoils of war,
Whom all the nations round with terror view'd,   30
Nor durst their godlike valour try?
Where'er they fought they certainly subdu'd,
And ev'ry combat gain'd a victory.
Ah! where's the house of the Eternal King,
The beauteous temple of the Lord of Hosts,   35
To whose large treasuries our fleets did bring
The gold and jewels of remotest coasts?
There had the infinite Creator plac'd
His terrible, amazing name,
And with his more peculiar presence grac'd   40
That heav'nly *sanctum* where no mortal came,
The high priest only; he but once a-year
In that divine apartment might appear;
So full of glory, and so sacred, then;
But now corrupted with the heaps of slain   45
Which, scatter'd round with blood, defile the mighty

III.   [fane.

Alas! Jerusalem! each spacious street
Was once so fill'd, the num'rous throng
Was forc'd to jostle as they pass'd along,
And thousands did with thousands meet;   50
The darling then of God, and man's belov'd retreat.

F iij

In thee was the bright throne of Justice fix'd,
Justice impartial, and with fraud unmix'd.
She scorn'd the beauties of fallacious gold,
Despising the most wealthy bribes,   55
But did the sacred balance hold
With godlike faith to all our happy tribes.
Thy well-built streets and ev'ry noble square
Were once with polish'd marble laid,
And all thy lofty bulwarks made   60
With wondrous labour and with artful care.
Thy pond'rous gates, surprising to behold,
Were cover'd o'er with solid gold,
Whose splendour did so glorious appear,
It ravish'd and amaz'd the eye,   65
And strangers passing, to themselves would cry,
" What mighty heaps of wealth are here !
" How thick the bars of massy silver lie !
" O happy people ! and still happy be,
" Celestial city ! from destruction free,   70
" May'st thou enjoy a long entire prosperity !"
                    IV.
But now, O ! wretched, wretched place !
Thy streets and palaces are spread
With heaps of carcasses, and mountains of the dead,
The bleeding relics of the Jewish race :   75.
Each corner of the town, no vacant space,
But is with breathless bodies fill'd,
Some by the sword and some by famine kill'd.
Natives and strangers are together laid :

Death's arrows all at random flew   80
Amongst the crowd, and no diftinction made,
But both the coward and the valiant flew.
All in one difmal ruin join'd,
(For fwords and peftilence are blind)
The fair, the good, the brave, no mercy find.   85
Thofe that from far, with joyful hafte,
Came to attend thy feftival,
Of the fame bitter poifon tafte,
And by the black deftructive poifon fall,
For the avenging fentence pafs'd on all.   90
Oh! fee how the delight of human eyes
In horrid defolation lies!
See how the burning ruins flame,
Nothing now left but a fad empty name,
And the triumphant victor cries,   95
" This was the fam'd Jerufalem!"
                    V.
The moft obdurate creature muft
Be griev'd to fee thy palaces in duft,
Thofe ancient habitations of the juft;
And could the marble rocks but know   100
The mis'ries of thy fatal overthrow,
They'd ftrive to find fome fecret way unknown,
Maugre the fenfelefs nature of the ftone,
Their pity and concern to fhow :
For now where lofty buildings ftood   105
Thy fons' corrupted carcaffes are laid,
And all by this deftruction made
One common Golgotha, one field of blood.

See how thefe ancient men who rul'd thy ftate,
And made thee happy, made thee great,   110
Who fat upon the awful chair
Of mighty Mofes, in long fcarlet clad,
The good to cherifh and chaftife the bad,
Now fit in the corrupted air,
In filent melancholy, and in fad defpair!   115
See how their murder'd children round 'em lie!
Ah! difmal fcene! hark, how they cry!
" Woe! woe! one beam of mercy give,
" Good Heav'n! Alas! for we would live!
" Be pitiful, and fuffer us to die!"   120
Thus they lament, thus beg for eafe,
While in their feeble aged arms they hold
The bodies of their offspring ftiff and cold,
To guard 'em from the rav'nous favages,
Till their increafing forrows Death perfuade   125
(For Death muft fure with pity fee
The horrid defolation he has made)
To put a period to their mifery.
Thy wretched daughters that furvive
Are by the Heathen kept alive   130
Only to gratify their luft,
And then be mixed with the common duft.
Oh! infupportable, ftupendous woe!
What fhall we do? ah! whither fhall we go?
Down to the grave, down to thofe happy fhades below
Where all our brave progenitors are bleft   136
With endlefs triumph and eternal reft.

VI.

But who, without a flood of tears, can see
Thy mournful sad cataftrophe?
Who can behold thy glorious Temple lie   140
In afhes, and not be in pain to die?
Unhappy, dear Jerufalem! thy woes
Have rais'd my griefs to fuch a vaft excefs,
Their mighty weight no mortal knows,
Thought cannot comprehend, or words exprefs; 145
Nor can they poffibly, while I furvive, be lefs.
Good Heav'n had been extremely kind
If it had ftruck me dead, or ftruck me blind,
Before this curfed time, this worft of days.
Is Death quite tir'd? are all his arrows fpent?   150
If not, why then fo many dull delays?
Quick, quick, let the obliging dart be fent!
Nay, at me only let ten thoufand fly,
Whoe'er fhall wretchedly furvive, that I
May, happily, be fure to die.   155
Yet ftill we live, live in excefs of pain;
Our friends and relatives are flain;
Nothing but ruins round us fee,
Nothing but defolation, woe, and mifery!
Nay, while we thus with bleeding hearts complain,
Our enemies without prepare   161
Their direful engines to purfue the war,
And you may flavifhly preferve your breath,
Or feek for freedom in the arms of Death.

VII.

Thus then refolve, nor tremble at the thought;   165
Can glory be too dearly bought?
Since the Almighty wifdom has decreed
That we and all our progeny fhould bleed,
It fhall be after fuch a noble way,
Succeeding ages will with wonder view   170
What brave defpair compell'd us to :
No, we will ne'er furvive another day.
Bring then your wives, your children, all
That's valuable, good, or dear,
With ready hands, and place 'em here ;   175
They fhall unite in one vaft funeral.
I know your courages are truly brave,
And dare do any thing but ill :
Who would an aged father fave,
That he may live in chains, and be a flave,   180
Or for remorfelefs enemies to kill?
Let your bold hands then give the fatal blow ;
For what at any other time would be
The dire effect of rage and cruelty,
Is mercy, tendernefs, and pity, now.   185
This, then, perform'd, we'll to the battle fly,
And there, amidft our flaughter'd foes, expire.
If 'tis revenge and glory you defire,
Now you may have them if you dare but die;
Nay, more, ev'n freedom and eternity.   190

REASON.

Unhappy man! who, thro' fucceffive years,
From early youth to life's laft childhood errs;
No fooner born but proves a foe to truth,
For infant Reafon is o'erpow'r'd in youth.
The cheats of fenfe will half our learning fhare, 5
And preconceptions all our knowledge are.
Reafon, 'tis true, fhould over fenfe prefide,
Correct our notions, and our judgments guide;
But falfe opinions, rooted in the mind,
Hoodwink the foul, and keep our reafon blind. 10
Reafon's a taper which but faintly burns;
A languid flame, that glows and dies by turns:
We fee't a little while, and but a little way;
We travel by its light, as men by day;
But quickly dying, it forfakes us foon. 15
Like morning-ftars, that never ftay till noon.
  The foul can fcarce above the body rife,
And all we fee is with corporeal eyes.
Life now does fcarce one glimpfe of light difplay;
We mourn in darknefs, and defpair of day : 20
That nat'ral light, once drefs'd with orient beams,
Is now diminifh'd, and a twilight feems;
A mifcellaneous compofition, made
Of night and day, of funfhine and of fhade.

Thro' an uncertain medium now we look,   25
And find that falfehood which for truth we took :
So rays projected from the eaftern fkies
Shew the falfe day before the fun can rife.
  That little knowledge now which man obtains,
From outward objects and from fenfe he gains :   30
He, like a wretched flave, muft plod and fweat,
By day muft toil, by night that toil repeat ;
And yet at laft what little fruit he gains!
A beggar's harveft, glean'd with mighty pains.
  The paffions ftill predominant will rule,   35
Ungovern'd, rude, not bred in Reafon's fchool ;
Our underftanding they with darknefs fill,
Caufe ftrong corruptions, and pervert the will :
On thefe the foul, as on fome flowing tide,
Muft fit, and on the raging billows ride,   40
Hurry'd away ; for how can be withftood
Th' impetuous torrent of the boiling blood ?
Be gone, falfe hopes! for all our learning's vain ;
Can we be free where thefe the rule maintain ?
Thefe are the tools of knowledge which we ufe ;   45
The fpirits heated will ftrange things produce.
Tell me who e'er the paffions could control,
Or from the body difengage the foul :
Till this is done our beft purfuits are vain
To conquer truth, and unmix'd knowledge gain.   50
Thro' all the bulky volumes of the dead,
And thro' thofe books that modern times have bred,

I

With pain we travel, as thro' moorifh ground,
Where fcarce one ufeful plant is ever found;
O'er-run with errors, which fo thick appear, 55
Our fearch proves vain, no fpark of truth is there.
    What's all the noify jargon of the fchools
But idle nonfenfe of laborious fools,
Who fetter Reafon with perplexing rules?
What in Aquinas' bulky works are found 60
Does not enlighten Reafon, but confound.
Who travels Scotus' fwelling tomes fhall find
A cloud of darknefs rifing on the mind.
In controverted points can Reafon fway,
When paffion or conceit ftill hurries us away? 65
Thus his new notions Sherlock would inftill,
And clear the greateft myfteries at will,
But by unlucky wit perplex'd them more,
And made them darker than they were before.
South foon oppos'd him, out of Chriftian zeal, 70
Shewing how well he could difpute and rail.
How fhall we e'er difcover which is right,
When both fo eagerly maintain the fight?
Each does the other's arguments deride;
Each has the church and Scripture on his fide: 75
The fharp ill-natur'd combat's but a jeft:
Both may be wrong; one, perhaps, errs the leaft.
How fhall we know which Articles are true,
The Old one's of the charch, or Burnet's New?

G

In paths uncertain and unfafe he treads,   80
Who blindly follows others' fertile heads.
What fure, what certain, mark have we to know
The right or wrong 'twixt Burgefs, Wake, and Howe!

    Should untun'd Nature crave the medic art,
What health can that contentious tribe impart ?   85
Ev'ry phyfician writes a diff'rent bill,
And gives no other reafon but his will.
No longer boaft your art, ye impious race !
Let wars 'twixt alcalies and acids ceafe,
And proud G—ll with Colbatch be at peace.   90
Gibbons and Radcliffe do but rarely guefs ;
To-day they've good, to-morrow no fuccefs.
Ev'n Garth and Maurus * fometimes fhall prevail,
When Gibfon, learned Hannes, and Tyfon, fail.   94
And, more than once, we've feen that blund'ring
Miffing the gout, by chance has hit the ftone; [S—ne,
The patient does the lucky error find ;
A cure he works, tho' not the cure defign'd.

    Cuftom, the world's great idol, we adore,
And knowing this we feek to know no more.   100
What education did at firft receive,
Our ripen'd age confirms us to believe :
The careful nurfe and prieft are all we need,
To learn opinions and our country's creed :
The parents' precepts early are inftill'd,   105
And fpoil the man, while they inftruct the child.

        * Sir Richard Blackmore.

To what hard fate is human-kind betray'd,
When thus implicit faith's a virtue made,
When education more than truth prevails,
And nought is current but what custom seals? 110
Thus from the time we firſt began to know
We live and learn, but not the wiſer grow.

We ſeldom uſe our liberty aright,
Nor judge of things by univerſal light;
Our prepoſſeſſions and affections bind   115
The ſoul in chains, and lord it o'er the mind;
And if ſelf-int'reſt be but in the caſe,
Our unexamin'd principles may paſs.
Good Heav'ns! that man ſhould thus himſelf deceive,
To learn on credit, and on truſt believe!   120
Better the mind no notions had retain'd,
But ſtill a fair unwritten blank remain'd:
For now, who truth from falſehood would diſcern,
Muſt firſt diſrobe the mind, and all unlearn.
Errors, contracted in unmindful youth,   125
When once remov'd, will ſmooth the way to truth.
To diſpoſſeſs the child the mortal lives,
But death approaches ere the man arrives.

Thoſe who would learning's glorious kingdom find,
The dear-bought purchaſe of the trading mind, 130
From many dangers muſt themſelves acquit,
And more than Scylla and Charybdis meet.
Oh! what an ocean muſt be voyag'd o'er
To gain a proſpect of the ſhining ſhore?

Refifting rocks oppofe th'inquiring foul,   135
And adverfe waves retard it as they roll.

   Does not that foolifh deference we pay
To men that liv'd long fince our paffage ftay?
What odd prepoft'rous paths at firft we tread,
And learn to walk by ftumbling on the dead?   140
Firft we a blefling from the grave implore,
Worfhip old urns, and monuments adore;
The rev'rend fage, with vaft efteem, we prize;
He liv'd long fince, and muft be wondrous wife.
Thus are we debtors to the famous dead   145
For all thofe errors which their fancies bred:
Errors indeed! for real knowledge ftay'd
With thofe firft times, not farther was convey'd,
While light opinions are much lower brought,
For on the waves of ignorance they float;   150
But folid truth fcarce ever gains the fhore,
So foon it finks, and ne'er emerges more.

   Suppofe thofe many dreadful dangers paft,
Will knowledge dawn, and blefs the mind at laft?
Ah! no; 'tis now environ'd from our eyes,   155
Hides all its charms, and undifcover'd lies.
Truth, like a fingle point, efcapes the fight,
And claims attention to perceive it right:
But what refembles truth is foon defcry'd,
Spread like a furface and expanded wide.   160
The firft man rarely, very rarely, finds
The tedious fearch of long inquiring minds:

But yet what's worfe, we know not when we err;
What mark does truth, what bright diftinction, bear?
How do we know that what we know is true?   165
How fhall we falfehood fly, and truth purfue?
Let none then here his certain knowledge boaft,
'Tis all but probability at moft:
This is the eafy purchafe of the mind,
The vulgar's treafure, which we foon may find: 170
But truth lies hid, and ere we can explore
The glitt'ring gem, our fleeting life is o'er.   172

PINDARIC ESSAYS.

A PROSPECT OF DEATH.

A PINDARIC ESSAY.

-------- Sed omnes una manet nox,
Et calcanda femel via lethi.   HOR.

I.

SINCE we can die but once, and after death
Our ftate no alteration knows,
But when we have refign'd our breath
Th' immortal fpirit goes
To endlefs joys or everlafting woes,   5
Wife is the man who labours to fecure
That mighty and important ftake,
And by all methods ftrives to make
His paffage fafe and his reception fure.
Merely to die no man of reafon fears,   10
For certainly we muft,
As we are born, return to duft;
'Tis the laft point of many ling'ring years:
But whither then we go,
Whither we fain would know;   15
But human underftanding cannot fhow:

This makes us tremble, and creates
Strange apprehenfions in the mind,
Fills it with reftlefs doubts and wild debates
Concerning what we living cannot find.   20
None know what death is but the dead,
Therefore we all, by nature, dying dread,
As a ftrange doubtful way we know not how to tread.

II.

When to the margin of the grave we come,
And fcarce have one black painful hour to live,   25
No hopes, no profpect, of a kind reprieve
To ftop our fpeedy paffage to the tomb,
How moving and how mournful is the fight!
How wondrous pitiful, how wondrous fad!
Where then is refuge, where is comfort, to be had   30
In the dark minutes of the dreadful night
To cheer our drooping fouls for their amazing flight?
Feeble and languifhing in bed we lie,
Defpairing to recover, void of reft,
Wifhing for death, and yet afraid to die;   35
Terrors and doubts diftract our breaft,
With mighty agonies and mighty pains oppreft.

III.

Our face is moiften'd with a clammy fweat,
Faint and irregular the pulfes beat;
The blood unactive grows,   40
And thickens as it flows,
Depriv'd of all its vigour, all its vital heat:

Our dying eyes roll heavily about,
Their light juft going out,
And for fome kind affiftance call ;   45
But pity, ufelefs pity, 's all
Our weeping friends can give
Or we receive ;
Tho' their defires are great their pow'rs are fmall.
The tongue's unable to declare   50
The pains and griefs, the miferies, we bear,
How infupportable our torments are.
Mufic no more delights our deaf'ning ears,
Reftores our joys, or diffipates our fears,
But all is melancholy, all is fad,   55
In robes of deepeft mourning clad ;
For ev'ry faculty and ev'ry fenfe
Partakes the woe of this dire exigence.

IV.

Then we are fenfible, too late,
'Tis no advantage to be rich or great ;   60
For all the fulfome pride and pageantry of ftate
No confolation brings ;
Riches and honours then are ufelefs things,
Taftelefs or bitter all,
And like the book which the Apoftle ate,   65
To the ill-judging palate fweet,
But turn at laft to naufeoufnefs and gall.
Nothing will then our drooping fpirits cheer
But the remembrance of good actions paft :
Virtue's a joy that will for ever laft,   70

And makes pale Death lefs terrible appear,
Takes out his baneful fting, and palliates our fear.
In the dark antichamber of the grave
What would we give (ev'n all we have,
All that our care and induftry hath gain'd,   75
All that our policy, our fraud, our art, obtain'd)
Could we recall thofe fatal hours again
Which we confum'd in fenfelefs vanities,
Ambitious follies, or luxurious cafe;
For then they urge our terrors and increafe our pain.80
V.
Our friends and relatives ftand weeping by,
Diffolv'd in tears, to fee us die,
And plunge into the deep abyfs of wide eternity.
In vain they mourn, in vain they grieve,
Their forrows cannot ours relieve: 85
They pity our deplorable eftate;
But what, alas! can pity do
To foften the decrees of Fate?
Befides, the fentence is irrevocable too.
All their endeavours to preferve our breath,   90
Tho' they do unfuccefsful prove,
Shew us how much, how tenderly, they love,
But cannot cut off the entail of death.
Mournful they look, and crowd about our bed;
One, with officious hafte,   95
Brings us a cordial we want fenfe to tafte;
Another foftly raifes up our head;

This wipes away the fweat; that, fighing, cries,
" See what convulfions, what ftrong agonies,
" Both foul and body undergo!   100
" His pains no intermiffion know;
" For ev'ry gafp of air he draws returns in fighs."
Each would his kind affiftance lend
To fave his dear relation or his dearer friend,
But ftill in vain with Deftiny they all contend. 105

VI.

Our father, pale with grief and watching grown,
Takes our cold hand in his, and cries, " Adieu!
" Adieu, my child! now I muft follow you;"
Then weeps, and gently lays it down.
Our fons, who in their tender years   110
Were objects of our cares and of our fears,
Come trembling to our bed, and, kneeling, cry,
" Blefs us, O Father! now before you die;
" Blefs us, and be you blefs'd to all eternity."
Our friend, whom equal to ourfelves we love,   115
Compaffionate and kind,
Cries, " Will you leave me here behind?
" Without me fly to the blefs'd feats above?
" Without me, did I fay? ah! no;
" Without thy friend thou canft not go;   120
" For tho' thou leav'ft me grov'lling here below,
" My foul with thee fhall upward fly,
" And bear thy fpirit company
" 'Thro' the bright paffage of the yielding fky.

" Ev'n death, that parts thee from thyfelf, fhall be
" Incapable to feparate   126
" (For 'tis not in the pow'r of Fate)
" My friend, my beft, my deareft, friend and me ;
" But fince it muft be fo, farewell,
" For ever! No ; for we fhall meet again,   130
" And live like gods, tho' now we die like men,
" In the eternal regions where juft fpirits dwell.

VII.

The foul, unable longer to maintain
The fruitlefs and unequal ftrife,
Finding her weak endeavours vain   135
To keep the counterfcarpe of life,
By flow degrees retires towards the heart,
And fortifies that little fort
With all the kind artilleries of art,
Botanic legions guarding ev'ry port;   140
But Death, whofe arms no mortal can repel,
A formal fiege difdains to lay,
Summons his fierce battalions to the fray,
And in a minute ftorms the feeble citadel.
Sometimes we may capitulate, and he   145
Pretends to make a folid peace ;
But 'tis all fham, all artifice,
That we may negligent and carelefs be;
For if his armies are withdrawn to-day,
And we believe no danger near,   150
But all is peaceable and all is clear,
His troops return fome unfufpected way;

While in the foft embrace of Sleep we lie,
The fecret murd'rers ftab us and we die.

VIII.

Since our firft parents' fall   155
Inevitable death defcends on all,
A portion none of human race can mifs;
But that which makes it fweet or bitter is
The fears of mifery or certain hopes of blifs:
For when th' impenitent and wicked die,   160
Loaded with crimes and infamy,
If any fenfe at that fad time remains,
They feel amazing terrors, mighty pains,
The carneft of that vaft ftupendous woe
Which they to all eternity muft undergo,   165
Confin'd in hell with everlafting chains.
Infernal fpirits hover in the air,
Like rav'nous wolves, to feize upon the prey,
And hurry the departed fouls away
To the dark receptacles of defpair,   170
Where they muft dwell till that tremendous day
When the loud trump fhall call them to appear
Before a Judge moft terrible and moft fevere,
By whofe juft fentence they muft go
To everlafting pains and endlefs woe.   175

IX.

But the good man, whofe foul is pure,
Unfpotted, regular, and free

From all the ugly ftains of luft and villany,
Of mercy and of pardon fure,
Looks thro' the darknefs of the gloomy night,   180
And fees the dawning of a glorious day ;
Sees crowds of angels ready to convey
His foul whene'er fhe takes her flight
To the furprifing manfions of immortal light :
Then the celeftial guards around him ftand,   185
Nor fuffer the black demons of the air
T" oppofe his paffage to the promis'd land,
Or terrify his thoughts with wild defpair,
But all is calm within, and all without is fair.
His pray'rs, his charity, his virtues, prefs   190
To plead for mercy when he wants it moft ;
Not one of all the happy number's loft,
And thofe bright advocates ne'er want fuccefs :
But when the foul's releas'd from dull mortality,
She paffes up in triumph thro' the fky,   195
Where fhe 's united to a glorious throng
Of angels, who, with a celeftial fong,
Congratulate her conqueft as fhe flies along.

X.

If, therefore, all muft quit the ftage,
When or how foon we cannot know,   200
But late or early we are fure to go,
In the frefh bloom of youth or wither'd age,
We cannot take too fedulous a care
In this important grand affair,

For as we die we muſt remain;   205
Hereafter all our hopes are vain,
To make our peace with Heav'n, or to return again.
The Heathen, who no better underſtood
Than what the light of Nature taught, declar'd
No future miſery could be prepar'd   210
For the ſincere, the merciful, the good;
But if there was a ſtate of reſt,
They ſhould with the ſame happineſs be bleſt
As the immortal gods, if gods there were, poſſeſt.
We have the promiſe of eternal Truth,   215
Thoſe who live well, and pious paths purſue,
To man and to their Maker true,
Let 'em expire in age or youth,
Can never miſs
Their way to everlaſting bliſs;   220
But from a world of miſery and care
To manſions of eternal eaſe repair,
Where joy in full perfection flows,
And in an endleſs circle moves
Thro' the vaſt round of beatific love,
Which no ceſſation knows.   226

GENERAL CONFLAGRATION,

AND

ENSUING JUDGMENT.

A PINDARIC ESSAY.

Effe quoque in fatis, reminifcitur, affore tempus
Quo mare, quo tellus, correptaque regia cœli
Ardeat, et mundi moles operofa laboret.　　OVID. MET.

I.

Now the black days of univerfal doom,
Which wondrous prophefies foretold, are come:
What ftrong convulfions, what ftupendous woe,
Muft finking Nature undergo,
Amidft the dreadful wreck and final overthrow!　　5
Methinks I hear her, confcious of her fate,
With fearful groans and hideous cries
Fill the prefaging fkies,
Unable to fupport the weight
Or of the prefent or approaching miferies.　　10
Methinks I hear her fummon all
Her guilty offspring, raving with defpair,
And trembling, cry aloud, " Prepare,
" Ye fublunary Pow'rs! t' attend my funeral."

II.

See! fee the tragical portents,　　15
Thofe difmal harbingers of dire events,

Loud thunders roar, and darting lightnings fly
'Thro' the dark-concave of the troubled sky;
The fiery ravage is begun, the end is nigh.
See how the glaring meteors blaze!   20
Like baleful torches, O, they come,
To light diffolving Nature to her tomb!
And, scatt'ring round their pestilential rays,
Strike the affrighted nations with a wild amaze.
Vast sheets of flame and globes of fire,   .   25
By an impetuous wind, are driven
Thro' all the regions of th' inferior heav'n,
Till hid in sulph'rous smoke they seemingly expire.

III.

Sad and amazing 'tis to see
What mad confusion rages over all   ·   30
This scorching ball!
No country is exempt, no nation free,
But each partakes the epidemic misery.
What dismal havoc of mankind is made
By wars, and pestilence, and dearth,   ···   35
Thro' the whole mournful earth,
Which with a murd'ring fury they invade,
Forsook by Providence and all propitious aid!
Whilst fiends let loose their utmost rage employ
To ruin all things here below;   40
Their malice and revenge no limits know,
But in the universal tumult all destroy.

IV.

Diſtracted mortals from their cities fly
For ſafety to their champaign ground;
But there no ſafety can be found;   45
The vengeance of an angry Deity,
With unrelenting fury, does incloſe them round:
And whilſt for mercy ſome aloud implore
The God they ridicul'd before;
And others, raving with their woe,   50
(For hunger, thirſt, deſpair, they undergo)
Blaſpheme and curſe the pow'r they ſhould adore:
The earth, parch'd up with drought, her jaws extends,
And op'ning wide a dreadful tomb,
The howling multitude at once deſcends   55
Together all into her burning womb.

V.

The trembling Alps abſcond their aged heads
In mighty pillars of infernal ſmoke,
Which from their bellowing caverns broke,
And ſuffocates whole nations where it ſpreads.   60
Sometimes the fire within divides
The maſſy rivers of thoſe ſecret chains
Which hold together their prodigious ſides,
And hurls the ſhatter'd rocks o'er all the plains,
While towns and cities, ev'ry thing below,   65
Is overwhelm'd with the ſame burſt of woe.

VI.

No fhow'rs defcend from the malignant fky
To cool the burning of the thirfty field;
The trees no leaves, no grafs the meadows, yield,
But all is barren, all is dry.   70
The little rivulets no more
To larger ftreams their tribute pay,
Nor to the ebbing ocean they,
Which, with a ftrange unufual roar,   74
Forfakes thofe ancient bounds it would have pafs'd be-
And to the monftrous deep in vain retires: [fore,
For ev'n the deep itfelf is not fecure,
But, belching fubterraneous fires,
Increafes ftill the fcalding calenture,
Which neither earth, nor air, nor water, can endure.

VII.

The fun, by fympathy, concern'd   81
At thofe convulfions, pangs, and agonies,
Which on the whole creation feize,
Is to fubftantial darknefs turn'd.
The neighb'ring moon, as if a purple flood   85
O'erflow'd her tott'ring orb, appears
Like a huge mafs of black corrupting blood,
For fhe herfelf a diffolution fears.
The larger planets, which once fhone fo bright
With the reflected rays of borrow'd light,   90
Shook from their centre, without motion lie
Unwieldy globes of folid night,
And ruinous lumber of the fky.

VIII.

Amidst this dreadful hurricane of woes
(For fire, confusion, horror, and despair,   95
Fill ev'ry region of the tortur'd earth and air)
The great archangel his loud trumpet blows;
At whose amazing sound fresh agonies
Upon expiring Nature seize:
For now she'll in few minutes know   100
'Th' ultimate event and fate of all below.
Awake, ye dead! awake! he cries;
(For all must come)
All that had human breath, arise,
To hear your last unalterable doom!   105

IX.

At this the ghastly tyrant, who had sway'd
So many thousand ages uncontroll'd,
No longer could his sceptre hold,
But gave up all, and was himself a captive made.
The scatter'd particles of human clay,   110
Which in the silent grave's dark chambers lay,
Resume their pristine forms again,
And now from mortal grow immortal men.
Stupendous energy of sacred pow'r!
Which can collect, wherever cast,   ·   115
The smallest atoms, and that shape restore
Which they had worn so many years before,
That thro' strange accidents and num'rous changes
          past.

X.

See how the joyful angels fly
From ev'ry quarter of the sky,   120
To gather and to convoy all
The pious sons of human race
To one capacious place,
Above the confines of this flaming ball.
See with what tenderness and love they bear   125
Thofe righteous fouls thro' the tumultuous air,
Whilft the ungodly ftand below,
Raging with fhame, confufion, and defpair,
Amidft the burning overthrow,
Expecting fiercer torments and acuter woe.   130
Round them infernal fpirits howling fly;
" O horror! curfes! tortures! chains!" they cry,
And roar aloud with execrable blafphemy.

XI.

Hark! how the daring fons of Infamy,
Who once diffolv'd in pleafures lay,   135
And laugh'd at this tremendous day,
To rocks and mountains now to hide 'em cry;
But rocks and mountains all in afhes lie.
Their fhame's fo mighty, and fo ftrong their fear,
That, rather than appear   140
Before a God incens'd, they would be hurl'd
Amongft the burning ruins of the world,
And lie conceal'd, if poffible, for ever there.
Time was they would not own a Deity,

Nor after death a future state;   145
But now, by sad experience, find too late,
There is, and terrible to that degree,
That rather than behold his face they'd cease to be.
And sure 'tis better, if Heav'n would give consent,
To have no being; but they must remain   150
For ever, and for ever be in pain:
O inexpreffible, stupendous punishment,
Which cannot be endur'd, yet must be underwent!

XII.

But now the eastern skies expanding wide,
The glorious Judge omnipotent descends,   155
And to the sublunary world his paffage bends,
Where, cloath'd with human nature, he did once reside.
Round him the bright ethereal armies fly,
And loud triumphant hallelujahs sing,
With songs of praise, and hymns of victory,   160
To their celestial King;
"All glory, pow'r, dominion, majesty,
"Now, and for everlasting ages, be
"To the essential One and co-eternal Three.
"Perish that world, as 'tis decreed,   165
"Which saw the God incarnate bleed!
"Perish, by thy almighty vengeance, those
"Who durst thy person or thy laws expose;
"The curfed refuse of mankind, and hell's proud seed.
"Now to the unbelieving nations show   170
"Thou art a God from all eternity;
"Not titular, or but by office so;

" And let 'em the myfterious union fee
" Of human nature with the Deity."

XIII.

With mighty tranfports, yet with awful fears,   175
The good behold this glorious fight;
Their God in all his majefty appears,
Ineffable, amazing bright,
And feated on a throne of everlafting light.
Round the tribunal, next to the moft High,   180
In facred difcipline and order, ftand
The peers and princes of the fky,
As they excel in glory or command.
Upon the right hand that illuftrious crowd,
In the white bofom of a fhining cloud,   185
Whofe fouls, abhorring all ignoble crimes,
Did, with a fteady courfe, purfue
His holy precepts in the worft of times,
Maugre what earth or hell, what men or devils,
        could do.
And now that God they did to death adore,   190
For whom fuch torments and fuch pains they bore,
Returns to place them on thofe thrones above,
Where, undifturb'd, uncloy'd, they will poffefs
Divine fubftantial happinefs,
Unbounded as his pow'r, and lafting as his love. 195

XIV.

" Go, bring," the Judge impartial, frowning, cries,
" Thofe rebel fons who did my laws defpife;

" Whom neither threats nor promifes could move,
" Not all my fufferings, nor all my love,
" To fave themfelves from everlafting miferies." 200
At this ten millions of archangels flew
Swifter than lightning, or the fwifteft thought,
And lefs than in an inftant brought
The wretched, curs'd, infernal, crew;
Who, with diftorted afpects, come   205
To hear their fad intolerable doom.
" Alas!" they cry, " one beam of mercy fhow,
" Thou all-forgiving Deity!
" To pardon crimes is natural to thee;
" Crufh us to nothing, or fufpend our woe: 210
" But if it cannot, cannot be,
" And we muft go into a gulf of fire,
" (For who can with Omnipotence contend?)
" Grant, for thou art a God, it may at laft expire,
" And all our tortures have an end.   215
" Eternal burnings, O! we cannot bear,
" 'Tho' now our bodies too immortal are.
" Let 'em be pungent to the laft degree;
" And let our pains innumerable be;
" But let 'em not extend to all eternity!"   220

XV.

Lo! now there does no place remain
For penitence and tears, but all
Muft by their actions ftand or fall:
To hope for pity is in vain;
The die is caft, and not to be recall'd again.   225

Two mighty books are by two angels brought:
In this, impartially recorded, stands
The law of Nature, and divine commands;
In that, each action, word, and thought,
Whate'er was said in secret, or in secret wrought. 230
Then first the virtuous and the good,
Who all the fury of temptation stood,
And bravely pafs'd thro' ignominy, chains, and blood,
Attended by their guardian angels, come
To the tremendous bar of final doom. 235
In vain the grand Accufer, railing, brings
A long indictment of enormous things,
Whofe guilt wip'd off by penitential tears,
And their Redeemer's blood and agonies,
No more to their aftonifhment appears, 240
But in the fecret womb of dark Oblivion lies.

XVI.

" Come now, my Friends!" he cries; " ye fons of Grace,
" Partakers once of all my wrongs and fhame,
" Defpis'd and hated for my name;
" Come to your Saviour's and your God's embrace!
" Afcend, and thofe bright diadems poffefs, 246
" For you by my eternal Father made
" Ere the foundation of the world was laid;
" And that furprifing happinefs,
" Immenfe as my own Godhead, and will ne'er be lefs.
" For when I languifhing in prifon lay, 251
" Naked, and ftarv'd almoft for want of bread,

" You did your kindly vifits pay,
" Both cloath'd my body, and my hunger fed.
" Weary'd with ficknefs, or opprefs'd with grief,
" Your hand was always ready to fupply;   256
" Whene'er I wanted, you were always by
" To fhare my forrows or to give relief.
" In all diftrefs fo tender was your love,
" I could no anxious trouble bear;   .   260
" No black misfortune or vexatious care,
" But you were ftill impatient to remove,
" And mourn'd your charitable hand fhould unfuc-
" All this you did, tho' not to me   {cefsful prove.
" In perfon, yet to mine in mifery;   265
" And fhall for ever live
" In all the glories that a God can give,
" Or a created being's able to receive."
XVII.
At this the architects divine on high
Innumerable thrones of glory raife,   270
On which they, in appointed order, place
The human coheirs of eternity,
And with united hymns the God incarnate praife:
" O holy, holy, holy Lord,
" Eternal God, almighty One,   275
" Be thou for ever, and be thou alone,
" By all thy creatures conftantly ador'd!
" Ineffable coequal Three,
" Who from nonentity gave birth

I

" To angels and to men, to heav'n and to earth, 280
" Yet always waſt thyſelf, and wilt for ever be.
" But for thy mercy we had ne'er poſſeſt
" Theſe thrones, and this immenſe felicity
" Could ne'er have been ſo infinitely bleſt :
" Therefore all glory, pow'r, dominion, majeſty,
" To thee, O Lamb of God! to thee   286
" For ever, longer than for ever, be."

XVIII.

Then the incarnate Godhead turns his face
To thoſe upon the left, and cries,
(Almighty vengeance flaſhing in his eyes)   290
" Ye impious, unbelieving race!
" To thoſe eternal torments go,
" Prepar'd for thoſe rebellious ſons of light,
" In burning darkneſs and in flaming night,
" Which ſhall no limit or ceſſation know,   295
" But always are extreme, and always will be ſo."
The final ſentence paſs'd, a dreadful cloud
Incloſing all the miſerable crowd,
A mighty hurricane of thunder roſe,
And hurl'd 'em all into a lake of fire,   300
Which never, never, never, can expire,
The vaſt abyſs of endleſs woes ;
Whilſt with their God the righteous mount on high,
In glorious triumph paſſing thro' the ſky,
To joys immenſe, and everlaſting ecſtaſy. . .   305

DIES NOVISSIMA:

OR,

THE LAST EPIPHANY.

A PINDARIC ODE.

On Chrift's fecond appearance to judge the world.

I.

Adieu, ye toyifh reeds! that once could pleafe
My fofter lips, and lull my cares to eafe :
Be gone; I'll wafte no more vain hours with you;
And fmiling Sylvia too, adieu ;
A brighter pow'r invokes my Mufe,   5
And loftier thoughts and raptures does infufe.
See! beck'ning from yon' cloud, he ftands,
And promifes affiftance with his hands.
I feel the heavy rolling God,
Incumbent, revel in his frail abode.   10
How my breaft heaves and pulfes beat!
I fink, I fink, beneath the furious heat ;
The weighty blifs o'erwhelms my breaft,
And overflowing joys profufely wafte.
Some nobler bard, O facred Pow'r! infpire,   15
Or foul more large, th' elapfes to receive ;
And, brighter yet, to catch the fire,
And each gay following charm from death to fave !
—In vain the fuit—the God inflames my breaft;
I rave, with ecftafies oppreft ;.   20

I rise, the mountains leſſen and retire;
And now I mix, unſing'd, with elemental fire;
The leading Deity I have in view,
Nor mortal knows as yet what wonders will enſue.

II.

We paſs'd thro' regions of unſully'd light;   25
I gaz'd and ſicken'd at the blisful ſight;
A ſhudd'ring paleneſs ſeiz'd my look;
At laſt the peſt flew off, and thus I ſpoke:
" Say, ſacred Guide! ſhall this bright clime
" Survive the fatal teſt of time,   30
" Or periſh with our mortal globe below,
" When yon' ſun no longer ſhines?".
Straight I finiſh'd——veiling low:
The viſionary Pow'r rejoins,
" "Tis not for you to aſk, nor mine to ſay,   35
" The niceties of that tremendous day.
" Know, when o'er-jaded Time his round has run,
" And finiſh'd are the radiant journies of the ſun,
" The great deciſive morn ſhall riſe,
" And heav'n's bright Judge appear in op'ning ſkies;
" Eternal grace and juſtice he'll beſtow   41
" On all the trembling world below."

III.

He ſaid; I mus'd; and thus return'd:
" What enſigns, courteous Stranger! tell,
" Shall the brooding day reveal?"   45
He anſwer'd mild——

" Already, ſtupid with their crimes,

" Blind mortals proſtrate to their idols lie :

" Such were the boding times,

" Ere ruin blaſted from the ſluicy ſky ;　　　　50

" Diſſolv'd they lay in fulſome eaſe,

" And revell'd in luxuriant peace ;

" In Bacchanals they did their hours conſume,

" And Bacchanals led on their ſwift advancing doom.

IV.

" Adult'rate chriſts already riſe,　　　　55

" And dare t' aſſwage the angry ſkies ;

" Erratic throngs their Saviour's blood deny,

" And from the croſs, alas ! he does neglected ſigh ;

" The antichriſtian pow'r has rais'd his hydra head,

" And ruin, only leſs than Jeſus' health, does ſpread.

" So long the gore thro' poiſon'd veins has flow'd, 61

" That ſcarcely ranker is a Fury's blood ;

" Yet ſpecious artifice and fair diſguiſe

" The monſter's ſhape and curs'd deſign belies :

" A fiend's black venom in an angel's mien　　　65

" He quaffs, and ſcatters the contagious ſpleen ;

" Straight, when he finiſhes his lawleſs reign,

" Nature ſhall paint the ſhining ſcene,

" Quick as the lightning which inſpires the train.

V.

" Forward Confuſion ſhall provoke the fray,　　70

" And Nature from her ancient order ſtray ;

" Black tempests, gath'ring from the seas around,
" In horrid ranges shall advance;
" And as they march, in thickest sables drown'd,
" The rival thunder from the clouds shall sound, 75
" And lightnings join the fearful dance:
" The blust'ring armies o'er the skies shall spread,
" And universal terror shed;
" Loud issuing peals and rising sheets of smoke
" Th' encumber'd region of the air shall choke; 80
" The noisy main shall lash the suff'ring shore,
" And from the rocks the breaking billows roar;
" Black thunder bursts, blue lightning burns,
" And melting worlds to heaps of ashes turns;
" The forests shall beneath the tempest bend, 85
" And rugged winds the nodding cedars rend.

VI.

" Reverse all Nature's web shall run,
" And spotless misrule all around
" Order, its flying foe, confound, 89
" Whilst backward all the threads shall haste to be un-
" Triumphant Chaos, with his oblique wand [spun.
" (The wand with which, ere time begun,
" His wand'ring slaves he did command,
" And made 'em scamper right, and in rude ranges
" The hostile harmony shall chace, [run)
" And as the nymph resigns her place, 96
" And, panting, to the neighb'ring refuge flies,
" The formless ruffian slarghters with his eyes,

" And following, ſtorms the perching dame's retreat,
" Adding the terror of his threat ; 100
" The globe ſhall faintly tremble round,
" And backward jolt, diſtorted with the wound.

VII.

" Swath'd in ſubſtantial ſhrowds of night,
" The ſick'ning ſun ſhall from the world retire,
" Stripp'd of his dazzling robes of fire, 105
" Which, dangling, once ſhed round a laviſh flood of
" No frail eclipſe, but all eſſential ſhade, [light ;
" Not yielding to primeval gloom,
" Whilſt day was yet an embryo in the womb ; 109
" Nor glimm'ring in its ſource with ſilver ſtreamers
" A jetty mixture of the darkneſs ſpread [play'd,
" O'er murm'ring Egypt's head ;
" And that which angels drew
" O'er Nature's face when Jeſus dy'd,
" Which ſleeping ghoſts for this miſtook, 115
" And riſing, off their hanging fun'rals ſhook,
" And fleeting paſs'd, expos'd their bloodleſs breaſts
      to view,
" Yet find it not ſo dark, and to their dormitories glide.

VIII.

" Now bolder fires appear,
" And o'er the palpable obſcurement ſport, 120
" Glaring and gay as falling Lucifer,
" Yet mark'd with fate, as when he fled th' ethereal
      court,

" And plung'd into the op'ning gulf of night :
" A fabre of immortal flame I bore,   124
" And with this arm his flour'fhing plume I tore,
" And ftraight the fiend retreated from the fight.

IX.

" Mean-time the lambent prodigies on high   .
" Take gamefome meafures in the fky;
" Joy'd with his future feaft the thunder roars
" In chorus to th' enormous harmony,   . .130
" And halloos to his offspring from fulphureous ftores,
" Applauding how they tilt and how they fly,
" And their each nimble turn and radiant embaffy.

X.

" The moon turns paler at the fight,
" And all the blazing orbs deny their light;   135
" The lightning with its livid tail,   .   .
" A train of glitt'ring terrors draws behind,
" Which o'er the trembling world prevail;
" Wing'd and blown on by ftorms of wind,
" They fhew the hideous leaps on either hand   140
" Of Night, that fpreads her ebon curtains-round,
" And there erects her royal ftand,
" In fev'n-fold winding jet her confcious temples

XI.   [bound.

" The ftars next, ftarting from their fphere,
" In giddy revolutions leap and bound;   145
" Whilft this with double fury glares,
" And meditates new wars,
" And wheels in fportive gyres around,

" Its neighbour shall advance to fight,
" And while each offers to enlarge its right, 150
" The gen'ral ruin shall increase,
" And banish all the votaries of peace.
" No more the stars, with paler beams,
" Shall tremble o'er the midnight streams,
" But travel downward to behold 155
" What mimics 'em so twinkling there,
" And, like Narciffus, as they gain more near,
" For the lov'd image straight expire,
" And agonize in warm desire,
" Or flake their luft as in the stream they roll. 160

XII.

" Whilft the world burns, and all the orbs below
" In their viperous ruins glow,
" They fink, and, unfupported, leave the fkies, [noife:
" Which fall abrupt, and tell their torment in the
" Then fee th' almighty Judge, fedate and bright, 165
" Cloath'd in imperial robes of light!
" His wings the wind, rough storms the chariot bear,
" And nimbler harbingers before him fly,
" And with officious rudenefs brufh the air;
" Halt as he halts, then doubling in their flight, 170
" In horrid fport with one another vie,
" And leave behind quick-winding tracks of light;
" Then urging, to their ranks they clofe,
" And fhiv'ring, left they ftart, a failing caravah
    compofe.

XIII.

" The mighty Judge rides in tempeftuous ftate,
" Whilft mighty guards his orders wait :   176
" His waving veftments fhine
" Bright as the fun, which lately did its beams refign,
" And burnifh'd wreaths of light fhall make his form
   divine.
" Strong beams of majefty around his temples play,
" And the tranfcendent gaiety of his face allay : 181
" His Father's rev'rend characters he'll wear,
" And both o'erwhelm with light and overawe with
" Myriads of angels fhall be there, · · [fear.
" And I, perhaps, clofe the tremendous rear : 185
" Angels, the firft and faireft fons of day,
" Clad with eternal youth, and as their veftments gay,

XIV.

" Nor for magnificence alone,
" To brighten and enlarge the pageant fcene,
" Shall we encircle his more dazzling throne,   90
" And fwell the luftre of his pompous train :
" The nimble minifters of blifs or woe
" We fhall attend, and fave or deal the blow,
" As he admits to joy or bids to pain.

XV.

" The welcome news   195
" Thro' ev'ry angel's breaft frefh raptures fhall diffufe.
" The day is come   [doom :
" When Satan, with his pow'rs, fhall fink to endlefs

" No more fhall we his hoftile troops purfue
" From cloud to cloud, nor the long fight renew. 200
XVI.

" Then Raphael, big with life, the trump fhall found;
" From falling fpheres the joyful mufic fhall rebound,
" And feas and fhores fhall catch and propagate it
    round:
" Louder he'll blow, and it fhall fpeak more fhrill,
" Than when, from Sinai's hill,   205
" In thunder, thro' the horrid redd'ning fmoke
" Th' Almighty fpoke.
" We'll fhout around with martial joy,
" And thrice the vaulted fkies fhall rend, and thrice our
" Then firft th' archangel's voice aloud [fhouts reply.
" Shall cheerfully falute the day and throng,   211
" And hallelujahs fill the crowd,
" And I, perhaps, fhall clofe the fong.
XVII.

" From its long fleep all human race fhall rife,   214
" And fee the morn and Judge advancing in the fkies;
" To their old tenements the fouls return,   [fcends.
" Whilft down the fteep of heav'n as fwift the Judge de-
" Thefe look illuftrious bright, no more to mourn;
" Whilft, fee! diftracted looks yon' ftalking fhades
" The faints no more fhall conflict on the deep, [attend.
" Nor rugged waves infult the lab'ring fhip,   221
" But from the wreck in triumph they arife,
" And borne to blifs fhall tread empyreal fkies." 223

UPON THE DIVINE ATTRIBUTES.

A PINDARIC ESSAY.

"Εις ἐςὶν Θεὸς
"Ος ἔρανον τέτυχε καὶ γαῖαν μακρὰν.   · ·SOPHOC.

I. UNITY. ETERNITY.

WHENCE sprung this glorious frame? or when began
Things to exift? they could not always be :
To what ftupendous energy
Shall we afcribe the origin of man ?
That caufe from whence all beings elfe arofe   5
Muft felf-exiftent be alone,
Entirely perfect, and but one ;
Nor equal nor fuperior knows :
Two Firfts, in reafon, we can ne'er fuppofe :
If that, in falfe opinion, we allow   10
That once there abfolutely nothing was,
Then nothing could be now ;
For by what inftrument, or how,
Shall nonexiftence to exiftence pafs?
Thus fomething muft from everlafting be,   15
Or matter or a deity.
If matter only uncreate we grant,
We fhall volition, wit, and reafon, want,
An agent infinite, and action free.
Whence does volition, whence does reafon, flow ? 20
How came we to reflect, defign, and know ?

I

This from a nobler nature springs,
Diftinct in effence from material things,
For thoughtlefs matter cannot thought beftow :
But if we own a God fupreme,   25
And all perfection's poffible in him,
In him does boundlefs excellence refide,
Pow'r to create, and providence to guide;
Unmade himfelf, could no beginning have,
But to all fubftance prime exiftence gave ;   30
Can what he will deftroy, and what he pleafes fave.

II. POWER.

The undefigning hand of giddy Chance
Could never fill with globes of light,
So beautiful and fo amazing bright,
The lofty concave of the vaft expanfe :   35
Thefe could proceed from no lefs pow'r than infinite.
There's not one atom of this wondrous frame,
Nor effence intellectual, but took
Exiftence when the great Creator fpoke,
And from the common womb of empty nothing came.
" Let fubftance be," he cry'd, and ftraight arofe   41
Angelic and corporeal too ;
All that material nature fhows,
And what does things invifible compofe,
_ * the fame inftant fprung, and into being flew.   45
Mount to the convex of the higheft fphere,
Which draws a mighty circle round,
Th' interior orbs, as their capacious bound,

K

There millions of new miracles appear;
There dwell the eldeft fons of Pow'r immenfe,   50
Who firft were to perfection wrought,
Firft to complete exiftence brought,
'To whom their Maker did difpenfe
The largeft portions of created excellence:
Eternal now, not of neceffity,   55
As if they could not ceafe to be,
Or were from poffible deftruction free,
But on the will of God depend;
For that which could begin can end:
Who when the lower worlds were made,   60
Without the leaft mifcarriage or defect,
By the almighty Architect,
United adoration paid,
And with ecftatic gratitude his laws obey'd.

III.

Philofophy of old in vain effay'd   65
To tell us how this mighty frame
Into fuch beauteous order came,
But by falfe reas'nings falfe foundations laid:
She labour'd hard, but ftill the more fhe wrought
The more was wilder'd in the maze of thought.   70
Sometimes fhe fancy'd things to be
Coeval with the Deity,
And in the form which now they are
From everlafting ages were.

Sometimes the cafual event   75
Of atoms floating in a fpace immenfe,
Void of all wifdom, rule, and fenfe,
But by a lucky accident
Jumbled into this fcheme of wondrous excellence.
'Twas an eftablifh'd article of old,   80
Chief of the philofophic creed,
And does in natural productions hold,
That from mere nothing nothing could proceed.
Material fubftance never could have rofe
If fome exiftence had not been before,   85
In wifdom infinite, immenfe in pow'r.
Whate'er is made a maker muft fuppofe,
As an effect a caufe that could produce it fhows.
Nature and art, indeed, have bounds affign'd,
And only forms to things, not being, give;   90
That from Omnipotence they muft receive:
But the eternal felf-exiftent Mind
Can, with a fingle fiat, caufe to be
All that the wondrous eye furveys,
And all it cannot fee.   95
Nature may fhape a beauteous tree,
And art a noble palace raife,
But muft not to creative pow'r afpire;
  That their God alone can claim,
     pre-exifting fubftance doth require;   100
So where they nothing find can nothing frame.

IV. WISDOM.

Matter produc'd had still a chaos been,
For jarring elements engag'd
Eternal battles would have wag'd,
And fill'd with endless horror the tumultuous scene,
If Wisdom infinite, for less   106
Could not the vast prodigious embryo wield,
Or strength complete to lab'ring Nature yield,
Had not, with actual address,
Compos'd the bellowing hurry and establish'd peace.
Whate'er this visible creation shows   111
That's lovely, uniform, and bright,
That gilds the morning or adorns the night,
To her its eminence and beauty owes.
By her all creatures have their ends assign'd,   115
Proportion'd to their nature and their kind,
To which they steadily advance,
Mov'd by right Reason's high command,
Or guided by the secret hand
Of real instinct or imaginary chance.   120
Nothing but men reject her sacred rules,
Who from the end of their creation fly,
And deviate into misery ;
As if the liberty to act like fools
Were the chief cause that Heav'n made 'em free. 125

V. PROVIDENCE.

Bold is the wretch, and blasphemous the man,
Who, finite, will attempt to scan

The works of Him that's infinitely wife,
And thofe he cannot comprehend denies;
As if a fpace immenfe were meafurable by a fpan.
Thus the proud fceptic will not own   131
That Providence the world directs,
Or its affairs infpects,
But leaves it to itfelf alone.
How does it with almighty grandeur fuit,   135
To be concern'd with our impertinence,
Or interpofe his pow'r for the defence
Of a poor mortal or a fenfelefs brute?
Villains could never fo fuccefsful prove,
And unmolefted in thofe pleafures live,   140
Which honour, eafe, and affluence, give,
While fuch as Heav'n adore, and virtue love,
And moft the care of Providence deferve,
Opprefs'd with pain and ignominy ftarve.
What reafon can the wifeft fhow   145
Why murder does unpunifh'd go,
If the Moft High, that's juft and good,
Intends and governs all below,
And yet regards not the loud cries of guiltlefs blood?
But fhall we things unfearchable deny,   150
Becaufe our reafon cannot tell us why
They are allow'd or acted by the Deity?
'Tis equally above the reach of thought
To comprehend how matter fhould be brought

K iij

From nothing, as exiſtent be   155
From all eternity,   .
And yet that matter is we feel and ſee;
Nor is it eaſier to define
What ligatures the ſoul and body join,
Or how the mem'ry does th' impreſſion take   160
Of things, and to the mind reſtores 'em back.

VI.

Did not th' Almighty, with immediate care,
Direct and govern this capacious all,
How ſoon would things into confuſion fall!
Earthquakes the trembling ground would tear,   165
And blazing comets rule the troubled air;
Wide inundations, with reſiſtleſs force,
The lower provinces o'erflow,
In ſpite of all that human ſtrength could do,
To ſtop the raging ſea's impetuous courſe: 170
Murder and rapine ev'ry place would fill,
And ſinking Virtue ſtoop to proſp'rous Ill;
Devouring peſtilence rave,
And all that part of nature which has breath
Deliver to the tyranny of death,   175
And hurry to the dungeons of the grave,
If watchful Providence were not concern'd to ſave.
Let the brave ſoldier ſpeak, who oft' has been
In dreadful ſieges, and fierce battles ſeen,
'How he's preſerv'd, when bombs and bullets fly 180
So thick, that ſcarce one inch of air is free;

And tho' he does ten thoufand fee
Fall at his feet, and in a moment die,
Unhurt retreats, or gains unhurt the victory.
Let the poor fhipwreck'd failor fhow   185
To what invifible protecting pow'r
He did his life and fafety owe
When the loud ftorm his well-built veffel tore,
And half a fhatter'd plank convey'd him to the fhore,
Nay; let th' ungrateful fceptic tell us how   190
His tender infancy protection found,
And helplefs childhood was with fafety crown'd,
If he 'll no Providence allow;
When he had nothing but his nurfe's arms
To guard him from innumerable fatal harms;   195
From childhood how to youth he ran
Securely, and from thence to man;
How in the ftrength and vigour of his years
The feeble bark of life he faves,
Amidft the fury of tempeftuous waves,   200
From all the dangers he forefees or fears,
Yet ev'ry hour 'twixt Scylla and Charybdis fteers,
If Providence, which can the feas command,
Held not the rudder with a fteady hand.

VII. OMNIPRESENCE.

'Tis happy for the fons of men that He   205
Who all exiftence out of nothing made
Supports his creatures by immediate aid;

But then this all-intending Deity
Muſt omnipreſent be :
For how ſhall we, by demonſtration, ſhow   210
The Godhead is this moment here,
If he 's not preſent ev'rywhere,
And always ſo ?
What 's not perceptible by ſenſe may be
'Ten thouſand miles remote from me,   215
Unleſs his nature is from limitation free.
In vain we for protection pray,
For benefits receiv'd high altars raiſe,
And offer up our hymns and praiſe,
In vain his anger dread or laws obey ;   220
An abſent God from ruin can defend
No more than can an abſent friend ;
No more is capable to know
How gratefully we make returns,
When the loud muſic ſounds or victim burns,   225
Than a poor Indian ſlave of Mexico.
If ſo, 'tis equally in vain
The proſp'rous ſings and wretched mourns ;
He cannot hear the praiſe or mitigate the pain.
But by what being is confin'd   230
The Godhead we adore ?
He muſt have equal or ſuperior pow'r :
If equal only, they each other bind ;
So neither 's God, if we define him right,
For neither 's infinite :   235
But if the other have ſuperior might,

Then he we worſhip can't pretend to be
Omnipotent, and free
From all reſtraint, and ſo no deity.
If God is limited in ſpace, his view,   240
His knowledge, pow'r, and wiſdom, is ſo too;
Unleſs we 'll own that theſe perfections are
At all times preſent ev'ry where,
Yet he himſelf not actually there ;
Which to ſuppoſe, that ſtrange concluſion brings, 245
His eſſence and his attributes are diff'rent things.

VIII. IMMUTABILITY.

As the ſupreme omniſcient Mind
Is by no boundaries confin'd,
So reaſon muſt acknowledge him to be
From poſſible mutation free ;   250
For what he is he was from all eternity.
Change, whether the effect of force or will,
Muſt argue imperfection ſtill;
But imperfection in a deity,
That 's abſolutely perfect, cannot be.   255
Who can compel, without his own conſent,
A God to change that is omnipotent ?
And ev'ry alteration without force
Is for the better or the worſe.
He that is infinitely wiſe .   260
To alter for the worſe will never chuſe;
That a depravity of nature ſhews :
And he, in whom all true perfection lies,
Cannot, by change, to greater excellencies riſe.

If God be mutable, which way, or how,   265
Shall we demonstrate that will please him now
Which did a thousand years ago?
And 'tis impossible to know
What he forbids or what he will allow.
Murder, inchantment, lust, and perjury,   270
Did in the foremost rank of vices stand,
Prohibited by an express command;
But whether such they still remain to be
No argument will positively prove,
Without immediate notice from above,   275
If the almighty Legislator can
Be chang'd, like his inconstant subject man.
Uncertain thus what to perform or shun,
We all intolerable hazards run,
When an eternal stake is to be lost or won.   280

IX. JUSTICE.

Rejoice, ye sons of Piety! and sing
Loud hallelujahs to his glorious name,
Who was, and will for ever be the same:
Your grateful incense to his temples bring,
That from the smoaking altars may arise   285
Clouds of perfumes to the imperial skies.
His promises stand firm to you,
And endless joy will be bestow'd,
As sure as that there is a God,
On all who virtue chuse, and righteous paths pursue.
Nor should we more his menaces distrust,   291

For while he is a deity he muſt
(As infinitely good) be infinitely juſt.
But does it with a gracious Godhead ſuit,
Whoſe mercy is his darling attribute,   295
To puniſh crimes that temporary be,
And thoſe but trivial offences too,
Mere ſlips of human nature, ſmall and few,
With everlaſting miſery?   299
This ſhocks the mind, with deep reflections fraught,
And reaſon bends beneath the pond'rous thought.
Crimes take their eſtimate from guilt, and grow
More heinous ſtill, the more they do incenſe
That God to whom all creatures owe
Profoundeſt reverence;   305
Tho', as to that degree they raiſe
The anger of the merciful moſt High,
We have no ſtandard to diſcern it by
But the infliction he on the offender lays:
So that, if endleſs puniſhment on all   310
Our unrepented ſins muſt fall,
None, not the leaſt, can be accounted ſmall.
That God is in perfection juſt, muſt be
Allow'd by all that own a deity:
If ſo, from equity he cannot ſwerve,   315
Nor puniſh ſinners more than they deſerve.
His will reveal'd is both expreſs and clear:
" Ye curſed of my Father! go
" To everlaſting woe."
If everlaſting means eternal here,   320

Duration abfolutely without end,
Againſt which fenſe ſome zealouſly contend,
That, when apply'd to pains, it only means
They ſhall ten thouſand ages laſt,
Ten thouſand more, perhaps, when they are paſt,
But not eternal, in a lit'ral fenſe :   326
Yet own the pleaſures of the juſt remain
So long as there's a God exiſts to reign :
Tho' none can give a ſolid reaſon why
The word Eternity,   330
To heav'n and hell indifferently join'd,
Should carry fenſe of a different kind ;
And 'tis a ſad experiment to try.

X. GOODNESS.

But if there be one attribute divine
With greater luſtre than the reſt can ſhine   335
'Tis goodneſs, which we ev'ry moment fee
The Godhead exerciſe with ſuch delight,
It ſeems, it only ſeems, to be
The beſt-belov'd perfection of the Deity,
And more than infinite :   340
Without that he could never prove
The proper object of our praiſe or love.
Were he not good, he'd be no more concern'd
To hear the wretched in affliction cry,
Or fee the guiltleſs for the guilty die,   345
Than Nero, when the flaming city burn'd,
And weeping Romans o'er its ruins mourn'd.

4

Eternal juftice then would be
But everlafting cruelty ;
Pow'r unreftrain'd almighty violence,   350
And wifdom unconfin'd but craft immenfe.
'Tis goodnefs conftitutes him that he is,
And thofe
Who will deny him this
A God without a Deity fuppofe.   355
When the lewd Atheift blafphemoufly fwears,
By his tremendous name,
There is no God, but all 's a fham,
Infipid tattle praife and pray'rs,
Virtue, pretence ; and all the facred rules   360
Religion teaches tricks to cully fools;
Juftice would ftrike th' audacious villain dead,
But mercy boundlefs faves his guilty head;
Gives him protection, and allows him bread.
Does not the finner, whom no danger awes,   365
Without reftraint his infamy purfue,
Rejoice and glory in it too,
Laugh at the pow'r divine, and ridicule his laws,
Labour in vice his rivals to excel,
That when he 's dead they may their pupils tell 370
How wittily the fool was damn'd, how hard he fell?
Yet this vile wretch in fafety lives,
Bleffings in common with the beft receives,
Tho' he is proud t' affront the God thofe bleffings gives.

L

The cheerful fun his influence fheds on all,   375
Has no refpect to good or ill;
And fruitful fhow'rs without diftinction fall,
Which fields with corn, with grafs the paftures, fill.
The bounteous hand of Heav'n beftows
Succefs and honour many times on thofe   380
Who fcorn his fav'rites and carefs his foes.

XI.

To this good God, whom my advent'rous pen
Has dar'd to celebrate
In lofty Pindar's ftrain,
'Tho' with unequal ftrength to bear the weight   385
Of fuch a pond'rous theme, fo infinitely great;
To this good God celeftial fpirits pay,
With ecftafy divine, inceffant praife,
While on the glories of his face they gaze,
In the bright regions of eternal day: 390
To him each rational exiftence here,
Whofe breaft one fpark of gratitude contains,
In whom there are the leaft remains
Of piety or fear,
His tribute brings of joyful facrifice,   395
For pardon prays, and for protection flies:
Nay, the inanimate creation give,
By prompt obedience to his word,
Inftinctive honour to their Lord,
And fhame the thinking world who in rebellion live.

With heav'n and earth, then, O my Soul! unite, 401
And the great God of both adore and blefs,
Who gives thee competence, content, and peace,
The only fountains of fincere delight;
That from the tranfitory joys below   405
Thou, by a happy exit, may'ft remove
To thofe ineffable above
Which from the vifion of the Godhead flow,
And neither end, decreafe, nor interruption, know.

EPISTLES.

CRUELTY AND LUST.

AN EPISTOLARY ESSAY *.

WHERE can the wretched'ſt of all creatures fly,
To tell the ſtory of her miſery ?
Where but to faithful Celia, in whoſe mind
A manly brav'ry's with ſoft pity join'd ?
I fear theſe lines will ſcarce be underſtood, 5
Blurr'd with inceſſant tears, and writ in blood :
But if you can the mournful pages read,
The ſad relation ſhews you ſuch a deed
As all the annals of th' infernal reign
Shall ſtrive to equal or exceed in vain. 10

Neronior's fame, no doubt, has reach'd your ears,
Whoſe cruelty has caus'd a ſea of tears,
Fill'd each lamenting town with fun'ral ſighs,
Deploring widows' ſhrieks and orphans' cries.
At ev'ry health the horrid monſter quaff'd 15
Ten wretches dy'd, and as they dy'd he laugh'd,
Till tir'd with acting devil, he was led,
Drunk with exceſs of blood and wine, to bed.

* This piece was occaſioned by the barbarity of Kirke. a
commander in the Weſtern rebellion, 1685, who debauched
a young lady, with a promiſe to ſave her huſband's life, but
hanged him the next morning.

Oh! curfed place!——I can no more command
My pen; fhame and confufion fhake my hand :   20
But I muft on, and let my Celia know
How barb'rous are my wrongs, how vaft my woe!
    Amongft the crowd of Weftern youths, who ran
To meet the brave betray'd unhappy man *,
My hufband, fatally uniting, went,   25
Unus'd to arms, and thoughtlefs of th' event :
But when the battle was by treach'ry won,
The chief and all but his falfe friend undone,
Tho' in the tumult of that defp'rate night
He.'fcap'd the dreadful flaughter of the fight,   30
Yet the fagacious blood-hounds, fkill'd too well
In all the murd'ring qualities of hell,
Each fecret place fo regularly beat,
They foon difcover'd his unfafe retreat.
As hungry wolves triumphing o'er their prey,   35
To fure deftruction hurry them away;
So the purveyors of fierce Mcloc's fon
With Charion to the common butch'ry run,
Where proud Neronior by his gibbet ftood,
To glut himfelf with frefh fupplies of blood.   40
Our friends, by pow'rful interceffion, gain'd
A fhort reprieve, but for three days obtain'd,
To try all ways might to compaffion move
The favage gen'ral; but in vain they ftrove.

* The Duke of Monmouth.

L iij

When I perceiv'd that all addresses fail'd,   45
And nothing o'er his stubborn soul prevail'd,
Distracted almost, to his tent I flew,
To make the last effort what tears could do.
Low on my knees I fell, then thus began:
" Great genius of success! thou more than man!   50
" Whose arms to ev'ry clime have terror hurl'd,
" And carry'd conquest round the trembling world;
" Still may the brightest glories Fame can lend,
" Your sword, your conduct, and your cause, attend.
" Here now the arbiter of Fate you sit,   55
" While suppliant slaves their rebel heads submit.
" Oh! pity the unfortunate, and give
" But this one thing; oh! let but Charion live!
" And take the little all that we possess;
" I'll bear the meagre anguish of distress;   60
" Content, nay, pleas'd, to beg or earn my bread,
" Let Charion live, no matter how I'm fed:
" The fall of such a youth no lustre brings [things,
" To him whose sword performs such wondrous
" As saving kingdoms and supporting kings.   65
" That triumph only with true grandeur shines
" Where godlike courage godlike pity joins.
" Cæsar, the eldest favourite of War,
" Took not more pleasure to subdue than spare;
" And since in battle you can greater be,   70
" That over, ben't less merciful than he.
" Ignoble spirits by revenge are known,
" And cruel actions spoil the conqu'ror's crown,

" In future hift'ries fill each mournful page
" With tales of blood and monuments of rage ;⁣   75
" And while his annals are with horror read,
" Men curfe him living, and deteft him dead.
" Oh! do not fully, with a fanguine dye,
" (The fouleft ftain) fo fair a memory !
" Then, as you 'll live the glory of our Ifle,⁣   80
" And Fate on all your expeditions fmile ;
" So, when a noble courfe you 've bravely ran,
" Die the beft foldier and the happieft man.
" None can the turns of Providence forefee,
" Or what their own cataftrophe may be ;⁣   85
" Therefore to perfons lab'ring under woe,
" That mercy they may want fhould always fhow :
" For in the chance of war the flighteft thing
" May lofe the battle or the vict'ry bring :
" And how would you that gen'ral's honour prize,
" Should in cool blood his captive facrifice ?⁣   91
⁣   " He that with rebel arms to fight is led,
" To juftice forfeits his opprobrious head.
" But 'tis unhappy Charion's firft offence,
" Seduc'd by fome too plaufible pretence,⁣   95
" To take th' inj'ring fide by error brought ;
" He had no malice, tho' he has the fault.
" Let the old tempters find a fhameful grave,
" But the half-innocent, the tempted, fave.
" Vengeance divine, tho' for the greateft crime,⁣   100
" But rarely ftrikes the firft or fecond time ;

" And he beſt follows the Almighty's will
" Who ſpares the guilty he has pow'r to kill.
" When proud rebellions would unhinge a ſtate,
" And wild diſorders in a land create,   105
" 'Tis requiſite the firſt promoters ſhou'd
" Put out the flames they kindled with their blood;
" But ſure 'tis a degree of murder all
" That draw their ſwords ſhould undiſtinguiſh'd fall :
" And ſince a mercy muſt to ſome be ſhown,   110
" Let Charion 'mongſt the happy few be one;
" For as none guilty has leſs guilt than he,
" So none for pardon has a fairer plea.

   " When David's general had won the field,
" And Abſalom, the lov'd ungrateful, kill'd,   115
" The trumpets ſounding made all ſlaughter ceaſe,
" And miſled Iſr'elites return'd in peace.
" The action paſt, where ſo much blood was ſpilt,
" We hear of none arraign'd for that day's guilt,
" But all concludes with the deſir'd event,   120
" The monarch pardons, and the Jews repent.

   " As great example your high courage warms,
" And to illuſtrious deeds excites your arms,
" So when you inſtances of mercy view,
" They ſhould inſpire you with compaſſion too; 125
" For he that emulates the truly brave
" Would always conquer, and ſhould always ſave."

   Here, interrupting, ſtern Neronior cry'd,
(Swell'd with ſucceſs, and blubber'd up with pride)

" Madam, his life depends upon my will,   130
" For ev'ry rebel I can fpare or kill.
" I 'll think of what you 've faid : this night return
" At ten; perhaps you 'll have no caufe to mourn.
" Go, fee your hufband ; bid him not defpair;
" His crime is great; but you are wondrous fair." 135
   When anxious miferies the foul amaze,
And dire confufion in the fpirits raife,
Upon the leaft appearance of relief
Our hopes revive, and mitigate our grief;
Impatience makes our wifhes earneft grow,   140
Which thro' falfe optics our deliv'rance fhow;
For while we fancy danger does appear
Moft at a diftance, it is oft' too near ;
And many times, fecure from obvious foes,
We fall into an ambufcade of woes.   145
   Pleas'd with the falfe Neronior's dark reply,
I thought the end of all my forrows nigh,
And to the main-guard haften'd, where the prey
Of this blood-thirfty fiend in durance lay.
When Charion faw me, from his turfy bed   150
With eagernefs he rais'd his drooping head :
" Oh! fly, my Dear! this guilty place," he cry'd,
" And in fome diftant clime thy virtue hidé :
" Here nothing but the fouleft demons dwell,
" The refufe of the damn'd, and mob of hell :   155
" The air they breathe is ev'ry atom curft;
" There's no degree of ills, for all are worft ;

" In rapes and murders they alone delight,
" And villanies of lefs importance flight;
" Act 'em indeed, but fcorn they fhould be nam'd,
" For all their glory's to be more than damn'd. 161
" Neronior's chief of this infernal crew
" And feems to merit that high ftation too;
" Nothing but rage and luft infpire his breaft,
" By Afmodai and Moloc both poffeft.   165
" When told you went to intercede for me,
" It threw my foul into an agony:
" Not that I would not for my freedom give
" What's requifite, or do not wifh to live;
" But for my fafety I can ne'er be bafe,   170
" Or buy a few fhort years with long difgrace:
" Nor would I have your yet unfpotted fame
" For me expos'd to an eternal fhame.
" With ignominy to preferve my breath
" Is worfe, by infinite degrees, than death.   175
" But if I can't my life with honour fave,
" With honour I'll defcend into the grave:
" For tho' Revenge and Malice both combine,
" (As both to fix my ruin feem to join)
" Yet, maugre all their violence and fkill,   180
" I can die juft, and I'm refolv'd I will.
     " But what is death we fo unwifely fear?
" An end of all our bufy tumults here;
" The equal lot of Poverty and State,
" Which all partake of by a certain fate.   185

" Whoe'er the profpect of mankind furveys

" At diverfe ages, and by diverfe ways,

" Will find them from this noify fcene retire;

" Some the firft minute that they breathe expire;

" Others, perhaps, furvive to talk and go,   190

" But die before they good or evil know.

" Here one to puberty arrives, and then

" Returns lamented to the duft again;

" Another there maintains a longer ftrife

" With all the pow'rful enemies of life,   195

" Till, with vexation tir'd, and threefcore years,

" He drops into the dark, and difappears.

" I' m young, indeed, and might expect to fee

" Times future long, and late pofterity;

" 'Tis what with reafon I could wifh to do,   200

" If to be old were to be happy too:

" But fince fubftantial grief fo foon deftroys

" The guft of all imaginary joys,

" Who would be too importunate to live,

" Or more for life than it can merit give?   205

   " Beyond the grave ftupendous regions lie,

" The boundlefs realms of vaft eternity!

" Where minds, remov'd from earthly bodies, dwell,

" But who their government or laws can tell?

" What 's their employment till the final doom,   210

" And time 's eternal period fhall come?

" Thus much the facred Oracles declare,

" That all are blefs'd or miferable there;

" Tho' if there's such variety of fate,

" None good expire too soon, nor bad too late.   215

" For my own part, with resignation still

" I can submit to my Creator's will;

" Let him recall the breath from him I drew

" When he thinks fit, and when he pleases too.

" The way of dying is my least concern;   220

" That will give no disturbance to my urn.

" If to the seats of happiness I go,

" There end all possible returns of woe;

" And when to those bless'd mansions I arrive,

" With pity I'll behold those that survive.   225

" Once more I beg you'd from these tents retreat,

" And leave me to my innocence and fate."

    " Charion," said I, " oh! do not urge my flight!

" I'll see th' event of this important night;

" Some strange presages in my soul forebode   230

" The worst of mis'ries or the greatest good.

" Few hours will shew the utmost of my doom,

" A joyful safety, or a peaceful tomb.

" If you miscarry I'm resov'd to try

" If gracious Heav'n will suffer me to die;   235

" For when you are to endless raptures gone,

" If I survive 'tis but to be undone.

" Who will support an injur'd widow's right,

" From sly Injustice or oppressive Might?

" Protect her person, or her cause defend?   240

" She rarely wants a foe or finds a friend.

" I 've no diftruft of Providence; but ftill
" 'Tis beft to go beyond the reach of ill;
" And thofe can have no reafon to repent,
" Who, tho' they die betimes, die innocent.   245
" But to a world of everlafting blifs
" Why would you go and leave me here in this?
" 'Tis a dark paffage; but our foes fhall view
" I 'll die as calm, tho' not fo brave, as you,
" That my behaviour to the laft may prove   250
" Your courage is not greater than my love."
The hour approach'd: as to Neronior's tent,
With trembling but impatient fteps I went,
A thoufand horrors throng'd into my breaft,
By fad ideas and ftrong fears poffeft: 255
Where'er I pafs'd the glaring lights would fhow
Frefh objects of defpair, and fcenes of woe.

Here, in a crowd of drunken foldiers, ftood
A wretched, poor, old man, befmear'd with blood,
And at his feet, juft thro' the body run,   260
Struggling for life, was laid his only fon,
By whofe hard labour he was daily fed,
Dividing ftill, with pious care, his bread;
And while he mourn'd, with floods of aged tears,
The fole fupport of his decrepit years,   265
The barb'rous mob, whofe rage no limit knows,
With blafphemous derifion mock'd his woes.

There, under a wide oak, difconfolate,
And drown'd in tears, a mournful widow fate;

M

High in the boughs the murder'd father hung;   270
Beneath the children round the mother clung :
They cry'd for food, but 'twas without relief,
For all they had to live upon was grief.
A sorrow so intense, such deep despair,
No creature merely human long could bear.   275
First in her arms her weeping babes she took,
And with a groan did to her husband look,
Then lean'd her head on theirs, and, sighing, cry'd,
" Pity me, Saviour of the world!" and dy'd.
    From this sad spectacle my eyes I turn'd,   280
Where sons their fathers, maids their lovers, mourn'd;
Friends for their friends, sisters for brothers, wept ;
Pris'ners of war in chains for slaughter kept :
Each ev'ry hour did the black message dread
Which should declare the person lov'd was dead. 285
Then I beheld, with brutal shouts of mirth,
A comely youth, and of no common birth,
To execution led, who hardly bore
The wounds in battle he receiv'd before ;
And as he pass'd I heard him bravely cry,   290
" I neither wish to live nor fear to die."
  ' At the curs'd tent arriv'd, without delay
They did me to the general convey,
Who thus began ——— ———
" Madam, by fresh intelligence I find   295
" That Charion's treason's of the blackest kind,

" And my commiffion is exprefs, to fpare
" None that fo deeply in rebellion are.
" New meafures therefore 'tis in vain to try;
" No pardon can be granted; he muft die :   300
" Muft, or I hazard all; which yet I'd do
" To be oblig'd in one requeft by you ;
" And, maugre all the dangers I forefee,
" Be mine this night, I'll fet your hufband free.
" Soldiers are rough, and cannot hope fuccefs   305
" By fupple flatt'ry and by foft addrefs :
" The pert gay coxcomb by thefe little arts
" Gains an afcendant o'er the ladies' hearts;
" But I can no fuch whining methods ufe :
" Confent he lives; he dies if you refufe."   310
      Amaz'd at this demand; faid I, " The brave
" Upon ignoble terms difdain to fave ;
" They let their captives ftill with honour live,
" No more require than what themfelves would give :
" For gen'rous victors, as they fcorn to do   315
" Difhoneft things, fcorn to propofe 'em too.
" Mercy, the brighteft virtue of the mind,
" Should with no devious appetite be join'd ;
" For if, when exercis'd, a crime it coft,
" Th' intrinfic luftre of the deed is loft.   320
" Great men their actions of a piece fhould have,
" Heroic all, and each entirely brave :
" From the nice rules of honour none fhould fwerve,
" Done becaufe good, without a mean referve.

                    M ij

" 'The crimes new charg'd upon th' unhappy youth
" May have revenge and malice, but no truth.　326
" Suppose the accusation justly brought,
" And clearly prov'd to the minutest thought,
" Yet mercies next to infinite abate
" Offences next to infinitely great;　330
" And 'tis the glory of a noble mind
" In full forgiveness not to be confin'd.
" Your prince's frowns if you have cause to fear,
" This act will more illustrious appear,
" Tho' his excuse can never be withstood,　335
" Who disobeys but only to be good.
" Perhaps the hazard 's more than you express;
" The glory would be were the danger less:
" For he that, to his prejudice, will do
" A noble action and a gen'rous too,　340
" Deserves to wear a more resplendent crown
" Than he that has a thousand battles won.
" Do not invert divine compassion so
" As to be cruel, and no mercy show.
" Of what renown can such an action be,　345
" Which saves my husband's life but ruins me?
" Tho', if you finally resolve to stand
" Upon so vile, inglorious a demand,
" He must submit: if 'tis my fate to mourn　349
" His death, I 'll bathe with virt'ous tears his urn.".
　　" Well, Madam," haughtily, Neronior cry'd,
" Your courage and your virtue shall be try'd:

" But to prevent all profpect of a flight,

" Some of my Lambs * fhall be your guard to-night:

" By them, no doubt, you 'll tenderly be us'd;   355

" They feldom afk a favour that's refus'd:

" Perhaps you 'll find them fo genteelly bred,

" They 'll leave you but few virt'ous tears to fhed.

" Surrounded with fo innocent a throng,

" The night muft pafs delightfully along;   360

" And in the morning, fince you will not give

" What I require, to let your hufband live,

" You fhall behold him figh his lateft breath,

" And gently fwing into the arms of Death.

" His fate he merits, as to rebels due,   365

" And your's will be as much deferv'd by you."

    Oh! Celia, think, fo far as thought can fhow

What pangs of grief, what agonies of woe,

At this dire refolution, feiz'd my breaft,

By all things fad and terrible poffeft!   370

In vain I wept, and 'twas in vain I pray'd,

For all my pray'rs were to a tiger made;

A tiger! worfe; for 'tis beyond difpute

No fiend 's fo cruel as a reas'ning brute.

Encompafs'd thus, and hopelefs of relief,   375

With all the fquadrons of defpair and grief,

Ruin ——— it was not poffible to fhun :

What could I do? oh! what would you have done ?

    * Kirke ufed to call the moft inhuman of his foldiers his Lambs.

                M iij

The hours that pafs'd till the black morn return'd
With tears of blood fhould be for ever mourn'd; 380
When, to involve me with confummate grief,
Beyond expreffion, and above belief,
" Madam," the monfter cry'd, " that you may find
" I can be grateful to the fair that's kind,
" Step to the door, I'll fhew you fuch a fight   385
" Shall overwhelm your fpirits with delight.
" Does not that wretch, who would dethrone his king,
" Become the gibbet, and adorn the ftring ?
" You need not now an injur'd hufband dread;
" Living he might, he'll not upbraid you dead. 390
" 'Twas for your fake I feiz'd upon his life;
" He would, perhaps, have fcorn'd fo chafte a wife.
" And, Madam, you'll excufe the zeal I fhow
" To keep that fecret none alive fhould know."
    " Curs'd of all creatures! for, compar'd with thee,
" The devils," faid I, " are dull in cruelty.   396
" Oh! may that tongue eternal vipers breed,
" And, wafteless, their eternal hunger feed;
" In fires too hot for falamanders dwell,
" The burning earneft of a hotter hell !   400
" May that vile lump of execrable luft
" Corrupt alive, and rot into the duft !
" May'ft thou, defpairing, at the point of death,
" With oaths and blafphemies refign thy breath; 404
" And the worft torments that the damn'd fhould
" In thine own perfon all united bear!"   [fhare

Oh! Celia! oh! my Friend! what age can ſhow
Sorrows like mine, ſo exquiſite a woe?
Indeed it does not infinite appear,
Becauſe it can't be everlaſting here;　　　　　410
But 'tis ſo vaſt that it can ne'er increaſe,
And ſo confirm'd it never can be lefs.　　-　　412

STREPHON'S LOVE FOR DELIA JUSTIFIED.

IN AN EPISTLE TO CELADON.

ALL men have follies, which they blindly trace
Thro' the dark turnings of a dubious maze;
But happy thofe who, by a prudent care,
Retreat betimes from the fallacious fnare.
 The eldeft fons of Wifdom were not free   5
From the fame failure you condemn in me;
They lov'd, and, by that glorious paffion led,
Forgot what Plato and themfelves had faid:
Love triumph'd o'er thofe dull pedantic rules
They had collected from the wrangling fchools,   10
And made 'em to his noble fway fubmit,
In fpite of all their learning, art, and wit;
Their grave ftarch'd morals then unufeful prov'd;
Thefe dufty characters he foon remov'd;
For when his fhining fquadrons came in view,   15
Their boafted reafon murmur'd and withdrew,
Unable to oppofe their mighty force
With flegmatic refolves and dry difcourfe.
 If, as the wifeft of the wife have err'd,
I go aftray, and am condemn'd unheard,   20
My faults you too feverely reprehend,
More like a rigid cenfor than a friend.
Love is the monarch paffion of the mind,
Knows no fuperior, by no laws confin'd,

But triumphs still, impatient of control,   25
O'er all the proud endowments of the soul.

You own'd my Delia, Friend! divinely fair,
When in the bud her native beauties were;
Your praise did then her early charms confess;
Yet you'd persuade me to adore her less.   30
You but the nonage of her beauty saw,
But might from thence sublime ideas draw,
And what she is by what she was conclude,
For now she governs those she then subdu'd.

Her aspect noble and mature is grown,   35
And ev'ry charm in its full vigour known;
There we may wond'ring view, distinctly writ,
The lines of goodness and the marks of wit;
Each feature, emulous of pleasing most,
Does justly some peculiar sweetness boast;   40
And her composure's of so fine a frame,
Pride cannot hope to mend nor Envy blame.

When the immortal beauties of the skies
Contended naked for the golden prize,
The apple had not fall'n to Venus' share   45
Had I been Paris, and my Delia there,
In whom alone we all their graces find.
The moving gaiety of Venus join'd
With Juno's aspect and Minerva's mind.

View but those nymphs whom other swains adore,
You'll value charming Delia still the more.   51

Dorinda's mien's majeſtic, but her mind
Is to revenge and peeviſhneſs inclin'd;
Myrtylla's fair, and yet Myrtylla's proud;
Chioe has wit, but noiſy, vain, and loud;   55
Melania dotes upon the ſillieſt things,
And yet Melania like an angel ſings:
But in my Delia all endowments meet,
All that is juſt, agreeable, or ſweet;
All that can praiſe and admiration move;   60
All that the wifeſt and the braveſt love.

In all diſcourſe ſhe's appoſite and gay,
And ne'er wants ſomething pertinent to ſay;
For if the ſubject's of a ſerious kind,
Her thoughts are manly, and her ſenſe refin'd;   65
But if divertive, her expreſſions fit,
Good language join'd with inoffenſive wit;
So cautious always, that ſhe ne'er affords
An idle thought the charity of words.

The vices common to her ſex can find   70
No room ev'n in the ſuburbs of her mind;
Concluding wiſely ſhe's in danger ſtill
From the mere neighb'rhood of induſtrious Ill;
Therefore at diſtance keeps the ſubtle foe,
Whoſe near approach would formidable grow;   75
While the unwary virgin is undone,
And meets the miſ'ry which ſhe ought to ſhun.

Her wit is penetrating, clear, and gay,
But lets true judgment and right reaſon ſway;

Modeſtly bold, and quick to apprehend,　　　　80
Prompt in replies, but cautious to offend.
Her darts are keen, but levell'd with ſuch care,
They ne'er fall ſhort, and ſeldom fly too far;
For when ſhe rallies 'tis with ſo much art,
We bluſh with pleaſure, and with rapture ſmart. 85
　　O, Celadon! you would my flame approve,
Did you but hear her talk, and talk of love;
That tender paſſion to her fancy brings
The prettieſt notions and the ſofteſt things,
Which are by her ſo movingly expreſt,　　　　90
They fill with ecſtaſy my throbbing breaſt:
'Tis then the charms of eloquence impart
Their native glories, unimprov'd by art:
By what ſhe ſays I meaſure things above,
And gueſs the language of ſeraphic love.　　　95
　　To the cool boſom of a peaceful ſhade,
By ſome wild beech or lofty poplar made,
When ev'ning comes, we ſecretly repair
To breathe in private, and unbend our care;
And while our flocks in fruitful paſtures feed,　100
Some well-deſign'd inſtructive poem read,
Where uſeful morals, with ſoft numbers join'd,
At once delight and cultivate the mind,
Which are by her to more perfection brought,
By wiſe remarks upon the poet's thought.　　　105
So well ſhe knows the ſtamp of eloquence,
The empty ſound of words from ſolid ſenſe,

The florid fuftian of a rhyming fpark,
Whofe random arrow ne'er comes near the mark,
Can't on her judgment be impos'd, and pafs   110
For ftandard gold, when 'tis but gilded brafs.
Oft' in the walks of an adjacent grove,
Where firft we mutually engag'd to love,
She, fmiling, afk'd me, " Whether I'd prefer
" An humble cottage on the plains with her,   115
" Before the pompous buildings of the great,
" And find content in that inferior ftate ?"
Said I, " The queftion you propofe to me
" Perhaps a matter of debate might be,
" Were the degrees of my affection lefs   120
" Than burning martyrs to the gods exprefs.
" In you I 've all I can defire below,
" That earth can give me, or the gods beftow;
" And, blefs'd with you, I know not where to find
" A fecond choice ; you take up all my mind.   125
" I 'd not forfake that dear delightful plain,
" Where charming Delia! Love and Delia reign,
" For all the fplendour that a court can give,
" Where gaudy fools and bufy ftatefmen live.
" Tho' youthful Paris, when his birth was known,
" (Too fatally related to a throne)   131
" Forfook Oenone and his rural fports,
" For dang'rous greatnefs and tumult'ous courts,
" Yet Fate fhould ftill offer its power in vain,   .
" For what is pow'r to fuch an humble fwain ? 135

" I would not leave my Delia, leave my fair,
" Tho' half the globe fhould be affign'd my fhare."
   And would you have me, Friend! reflect again,
Become the bafeft and the worft of men?
O, do not urge me, Celadon! forbear;   140
I cannot leave her; fhe's too charming fair!
Should I your counfel in this cafe purfue,
You might fufpect me for a villain too;
For fure that perjur'd wretch can never prove
Juft to his friend who's faithlefs to his love.   145

N

AN EPISTLE TO DELIA.

As thofe who hope hereafter heav'n to fhare,
A rig'rous exile here can calmly bear,
And with collected fpirits undergo
The fad variety of pain below,
Yet with intenfe reflections antedate   5
The mighty raptures of a future ftate,
While the bright profpect of approaching joy
Creates a blifs no trouble can deftroy;
So tho' I'm tofs'd by giddy Fortune's hand
Ev'n to the confines of my native land,   10
Where I can hear the ftormy ocean roar,
And break its waves upon the foaming fhore;
Tho' from my Delia banifh'd, all that's dear,
That's good, or beautiful, or charming, here,
Yet flatt'ring hopes encourage me to live,   15
And tell me Fate will kinder minutes give;
That the dark treafury of time contains
A glorious day will finifh all my pains;
And while I contemplate on joys to come,
My griefs are filent and my forrows dumb.   20
Believe me, Nymph! believe me, charming Fair!
(When truth's confpicuous we need not fwear;
Oaths would fuppofe a diffidence in you
That I am falfe, my flame fictitious too)
Were I condemn'd, by Fate's imperial pow'r,   25
Ne'er to return to your embraces more,

I'd fcorn whate'er the bufy world could give;
'Twould be the worft of miferies to live;
For all my wifhes and defires purfue,
All I admire or covet here, is you.   30
Were I poffefs'd of your furprifing charms,
And lodg'd again within my Delia's arms,
Then would my joys afcend to that degree,
Could angels envy, they would envy me.

  Oft', as I wander in a filent fhade,   35
When bold vexations would my foul invade, ·
I banifh the rough thought, and none purfue
But what inclines my willing mind to you:
The foft reflections on your facred love,
Like fov'reign antidotes, all cares remove;   40
Compofing ev'ry faculty to reft,
They leave a grateful flavour in my breaft.

  Retir'd fometimes into a lonely grove,
I think o'er all the ftories of our love.
What mighty pleafure have I oft' poffeft,   45
When, in a mafculine embrace, I preft
The lovely Delia to my heaving breaft!
Then I remember, and with vaft delight,
The kind expreffions of the parting night:
Methought the fun too quick return'd again,   50
And day feem'd ne'er impertinent till then.
Strong and contracted was our eager blifs;
An age of pleafure in each gen'rous kifs:
                              N ij

Years of delight in moments we compriz'd,
And heav'n itfelf was there epitomiz'd.   55
    But when the glories of the eaftern light
O'erflow'd the twinkling tapers of the night,
" Farewell, my Delia! O, farewell!" faid I,
" The utmoft period of my time is nigh;
" Too cruel Fate forbids my longer ftay,   60
" And wretched Strephon is compell'd away.
" But tho' I muft my native plains forego,
" Forfake thefe fields, forfake my Delia too,
" No change of fortune fhall for ever move
" The fettled bafe of my immortal love."   65
    " And muft my Strephon, muft my faithful fwain,
" Be forc'd," you cry'd, " to a remoter plain!
" The darling of my foul fo foon remov'd!
" The only valu'd, and the beft belov'd!
" Tho' other fwains to me themfelves addreft,   70
" Strephon was ftill diftinguifh'd from the reft;
" Flat and infipid all their courtfhip feem'd;
" Little themfelves, their paffions lefs, efteem'd;
" For my averfion with their flames increas'd,
" And none but Strephon partial Delia pleas'd.   75
" Tho' I'm depriv'd of my kind fhepherd's fight,
" Joy of the day, and bleffing of the night,
" Yet will you, Strephon! will you love me ftill?
" However flatter me, and fay you will;
" For fhould you entertain a rival love,   80
" Should you unkind to me or faithlefs prove,

" No mortal e'er could half so wretched be,
" For sure no mortal ever lov'd like me."
  "Your beauty, Nymph!" said I, "my faith secures;
" Those you once conquer must be always your's;
" For hearts subdu'd by your victorious eyes   86
" No force can storm, no stratagem surprise:
" Nor can I of captivity complain,
" While lovely Delia holds the glorious chain.
" The Cyprian queen, in young Adonis' arms,   90
" Might fear, at least, he would despise her charms,
" But I can never such a monster prove,
" To slight the blessings of my Delia's love.
" Would those who at celestial tables sit,
" Bless'd with immortal wine, immortal wit,   95
" Chuse to descend to some inferior board,
" Which nought but stum and nonsense can afford?
" Nor can I e'er to those gay nymphs address,
" Whose pride is greater and whose charms are less;
" Their tinsel beauty may, perhaps, subdue   100
" A gaudy coxcomb or a fulsome beau,
" But seem at best indifferent to me,
" Who none but you with admiration see.
  " Now would the rolling orbs obey my will,
" I'd make the sun a second time stand still,   105
" And to the lower world their light repay,
" When conqu'ring Joshua robb'd 'em of a day;
" Tho' our two souls would diff'rent passions prove,
" His was a thirst of glory, mine of love.

N iij

" It will not be; the fun makes hafte to rife,   110
" And take poffeffion of the eaftern fkies;
" Yet one more kifs, tho' millions are too few,
" And, Delia! fince we muft, muft part, adieu."
    As Adam, by an injur'd Maker driv'n
From Eden's groves the vicinage of heav'n,   115
Compell'd to wander, and oblig'd to bear
The harfh impreffions of a ruder air,
With mighty forrow and with weeping eyes
Look'd back, and mourn'd the lofs of Paradife;
With a concern like his did I review   120
My native plains, my charming Delia too;
For I left Paradife in leaving you.
    If, as I walk, a pleafant fhade I find,
It brings your fair idea to my mind :
Such was the happy place, I, fighing, fay,   125
Where I and Delia, lovely Delia! lay,
When firft I did my tender thoughts impart,
And made a grateful prefent of my heart :
Or if my friend in his apartment fhows
Some piece of Vandyke's or of Angelo's,   130
In which the artift has, with wondrous care,
Defcrib'd the face of one exceeding fair,
Tho' at firft fight it may my paffion raife,
And ev'ry feature I admire and praife,
Yet ftill methinks, upon a fecond view,   135
'Tis not fo beautiful, fo fair, as you.

If I converfe with thofe whom moft admit
To have a ready, gay, vivacious, wit,
They want fome amiable moving grace,
Some turn of fancy, that my Delia has;   140
For ten good thoughts amongft the crowd they vent,
Methinks ten thoufand are impertinent.

    Let other fhepherds that are prone to range,
With each caprice their giddy humours change;
They from variety lefs joys receive   145
Than you alone are capable to give :
Nor will I envy thofe ill-judging fwains
(What they enjoy's the refufe of the plains)
If, for my fhare of happinefs below,
Kind Heav'n upon me Delia would beftow;   150
Whatever bleffings it can give befide
Let all mankind among themfelves divide.   152

TO HIS FRIEND

UNDER AFFLICTION.

None lives in this tumultuous ftate of things,
Where ev'ry morning fome new trouble brings,
But bold inquietudes will break his reft,
And gloomy thoughts difturb his anxious breaft.
Angelic forms and happy fpirits are   5
Above the malice of perplexing care;
But that's a blefling too fublime, too high
For thofe who bend beneath mortality.
If in the body there was but one part
Subject to pain and fenfible of fmart,   10
And but one paffion could torment the mind,
That part, that paffion, bufy Fate would find:
But fince infirmities in both abound,
Since forrow both fo many ways can wound,
'Tis not fo great a wonder that we grieve   15
Sometimes, as 'tis a miracle we live.

　　The happieft man that ever breath'd on earth,
With all the glories of eftate and birth,
Had yet fome anxious care, to make him know
No grandeur was above the reach of woe.   20
To be from all things that difquiet free
Is not confiftent with humanity.
Youth, wit, and beauty, are fuch charming things,
O'er which if Affluence fpreads her gaudy wings,

We think the perfon who enjoys fo much   25
No care can move, and no affliction touch:
Yet could we but fome fecret method find
To view the dark receffes of the mind,
We there might fee the hidden feed of ftrife,
And woes in embryo rip'ning into life;   30
How fome fierce luft or boift'rous paffion fills
The lab'ring fpirit with prolific ills;
Pride, envy, or revenge, diftract the foul,
And all right reafon's godlike pow'rs control:
But if fhe muft not be allow'd to fway,   35
Tho' all without appears ferene and gay,
A cank'rous venom on the vitals preys,
And poifons all the comforts of his days.
    External pomp and vifible fuccefs
Sometimes contribute to our happinefs;   40
But that which makes it genuine, refin'd,
Is a good confcience and a foul refign'd:
Then to whatever end affliction 's fent,
To try our virtues, or for punifhment,
We bear it calmly, tho' a pond'rous woe,   45
And ftill adore the hand that gives the blow;
For in misfortune this advantage lies,
They make us humble and they make us wife;
And he that can acquire fuch virtues, gains
An ample recompenfe for all his pains.   50
    Too foft careffes of a profp'rous fate
The pious fervours of the foul abate,

Tempt to luxurious eafe our careless days,
And gloomy vapours round the fpirits raife :
Thus lull'd into a fleep, we dozing lie,   55
And find our ruin in fecurity,
Unlefs fome forrow comes to our relief,
And breaks th' inchantment by a timely grief.
But as we are allow'd, to cheer our fight,
In blackeft days fome glimmerings of light,   60
So in the moft dejected hours we may
The fecret pleafure have to weep and pray;
And thofe requefts the fpeedieft paffage find
To Heav'n which flow from an afflicted mind ;
And while to him we open our diftrefs,   65
Our pains grow lighter and our forrows lefs.
The fineft mufic of the grove we owe
To mourning Philomel's harmonious woe,
And while her grief's in charming notes expreft,
A thorny bramble pricks her tender breaft ;   70
In warbling melody fhe fpends the night,
And moves at once compaffion and delight.
　· No choice had e'er fo happy an event
But he that made it did that choice repent.
So weak's our judgment, and fo fhort's our fight, 75
We cannot level our own wifhes right;
And if fometimes we make a wife advance,
T' ourfelves we little owe, but much to chance :
So that when Providence, for fecret ends,
Corroding cares or fharp affliction fends,   80

We muſt conclude it beſt it ſhould be ſo,
And not deſponding or impatient grow:
For he that will his confidence remove
From boundleſs wiſdom and eternal love,
To place it on himſelf or human aid, 85
Will meet thoſe woes he labours to evade:
But in the keeneſt agonies of grief
Content's a cordial that ſtill gives relief.
Heav'n is not always angry when he ſtrikes,
But moſt chaſtiſes thoſe whom moſt he likes, 90
And if with humble ſpirits they complain,
Relieves the anguiſh, or rewards the pain. 92

TO ANOTHER FRIEND

UNDER AFFLICTION.

Sɪɴcᴇ the firſt man by diſobedience fell
An eaſy conqueſt to the pow'rs of hell,
There's none in ev'ry ſtage of life can be
From the inſults of bold Affliction free.
If a ſhort reſpite gives us ſome relief, 5
And interrupts the ſeries of our grief,
So quick the pangs of miſery return,
We joy by minutes, but by years we mourn.
 Reaſon refin'd, and to perfection brought,
By wiſe philoſophy and ſerious thought, 10

Supports the foul beneath the pond'rous weight
Of angry ftars and unpropitious Fate.
Then is the time fhe fhould exert her pow'r,
And make us practice what fhe taught before ;
For why are fuch volum'nous authors read,   15
The learned labours of the famous dead,
But to prepare the mind for its defence,
By fage refults and well-digefted fenfe,
That when the ftorm of mifery appears,
With all its real or fantaftic fears,   20
We either may the roiling danger fly,
Or ftem the tide before it fwells too high ?
    But tho' the theory of wifdom's known
With eafe, what fhould and what fhould not be done,
Yet all the labour in the practice lies,   25
To be in more than words and notion wife.
The facred truth of found philofophy
We ftudy early, but we late apply.
When ftubborn anguifh feizes on the foul,
Right reafon would its haughty rage control;   30
But if it may n't be fuffer'd, to endure
The pain is juft when we reject the cure :
For many men, clofe obfervation finds,
Of copious learning and exalted minds,
Who tremble at the fight of daring woes,   35
And ftoop ignobly to the vileft foes,
As if they underftoood not how to be
Or wife or brave but in felicity;

And by some action servile or unjust,
Lay all their former glories in the dust.   40
For wisdom first the wretched mortal flies,
And leaves him naked to his enemies;
So that, when most his prudence should be shown,
The most imprudent giddy things are done :
For when the mind's surrounded with distress,   45
Fear or inconstancy the judgment press,
And render it incapable to make
Wise resolutions, or good counsels take.
Yet there 's a steadiness of soul and thought,
By Reason bred, and by Religion taught,   50
Which, like a rock amidst the stormy waves,
Unmov'd remains, and all affliction braves.

   In sharp misfortunes some will search too deep
What Heav'n prohibits and would secret keep;
But those events 'tis better not to know   55
Which, known, serve only to increase our woe.
Knowledge forbid ('tis dang'rous to pursue)
With guilt begins, and ends with ruin too :
For had our earliest parents been content
Not to know more than to be innocent,   60
Their ignorance of evil had preserv'd
Their joys entire, for then they had not swerv'd ;
But they imagin'd (their desires were such)
They knew too little, till they knew too much.
E'er since by folly most to wisdom rise,   65
And few are but by sad experience wise.

O

Confider, Friend! who all your bleffings gave,
What are recall'd again, and what you have,
And do not murmur when you are bereft
Of little, if you have abundance left.   70
Confider, too, how many thoufands are
Under the worft of miferies, defpair,
And do n't repine at what you now endure;
Cuftom will give you eafe, or time will cure.
Once more; confider that the prefent ill,   75
'Tho' it be great, may yet be greater ftill;
And be not anxious; for to undergo
One grief is nothing to a num'rous woe.
But fince it is impoffible to be
Human and not expos'd to mifery,   80
Bear it, my Friend! as bravely as you can;
You are not more and be not lefs than man!

    Afflictions paft can no exiftence find
But in the wild ideas of the mind;
And why fhould we for thofe misfortunes mourn   85
Which have been fuffer'd, and can ne'er return?
Thofe that have weather'd a tempeftuous night,
And find a calm approaching with the light,
Will not, unlefs their reafon they difown,
Still make thofe dangers prefent that are gone.   90
What is behind the curtain none can fee;
It may be joy; fuppofe it mifery:
'Tis future ftill; and that which is not here   .
May never come, or we may never bear:

Therefore the prefent ill alone we ought   95
To view, in reafon, with a troubled thought;
But if we may the facred pages truft,
He's always happy that is always juft.   98

TO HIS FRIEND

INCLINED TO MARRY.

I would not have you, Strephon, chufe a mate
From too exalted or too mean a ftate,
For in both thefe we may expect to find
A creeping fpirit or a haughty mind.
Who moves within the middle region fhares   5
The leaft difquiets and the fmalleft cares.
Let her extraction with true luftre fhine;
If fomething brighter, not too bright for thine:
Her education liberal, not great;
Neither inferior nor above her ftate.   10
Let her have wit, but let that wit be free
From affectation, pride, and pedantry;
For the effect of woman's wit is fuch;
Too little is as dang'rous as too much.
But, chiefly, let her humour clofe with thine,   15
Unlefs where your's does to a fault incline;
The leaft difparity in this deftroys,
Like fulph'rous blafts, the very buds of joys.

O ij

Her perſon amiable, ſtraight, and free
From natural or chance deformity.   20
Let not her years exceed, if equal, thine,
For women paſt their vigour ſoon decline.
Her fortune competent; and if thy ſight
Can reach ſo far, take care 'tis gather'd right.
If thine's enough, then her's may be the leſs: 25
Do not aſpire to riches in exceſs;
For that which makes our lives delightful prove
Is a genteel ſufficiency and love.   28

TO A PAINTER

DRAWING DORINDA'S PICTURE.

Painter! the utmoſt of thy judgment ſhow;
Exceed ev'n Titian and great Angelo;
With all the livelineſs of thought expreſs
The moving features of Dorinda's face:
Thou canſt not flatter where ſuch beauty dwells;   5
Her charms thy colours and thy art excels.
Others, leſs fair, may from thy pencil have
Graces which ſparing Nature never gave;
But in Dorinda's aſpect thou wilt ſee
Such as will poſe thy famous art and thee :   10
So great, ſo many, in her face unite,
So well proportion'd, and ſo wondrous bright,

No human skill can ere expres 'em all,
But must do wrong to th' fair original.
An angel's hand alone the pencil fits,　　15
To mix the colours when an angel fits
　　Thy picture may as like Dorinda be
As art of man can paint a deity,
And justly may, perhaps, when she withdraws,
Excite our wonder, and deserve applause;　　20
But when compar'd, you 'll be oblig'd to own
No art can equal what's by Nature done.
Great Lely's noble hand, excell'd by few,
The picture fairer than the person drew:
He took the best that Nature could impart,　　25
And made it better by his pow'rful art:
But had he seen that bright surprising grace
Which spreads itself o'er all Dorinda's face,
Vain had been all the essays of his skill;
She must have been confess'd the fairest still.　　30
　　Heav'n in a landscape may be wondrous fine,
And look as bright as painted light can shine,
But still the real glories of that place
All art by infinite degrees surpass.　　34

TO THE PAINTER

AFTER HE HAD FINISHED DORINDA'S PICTURE.

PAINTER! thou haſt perform'd what man can do;
Only Dorinda's ſelf more charms can ſhow.
Bold are thy ſtrokes, and delicate each touch;
But ſtill the beauties of her face are ſuch
As cannot juſtly be deſcrib'd, tho' all   5
Confeſs 'tis like the bright original.
In her, and in thy picture, we may view
The utmoſt Nature or that Art can do;
Each is a maſterpiece, deſign'd ſo well,
That future times may ſtrive to parallel,
But neither Art nor Nature's able to excel.   11

CONTENTS.

EPISTLES.

From the APOLLO PRESS,
by the MARTINS,
July 22. 1779.

THE END.

BELL'S EDITION.
The POETS of GREAT BRITAIN
COMPLETE, FROM
CHAUCER to CHURCHILL.

ROSCOMMON.
Hail sacred Solitude! from this calm Bay
I view the World's tempestuous Sea.
Ode upon Solitude

London, Printed for J. Bell, at the British Library, Strand. May 16. 1778

THE

POETICAL WORKS

OF

WENT. DILLON,

EARL OF ROSCOMMON.

WITH THE LIFE OF THE AUTHOR.

The Grecians added verfe; their tuneful tongue
Made Nature firft, and Nature's God, their fong.----
------------------ -----Conqu'ring Rome,
With Grecian fpoils, brought Grecian numbers home,
Enrich'd by thefe Athenian Mufes more
Than all the vanquifh'd world could yield before.----
--- ------------ ----------Britain, laft,
In manly fweetnefs all the reft furpaft.
The wit of Greece, the gravity of Rome,
Appear exalted in the Britifh loom:
The Mufes' empire is reftor'd agen
In Charles's reign, and by ROSCOMMON's pen.   DRYDEN.

EDINBURG:

AT THE Apollo Prefs, BY THE MARTINS.
Anno 1780.

THE

POETICAL WORKS

OF

WENTWORTH DILLON,

EARL OF ROSCOMMON.

CONTAINING HIS

| MISCELLANIES, | TRANSLATIONS, |
| PROLOGUES, | IMITATIONS, |

&c. &c. &c.

Nor muft ROSCOMMON pafs negleĉted by,
That makes ev'n Rules a noble poetry;
Rules whofe deep fenfe and heav'nly numbers fhow
The beft of critics and of poets too.　　ADDISON.
------------------In all Charles's days
ROSCOMMON only boafts unfpotted lays.----
ROSCOMMON! not more learn'd than good,
With manners gen'rous as his noble blood;
To him the wit of Greece and Rome was known,
And ev'ry author's merit but his own.　　POPE.

EDINBURG:

AT THE Apollo Prefs, BY THE MARTINS.

Anno 1780.

WENTWORTH DILLON,

EARL OF ROSCOMMON.

This nobleman was fon of James Dillon Earl of Rof-common, and was born in Ireland during the Lieute-nancy of the Earl of Strafford, in the reign of King Charles I. Lord Strafford was his godfather, and na-med him by his own firname. He paffed fome of his firft years in his native country, till the Earl of Straf-ford imagining, when the rebellion firft broke out, that his father, who had been converted by Archbi-fhop Ufher to the Proteftant religion, would be ex-pofed to great danger, and be unable to protect his family, fent for his godfon, and placed him at his own feat in Yorkfhire under the tuition of Dr. Hall, after-wards Bifhop of Norwich, by whom he was inftruct-ed in Latin; and without learning the common rules of grammar, which he could never retain in his me-mory, he attained to write in that language with claffical elegance and propriety, and with fo much eafe, that he chofe it to correfpond with thofe friends who had learning fufficient to fupport the commerce. When the Earl of Strafford was profecuted, Lord Rofcommon went to Caen in Normandy by the ad-vice of Bifhop Ufher, to continue his ftudies under Bochart, where he is faid to have had an extraordi-nary impulfe of his father's death, which is related by

Mr. Aubrey in his Mifcellany; " Our Author, then a
" boy of about ten years of age, one day was as it were
" madly extravagant in playing, getting over the ta-
" bles, boards, &c. He was wont to be fober enough.
" They who obferved him faid, God grant this proves
" no ill luck to him. In the heat of this extravagant
" fit he cries out, My father is dead. A fortnight af-
" ter news came from Ireland that his father was
" dead. This account I had from Mr. Knowles who
" was his governor, and then with him, fince Secre-
" tary to the Earl of Strafford, and I have heard his
" Lordfhip's relations confirm the fame."

The ingenious author of Lord Rofcommon's Life,
publifhed in The Gentleman's Magazine for the month
of May 1748, has the following remarks on the above
relation of Aubrey's.

" The prefent age is very little inclined to favour
" any accounts of this fort, nor will the name of Au-
" brey much recommend it to credit; it ought not,
" however, to be omitted, becaufe better evidence of
" a fact is not eafily to be found than is here offered,
" and it muft be by preferving fuch relations that we
" may at leaft judge how much they are to be regard-
" ed. If we ftay to examine this account we fhall find
" difficulties on both fides; here is a relation of a fact
" given by a man who had no intereft to deceive him-
" felf; and here is, on the other hand, a miracle which
" produces no effect; the order of Nature is inter-

" rupted to difcover not a future but only a diftant
" event, the knowledge of which is of no ufe to him
" to whom it is revealed. Betwgen thefe difficulties
" what way fhall be found? Is reafon or teftimony to
" be rejected? I believe what Ofborne fays of an ap-
" pearance of fanctity may be applied to fuch impul-
" fes or anticipations; "Do not wholly flight them,
" becaufe they may be true; but do not eafily truft
" them, becaufe they may be falfe."

Some years after he travelled to Rome, where he
grew familiar with the moft valuable remains of An-
tiquity, applying himfelf particularly to the knowledge of medals, which he gained in great perfection,
and fpoke Italian with fo much grace and fluency
that he was frequently miftaken there for a native.
He returned to England upon the reftoration of King
Charles II. and was made Captain of the Band of Pen-
fioners, an honour which tempted him to fome extra-
vagancies. " In the gaieties of that age,"fays Fenton,
" he was tempted to indulge a violent paffion for ga-
" ming, by which he frequently hazarded his life in
" duels, and exceeded the bounds of a moderate for-
" tune." This was the fate of many other men whofe
genius was of no other advantage to them than that
it recommended them to employments, or to diftinction, by which the temptations to vice were multi-
plied, and their parts became foon of no other ufe than
that of enabling them to fucceed in debauchery.

A difpute about part of his eftate obliging him to return to Ireland, he refigned his poft, and upon his arrival at Dublin was made Captain of the guards to the Duke of Ormond.

When he was at Dublin he was as much as ever diftempered with the fame fatal affection for play, which engaged him in one adventure which well deferves to be related : " As he returned to his lodgings " from a gaming-table, he was attacked in the dark " by three ruffians who were employed to affaffinate " him. The Earl defended himfelf with fo much re-" folution that he difpatched one of the aggreffors, " while a gentleman accidentally paffing that way in-" terpofed and difarmed another; the third fecured " himfelf by flight. This generous affiftant was a dif-" banded officer of a good family and fair reputation, " who by what we call Partiality of Fortune, to avoid " cenfuring the iniquities of the times, wanted even a " plain fuit of clothes to make a decent appearance " at the Caftle ; but his Lordfhip on this occafion pre-" fenting him to the Duke of Ormond, with great " importunity prevailed with his Grace that he might " refign his poft of Captain of the guards to his friend, " which for about three years the gentleman enjoyed, " and upon his death the Duke returned the com-" miffion to his generous benefactor *.

His Lordfhip having finifhed his affairs in Ireland he returned to London, was made Mafter of the Horfe

* Fenton.

to the Duchefs of York, and married the Lady Fran-
ces, eldeft daughter of the Earl of Burlington, and
widow of Colonel Courtnay.

About this time, in imitation of thofe learned and
polite affemblies with which he had been acquainted
abroad, particularly one at Caen, (in which his tutor Bochartus died fuddenly while he was delivering
an oration) he began to form a fociety for refining
and fixing the ftandard of our language. In this defign his great friend Mr. Dryden was a particular
affiftant; " A defign," fays Fenton, " of which it is
" much more eafy to conceive an agreeable idea than
" any rational hope ever to fee it brought to perfec-
" tion." This excellent defign was again fet on foot
under the miniftry of the Earl of Oxford, and was
again defeated by a conflict of parties, and the neceffity of attending only to political difquifitions for de-
fending the conduct of the adminiftration, and forming parties in the parliament. Since that time it has
never been mentioned, either becaufe it has been hi-
therto a fufficient objection that it was one of the de-
figns of the Earl of Oxford, by whom Godolphin was
defeated, or becaufe the ftatefmen who fucceeded
him have not more leifure, and perhaps lefs tafte, for
literary improvements. Lord Rofcommon's attempts
were fruftrated by the commotions which were pro-
duced by King James's endeavours to introduce al-
terations in religion. He refolved to retire to Rome,

alleging " it was beft to fit next the chimney when
" the chamber fmoked."

It will no doubt furprife many of the prefent age,
and be a juft caufe of triumph to them, if they find
what Rofcommon and Oxford attempted in vain carried into execution, in the moft mafterly manner, by a
private gentleman, unaffifted and unpenfioned. The
world has feen this from the publication of an Englifh
Dictionary by Mr. Johnfon; a lafting monument of
the nation's honour and that writer's merit.

Lord Rofcommon's intended retreat into Italy,
already mentioned, on account of the troubles in
James II.'s reign, was prevented by the gout, of which
he was fo impatient that he admitted a repellent application from a French empyric; by which his di-
ftemper was driven up into his bowels, and put an
end to his life in 1684.

Mr. Fenton has told us that the moment in which
he expired he cried out, with a voice that expreffed
the moft intenfe fervour of devotion,

> My God! my Father, and my Friend!
> Do not forfake me at my end.

two lines of his own verfion of the Hymn, *Dies iræ,
Dies illa.*

The fame Mr. Fenton, in his notes upon Waller,
has given Rofcommon a character too general to be
critically juft. " In his Writings," fays he, "we view
" the image of a mind which was naturally ferious

" and folid, richly furnifhed and adorned with all the
" ornaments of art and fcience, and thofe ornaments
" unaffectedly difpofed in the moft regular and ele-
" gant order. His imagination might have probably
" been fruitful and fprightly if his judgment had
" been lefs fevere ; but that feverity (delivered in a
" mafculine, clear, fuccinct ftyle)contributed to make
" him fo eminent in the didactical manner, that no
" man with-juftice can affirm he was ever equalled
" by any of our nation, without confeffing at the fame
" time that he is inferior to none. In fome other
" kinds of writing his genius feems to have wanted
" fire to attain the point of perfection : but who can
" attain it ?"

From this account of the riches of his mind, who
would not imagine that they had been difplayed in
large volumes and numerous performances ? who
would not, after the perufal of this character, be fur-
prifed to find that all the proofs of this genius, and
knowledge and judgment, are hardlyfufficient to form
a fmall volume ? But thus it is that characters are generally written ; we know fomewhat, and we imagine the reft. The obfervation that his imagination
would have probably been more fruitful and fprightly
if his judgment had been lefs fevere, might, if we
were inclined to cavil, be anfwered by a contrary fup-
pofition, that his judgment would have been lefs fevere if his imagination had been more fruitful : it is

ridiculous to oppose judgment and imagination to each other, for it does not appear that men have necessarily less of the one as they have more of the other.

We must allow in favour of Lord Roscommon what Fenton has not mentioned so distinctly as he ought, and what is yet very much to his honour, that he is perhaps the only correct writer in verse before Addison; and that if there are not so many beauties in his compositions as in those of some of his contemporaries, there are at least fewer faults. Nor is this his highest praise; for Mr. Pope has celebrated him as the only moral writer in Charles II.'s reign.

> Unhappy Dryden——In all Charles's days
> Roscommon only boasts unspotted lays.

Mr. Dryden, speaking of Roscommon's Essay on Translated Verse, has the following observation; " It was that," says he, " that made me uneasy till " I tried whether or no I was capable of following " his rules, and of reducing the speculation into prac- " tice : for many a fair precept in poetry is like a " seeming demonstration in mathematics, very spe- " cious in the diagram, but failing in mechanic ope- " ration. I think I have, generally, observed his in- " structions : I am sure my reason is sufficiently con- " vinced both of their truth and usefulness, which, in " other words, is to confess no less a vanity than to " pretend that I have at least in some places made " examples to his rules."

6

This declaration of Dryden will be found no more than one of thofe curfory civilities which one author pays to another, and that kind of compliment for which Dryden was remarkable : for when the fum of Lord Rofcommon's precepts is collected, it will not be eafy to difcover how they can qualify their reader for a better performance of tranflation than might have been attained by his own reflections.

He that can abftract his mind from the elegance of the poetry, and confine it to the fenfe of the precepts, will find no other direction than that the author fhould be fuitable to the tranflator's genius; that he fhould be fuch as may deferve a tranflation; that he who intends to tranflate him fhould endeavour to un-derftand him; that perfpicuity fhould be ftudied, and unufual and uncouth names fparingly inferted; and that the ftyle of the original fhould be copied in its elevation and depreffion. Thefe are the rules that are celebrated as fo definite and important, and for the delivery of which to mankind fo much honour has been paid. Rofcommon has indeed deferved his praifes had they been given with difcernment, and beftowed not on the rules themfelves, but the art with which they are introduced, and the decorations with which they are adorned.

The Effay, though generally excellent, is not with-out its faults. The ftory of the Quack, borrowed from

B

Boileau, was not worth the importation : he has confounded the Britifh and Saxon mythology :

> I grant that from fome moffy idol oak,
> In double rhymes, our Thor and Woden fpoke.

The oak, as Gildon has obferved, belonged to the
Britifh druids, and Thor and Woden were Saxon dei-
ties. Of the double rhymes, which he fo liberally
fuppofes, he certainly had no knowledge.

His interpofition of a long paragraph of blank
verfes is unwarrantably licentious. Latin poets might
as well have introduced a feries of iambics among
their heroics.

His next work is the tranflation of The Art of
Poetry, which has perhaps received not lefs praife
than it deferves. Blank verfe, left merely to its numbers, has little operation either on the ear or mind :
it can hardly fupport itfelf without bold figures and
ftriking images. A poem frigidly didactic, without
ryhme, is fo near to profe, that the reader only fcorns
it for pretending to be verfe.

Having difentangled himfelf from the difficulties
of rhyme, he may juftly be expected to give the fenfe
of Horace with great exactnefs, and to fupprefs no
fubtilty of fentiment for the difficulty of expreffing it:
this demand, however, his tranflation will not fatisfy : what he found obfcure it is not obvious that
he has ever cleared.

Among his fmaller works the Eclogue of Virgil and the *Dies Iræ* are well tranflated; though the beft line in the *Dies Iræ* is borrowed from Dryden. In return, fucceeding poets have borrowed from Rofcommon.

In the verfes on the Lap-dog, the pronouns *thou* and *you* are offenfively confounded; and the turn at the end is from Waller.

His verfions of the two odes of Horace are made with great liberty, which is not recompenfed by much elegance or vigour.

His political verfes are fprightly, and when they were written muft have been very popular.

Of the fcene of Guarini, and the prologue to Pompey, Mrs. Philips, in her letters to Sir Charles Cotterel, has given the hiftory.

" Lord Rofcommon," fays fhe, " is certainly one " of the moft promifing young noblemen in Ireland. " He has paraphrafed a pfalm admirably, and a fcene " of *Paftor Fido* very finely, in fome places much bet- " ter than Sir Richard Fanfhaw. This was undertaken " merely in compliment to me, who happened to fay " that it was the beft fcene in Italian, and the worft " in Englifh. He was only two hours about it. It be- " gins thus:

" Dear happy groves! and you, the dark retreat
" Of filent Horror, Reft's eternal feat."

B ij

From thefe lines, which are fince fomewhat mended, it appears that he did not think a work of two hours fit to endure the eye of criticifm without revifal.

When Mrs. Philips was in Ireland, fome ladies that had feen her tranflation of Pompey refolved to bring it on the ftage at Dublin; and, to promote their defign, Lord Rofcommon gave them a prologue, and Sir Edward Dering an epilogue; " which," fays fhe, " are the beft performances of thofe kinds I ever faw." If this is not criticifm it is at leaft gratitude. The thought of bringing Cæfar and Pompey into Ireland, the only country over which Cæfar never had any power, is lucky.

Of Rofcommon's Works the judgment of the public feems to be right. He is elegant, but not great; he never labours after exquifite beauties, and he feldom falls into grofs faults. His verfification is fmooth, but rarely vigorous, and his rhymes are remarkably exact. He improved tafte if he did not enlarge knowledge, and may be numbered among the benefactors to Englifh literature.

TO THE EARL OF ROSCOMMON,

ON HIS EXCELLENT

ESSAY ON TRANSLATED VERSE.

WHETHER the fruitful Nile or Tyrian fhore
The feeds of arts and infant fcience bore,
'Tis fure the noble plant tranflated firft
Advanc'd its head in Grecian gardens nurft.
The Grecians added verfe; their tuneful tongue   5
Made Nature firft, and Nature's God, their fong.
Nor ftopp'd Tranflation here; for conqu'ring Rome,
With Grecian fpoils, brought Grecian numbers home,
Enrich'd by thofe Athenian Mufes more
Than all the vanquifh'd world could yield before, 10
'Till barb'rous nations and more barb'rous times
Debas'd the majefty of verfe to rhymes,
Thofe rude at firft, a kind of hobbling profe,
That limp'd along, and tinckled in the clofe;
But Italy reviving from the trance   15
Of Vandal, Goth, and Monkifh, ignorance,
With paufes, cadence, and well-vowell'd words,
And all the graces a good ear affords,

B iij

Made rhyme an art, and Dante's polifh'd page
Reftor'd a Silver not a Golden Age: 20
Then Petrarch follow'd, and in him we fee
What rhyme improv'd in all its hight can be;
At beft a pleafing found and fair barbarity.
The French purfu'd their fteps, and Britain, laft,
In manly fweetnefs all the reft furpaft.   25
The wit of Greece, the gravity of Rome,
Appear exalted in the Britifh loom:
The Mufes' empire is reftor'd agen
In Charles's reign, and by Rofcommon's pen.
Yet modeftly he does his work furvey,   30
And calls a finifh'd poem An Effay:
For all the needful rules are fcatter'd here,
Truth fmoothly told and pleafantly fevere;
(So well is Art difguis'd for Nature to appear.)
Nor need thofe rules to give Tranflation light,   35
His own example is a flame fo bright,
That he who but arrives to copy well
Unguided will advance, unknowing will excel:
Scarce his own Horace could fuch rules ordain,
Or his own Virgil fing a nobler ftrain.   40
How much in him may rifing Ireland boaft!
How much in gaining him has Britain loft!
Their ifland in revenge has our's reclaim'd;
The more inftructed we, the more we ftill are fham'd.
'Tis well for us his gen'rous blood did flow   45
Deriv'd from Britifh channels long ago;

'That here his conqu'ring anceftors were nurft,
And Ireland but tranflated England firft.
By this reprifal we regain our right,
Elfe muft the two contending nations fight;   50
A nobler quarrel for his native earth
'Than what divided Greece for Homer's birth.
To what perfection will our tongue arrive,
How will Invention and Tranflation thrive,
When authors nobly born will bear their part,   55
And not difdain th' inglorious praife of art!
Great gen'rals thus defcending from command,
With their own toil provoke the foldier's hand.
How will fweet Ovid's ghoft be pleas'd to hear
His fame augmented by an Englifh peer *,   60
How he embellifhes his Helen's loves,
Out-does his foftnefs, and his fenfe improves?
When thefe tranflate, and teach tranflators too,
Nor firftling kid nor any vulgar vow
Should at Apollo's grateful altar ftand;   65 ⎫
Rofcommon writes! to that aufpicious hand,   ⎬
Mufe! feed the bull that fpurns the yellow fand.   ⎭
Rofcommon! whom both court and camps commend,
True to his prince, and faithful to his friend.;
Rofcommon! firft in fields of honour known,   70 ⎫
Firft in the peaceful triumphs of the gown,   ⎬
Who both Minervas juftly makes his own.   ⎭

* The Earl of Mulgrave.

Now let the few belov'd by Jove, and they
Whom infus'd Titan form'd of better clay,
On equal terms with ancient Wit engage,   75
Nor mighty Homer fear, nor facred Virgil's page;
Our Englifh palace opens wide in ftate,
And without ftooping they may pafs the gate.   78

JOHN DRYDEN.

AD ILLUSTRISSIMUM VIRUM,

DOM. COMIT. DE ROSCOMMON,

In tentamen fuum five fpecimen de Poetis Transferendis.
  Carmen encomiafticon

ANGLIA fi claris pollet fæcunda poetis
Mundo præreptos jactans in pace triumphos;
Pallada nutrivit fi non minus ubere glebâ;
Augufto quam magna tulit fub Cæfare Roma;
Hoc tibi debeter comes illuftriffime fecli :   5
Nam poftquam per te patuit, populoque refulfit
Ars flacci, vatum furrexit vivida proles,
Divinus inftructa modis et carmine puro.
Jam non fola fequi veftigia facra Maronis
Sed transferre datur : vos O gaudete fuperbi   10
Angligenæ, meritifque virum redimite corollis
Quem penes arbitrium eft et jus et norma loquendi.
Nam duce te vatum feries æterna fequetur,
Qui tentare modos aufi immortalis Homeri,

Heroafque, deofque canent, plaufuque fecundo　15
Non male ceratis tendent fuper æthera pennis.
Et tua, docte Maro (ni fallor) carmina reddent
Majeftate pari; dum læta vagaberis umbra
Per facrum fpatiata nemus: verfuque Britanno
Æneadas mirata cani, bellumque, ducefque,　20
Et paftoris oves, his vocibus ora refolves.
Quam bene te poteram patulis amplectier ulnis,
Magne comes, noftræ O famæ defenfor et hæres;
Nunc licet infulfi vertant mea fcripta poetæ,
Mollior ac elegis Ovidî fonet Ilias, aufit　25
Mævius infælix calamo difperdere verfus,
Cuncta piat Silenus, et haud imitabile carmen
Prima quod infantis cecinit cunabula mundi,
Durabit, famamque per omne tuebitur ævum.
Grandibus ille modis et mirâ pingitur arte:　30
Per te, dulce decus, noftri viget ille laboris
Relliquiæ, multum celebrandus in orbe Britanno.
Tu genio da fræna tuo, nec voce beatam
Hâc triftere animam——cape dona extrema tuorum.
Carmina adhuc cineri exequias perfolve Maronis.　35
Pulchrior in tantâ fplendet mea gloria Musâ.
Plurimus Angligenum manibus verfabere, plebi
Sordebunt excufa ducum fimulacra tabellis;
Te melius vivo pingentem carmine cernent.
Dum Tranflatorum fudant ignobile vulgus,　40
Ut captent oculos phaleris, et imagine falfâ

Lactent lectorem, et vanâ dulcedine pascant;
Me mihi restituis versu, sensusque latentes
Eruis, et duplicem reddit tua charte Maronem. 44

E. Collegio S. S. et in-   CAROLUS DRYDEN.
dividuæ Trin. Cant.

TO THE EARL OF ROSCOMMON,

ON HIS EXCELLENT POEM.

As when by lab'ring stars new kingdoms rise,
The mighty mass in rude confusion lies,
A court unform'd, disorder'd at the bar,
And ev'n in peace the rugged mien of war,
' Till some wise statesman into method draws   5
The parts, and animates the frame with laws;
Such was the case when Chaucer's early toil
Founded the Muses' empire in our soil.
Spenser improv'd it with his painful hand,
But lost a noble Muse in Fairy-land.   10
Shakespeare said all that Nature could impart,
And Johnson added industry and art.
Cowley and Denham gain'd immortal praise;
And some who merit as they wear the bays,
Search'd all the treasuries of Greece and Rome,   15
And brought the precious spoils in triumph home.
But still our language had some ancient rust,
Our flights were often high, but seldom just;
There wanted one who licence could restrain,
Make civil laws o'er barb'rous usage reign;   20

One worthy in Apollo's chair to fit,
To hold the fcales, and give the ftamp of wit;
In whom ripe judgment and young fancy meet,
And force the poet's rage to be difcreet;
Who grows not naufeous whilft he ftrives to pleafe,
But marks the fhelves in the poetic feas;   26
Who knows and teaches what our clime can bear,
And makes the barren ground obey the lab'rer's care.

 Few could conceive, none the great work could do;
'Tis a frefh province, and referv'd for you.   30

 Thofe talents all are your's, of which but one
Were a fair fortune for a Mufe's fon;
Wit, reading, judgment, converfation, art,
A head well balanc'd, and a gen'rous heart.
While infect rhymes cloud the polluted fky,   35
Created to moleft the world and die, …
Your file does polifh what your fancy caft;
Works are long forming which muft always laft.
Rough iron fenfe, and ftubborn to the mould,
Touch'd by your chymic hand is turn'd to gold; 40
A fecret grace fafhions the flowing lines,
And infpiration thro' the labour fhines.
Writers in fpite of all their paint and art
Betray the darling paffion of their heart:
No fame you wound, give no chafte ears offence; 45
Still true to friendfhip, modefty, and fenfe.
So faints from heav'n, for our example fent,
Live to their rules, having nothing to repent.

Horace, if living, by exchange of fate,
Would give no laws, but only your's tranflate.   50

   Hoift fail, bold Writers! fearch, difcover far,
You have a compafs for a polar ftar:
Tune Orpheus' harp, and with enchanting rhymes
Soften the favage humour of the times.

   Tell all thofe untouch'd wonders which appear'd
When Fate itfelf for our great monarch fear'd,   55
Securely thro' the dang'rous foreft led
By guards of angels when his own were fled:
Heav'n kindly exercis'd his youth with cares,
To crown with unmix'd joys his riper years.   60

   Make warlike James's peaceful virtues known,
The fecond hope and genius of the throne:
Heav'n in compaffion brought him on our ftage
To tame the fury of a monftrous age.

   But what blefs'd voice fhall your Maria fing,   65
Or a fit off'ring to her altars bring?
In joys, in grief, in triumphs, in retreat,
Great always, without aiming to be great.
Beauty and Love fit awful in her face,
And ev'ry gefture form'd by ev'ry Grace.   70
Her glories are too heav'nly and refin'd
For the grofs fenfes of a vulgar mind.
It is your part (you poets can divine)
To prophefy how fhe by Heav'n's defign
Shall give an heir to the great Britifh line,   75

Who over all the Weſtern iſles ſhall reign,
Both awe the continent and rule the main;
It is your place to wait upon her name
Thro' the vaſt regions of eternal fame.

True poets' ſouls to princes are ally'd,   80
And the world's empire with its kings divide.
Heav'n truſts the preſent time to monarchs' care,
Eternity is the good writer's ſhare.   83

KNIGHTLY CHETWOOD.

TO THE EARL OF ROSCOMMON,

ON HIS EXCELLENT

ESSAY ON TRANSLATED VERSE.

WHILE ſatire pleas'd, and nothing elſe was writ,
But pure ill-nature paſs'd for nobleſt wit,
Some priv'leg'd climes the pois'nous weeds refuſe;
But when a gen'rous underſtanding Muſe
Does richer fruits from happier ſoils tranſlate,   5
We're ſent to Ireland by reverſe of fate;
Yet you, I know, with Plato would diſdain
To write and equal the Mæonian ſtrain,
If 't would debauch your humour ſo far forth
To think ſo mean a thing enhanc'd your worth: 10
For were that praiſe, and only that, your due,
Which Virgil too might claim no leſs than you,

C

Tho' that had merited my bare efteem,
I 'd leave to other pens the fingle theme :
But when I faw the candour of your mind,   15
A Mufe inur'd to camps in courts refin'd,
A foul ev'n capable of being a friend,
Free from thofe follies which the great attend,
I grant fuch excellence my foul did fire ;
Unable to commend I will admire.   20
  . " Happy the man when no concern is nigh
" But Nature 's wanton and his blood runs high,
".Who free from cares enjoys without control
" His Mufe, the darling miftrefs of his foul!
" No tedious court his appetite deftroys,   25
" Nor thoughts of gain pollute the rapt'rous joys;
" The dear Minerva 's form'd without a pain,
" And nothing lefs could fpring from fuch a brain;
" And yet his godlike pity he imparts   ⎫
" To thofe that drudge at duty 'gainft their hearts, ⎬
" And to illib'ral ufes wreft the lib'ral arts"— 31   ⎭
    When I obferve the wonders you explain, .
Too much the Ancients you commend—in vain ;
In vain you would endeavour to perfuade
That all our laws were in thofe archieves laid;   35
That poetry muft ever ftand unmov'd,
The only art experience han't improv'd.
But grant their rites were to religion grown,
Sure they concern no countries but their own;

For let Æneid pafs thro' others' hands, 40
The Æneid's felf a third-rate poet ftands;
Unfit to reach the heights that he has flown,
We wifely to our level bring him down :
Himfelf had writ lefs fweet and lefs fublime
In any other tongue or other time. 45

    And now, my Lord, on this account I grieve,
To think how diff'rent from yourfelf you 'll live.
When this inimitable Piece is fhown
In languages and empires yet unknown,
It will be learning then to know and hear
Not only what you wrote but what you were. 51

J. AMHERST.

UPON THE

EARL OF ROSCOMMON'S

TRANSLATION OF HORACE DE ARTE POETICA,

And of the Ufe of Poetry.

Rome was not better by her Horace taught,
Than we are here to comprehend his thought :
The poet writ to noble Pifo there ;
A noble Pifo does inftruct us here ;
Gives us a pattern in his flowing ftyle, 5
And with rich precepts does oblige our ifle :
Britain ! whofe genius is in verfe exprefs'd
Bold and fublime, but negligently drefs'd.

C ij

Horace will our fuperfluous branches prune,
Give us new rules, and fet our harp in tune;   10
Direct us how to back the winged horfe,
Favour his flight, and moderate his force.

Tho' poets may of infpiration boaft,
Their rage, ill-govern'd, in the clouds is loft.
He that proportion'd wonders can difclofe,   15
At once his fancy and his judgment fhows.
Chafte moral writing we may learn from hence,
Neglect of which no wit can recompenfe.
The fountain which from Helicon proceeds,
That facred ftream! fhould never water weeds,   20
Nor make the crop of thorns and thiftles grow,
Which envy or perverted nature fow.

Well-founding verfes are the charm we ufe,
Heroic thoughts and virtue to infufe:
Things of deep fenfe we may in profe unfold,   25
But they move more in lofty numbers told.
By the loud trumpet, which our courage aids,
We learn that found, as well as fenfe, perfuades.

The Mufe's friend, unto himfelf fevere,
With filent pity looks on all that err;   30
But where a brave, a public, action fhines,
That he rewards with his immortal lines.
Whether it be in council or in fight,
His country's honour is his chief delight;
Praife of great acts he fcatters as a feed   35
Which may the like in coming ages breed.

Here taught the fate of verfes, (always priz'd
With admiration, or as much defpis'd)
Men will be lefs indulgent to their faults,
And patience have to cultivate their thoughts.   40
Poets lofe half the praife they fhould have got,
Could it be known what they difcreetly blot,
Finding new words, that to the ravifh'd ear
May like the language of the gods appear,
Such as, of old, wife bards employ'd, to make   45
Unpolifh'd men their wild retreats forfake :
Law-giving heroes fam'd for taming brutes,
And raifing cities with their charming lutes :
For rudeft minds with harmony were caught,
And civil life was by the Mufes taught.   50
So wand'ring bees would perifh in the air,
Did not a found, proportion'd to their ear,
Appeafe their rage, invite them to the hive,
Unite their force, and teach them how to thrive :
To rob the flow'rs, and to forbear the fpoil,   55
Preferv'd in winter by their fummer's toil,
They give us food which may with nectar vie,
And wax that does the abfent fun fupply.   58

EDMUND WALLER.

*Cum Opus suum Manuscriptum, unà cum eleganti car-
mine Latino sibi mitteret illustrissimus Author, ita re-
spondit devotissimus suus, K. C.*

Aulæ dulce decus, quem culta Britannia vellet,
Scotia seque sibi vix peperisse putat;
Quid, mibi dum nunquam peritura volumina mittis,
Me, nisi mirari, dulcis amice, velis?
Scripta tua in melius qui fingere possit, Apellis   5
Is venerem, Phidiæ possit et ille Jovem :
Consilio ille juvet miscentem elementa tonantem,
Rectius et soli scribere possit iter.
Res sancta est, surgens vestra ad fastigia, vates,
Cui præsens semper pectora numen habet.   10
Quantum est victuris victuras condere leges,
In litem lauros et revocare novam!
Extinctis vitam dare res est quanta! sed ipse
Quantus! pars minima est Musa diserta tui.   14

AN ESSAY

ON TRANSLATED VERSE.

Happy that author whofe correct Effay *
Repairs fo well our old Horatian way;
And happy you who, by propitious fate,
On great Apollo's facred ftandard wait,
And with ftrict difcipline inftructed right,   5
Have learn'd to ufe your arms before you fight.

TENTAMEN, SIVE SPECIMEN

DE POETIS TRANSFERENDIS LATINE REDDITUM †.

Felix ille operis, digno qui carmine leges
Reftituit, facræ quas fixit Horatius arti.
Vos quoque felices, quibus indulgentia fati
Militiam tanto primam tolerare magiftro,
Vexillumque dedit facratum attollere Phœbi.   5
Egregiè inftructi miris ducis artibus, arma

---

* John Sheffield Duke of Buckinghamfhire.
† This Latin verfion of Lord Rofcommon's Effay on Tranflated Verfe is by the late Mr. Eufden of Cambridge.

But since the press, the pulpit, and the stage,
Conspire to censure and expose our age,
Provok'd too far, we resolutely must
To the few virtues that we have be just;   10
For who have long'd or who have labour'd more
To search the treasures of the Roman store,
Or dig in Grecian mines for purer ore?
The noblest fruits transplanted in our isle
With early hope and fragrant blossoms smile.   15
Familiar Ovid tender thoughts inspires,
And Nature seconds all his soft desires.
Theocritus does now to us belong,
And Albion's rocks repeat his rural song.

Exercere prius nôstis, quàm ad proelia ventum est.
At nunc cùm proelium, cùm pulpita, cumq; theatra
Stultitiam sæc'li rident, et stultiùs augent,
Sæpe lacessitis sumenda audacia; nobis   10
Virtutes paucæ; fas sit defendere paucas.
Qui nostris cupidi magis, aut qui plura ferendo
Certârunt vastas Romæ perquirere gazas,
Purius aut Graiis aurum exhaurire fodinis?
Translatus nostris fructus pulcherrimus oris   15
Spes det maturas, et amænis floribus halat.
Dulcè fluens Naso teneros inspirat amores,
Et quodcunque petit, sequitur natura petentem.
Nostra Syracosium referunt jam carmina vatem,
Illius agrestem rupes sonat Anglica Musam.   20

Who has not heard how Italy was bleſt   20
Above the Medes, above the wealthy Eaſt?
Or Gallus' ſong, ſo tender and ſo true,
As ev'n Lycoris might with pity view.
When mourning nymphs attend their Daphne's ſhearſe,
Who does not weep that reads the moving verſe! 25
But hear, oh! hear, in what exalted ſtrains ⎫
Sicilian Muſes thro' theſe happy plains   ⎬
Proclaim Saturnian times--our own Apollo reigns! ⎭
    When France had breath'd, after inteſtine broils,
And peace and conqueſt crown'd her foreign toils, 30
There, cultivated by a royal hand,
Learning grew faſt, and ſpread, and bleſs'd the land;

Quis neſcit, quanto felicior Itala tellus
Medorum ſylvis, gemmiſque Oriente ſuperbo?
Aut quæ cantavit Gallus molliſſima, cantus
Redditur en! qualem immoto nec corde Lycoris
Ipſa legat: vel cùm lugent tua funera, Daphni,   25
Nymphæ, quis ſiccis lugentes cernat ocellis?
En! verò numeris en! quàm ſublimibus arva
Fortunata per hæc ſiculæ Saturnia Muſæ
Tempora jam reſonant; noſter jam regnat Apollo.
    Libera civili requieſcere Gallia bello   30
Ut cæpit, pacemque domi palmaſque labores
Externi peperêre, illic doctrina vigebat
Regali nutrita manu, latèque beabat

The choiceſt books that Rome or Greece have known
Her excellent tranſlators made her own ;
And Europe ſtill conſiderably gains   .   ' 35
Both by their good example and their pains.
From hence our gen'rous emulation came,
We undertook, and we perform'd, the ſame.
But now we ſhew the world a nobler way,
And in Tranſlated Verſe do more than they ;   40
Serene and clear harmonious Horace flows,
With ſweetneſs not to be expreſs'd in proſe ;
Degrading proſe explains his meaning ill,
And ſhews the ſtuff, but not the workman's ſkill :

Omnia diffundens ſeſe : tum Græcia quicquid,
Aut quicquid Latium jactaret amabile, ſolers,   35
Dum digne vertit, proprium ſibi Gallia fecit.
Et quòd adhuc noſtro, tu jure fateberis, orbi
Multùm operæ illius, multùm exemplaria proſint.
Hinc ille illuſtris nobis, hinc æmulus ardor ;
Rem libuit tentare, et quæ tentata placebat,   40
Sortita eventum votis ſucceſſit amicè.   . ﹐ ·
At nunc nobilior monſtratur ſemita, verſo
Carmine præſtamus nos, quod nec Gallia præſtet.
Hìc, numeroſe, nites ſine nube ſerenus, Horati,
Nil perit hìc, numeris et iiſdem redderis idem.   45
Vim nemo hanc dulcem ſperet ſermone ſoluto.
Vulgaris ſermo vatis nudè edere ſenſum
Iſte valet ; tibi materiam, non explicat ingens

I, who have ferv'd him more than twenty years, 45
Scarce know my mafter as he there appears.
Vain are our neighbours' hopes, and vain their cares;
The fault is more their language's than theirs:
'Tis courtly, florid, and abounds in words
Of fofter found than ours perhaps affords;   50
But who did ever in French authors fee
The comprehenfive Englifh energy?
The weighty bullion of one fterling line,
Drawn to French-wire, would thro' whole pages
I fpeak my private but impartial fenfe   [fhine.
With freedom, and, I hope, without offence;   56
For I'll recant when France can fhew me wit
As ftrong as ours, and as fuccinctly writ.

Artis opus: colui multos quem fedulus annos
Ipfe ego, qualis ibì legitur mutatus in ora   50
Planè aliena, meum jam vix agnofco magiftrum.
Fruftrà finitimi tendunt, fruftràque laborant,
Des linguæ vitio, haud illis: hæc culta videtur,
Florida, verborumque ferax, quæ fortè tenellas
Titillent leviore fono, quàm poffumus, aures.   55
Efto; at quis nobis oftendat Gallicus autor
Angliacæ nervos fimul, et compendia linguæ?
Carminis unius nitidus cum pondere fenfus
Deductus tenùi per tota pöemata filo
Ornaret Gallos: quæ fit fententia nobis   · 60

'Tis true compoſing is the nobler part,
But good Tranſlation is no eaſy art;   60
For tho' materials have long ſince been found,
Yet both your fancy and your hands are bound;
And by improving what was writ before
Invention labours leſs, but judgment more.

The ſoil intended for Picrian ſeeds   65
Muſt be well purg'd from rank pedantic weeds.
Apollo ſtarts, and all Parnaſſus ſhakes
At the rude rumbling Baralipton makes:

(Æqua licèt privata) libet veram edere apertè,
Nec cuiquam nocuiſſe velim, nam dicta retracto,
Si brevitate pari ſenſus includere nôrint
Tam crebros, acreſque, et molli ſtringere nodo.

Pulchrior illa quidem eſt fæcundo pectore primùm
Rem tibi vis promens, felicique ubere vena,   66
Sed genio haud caret et bene vertere; nam tibi quamvis
Tradita materies aliunde hæc ſuppetat, extrà
Libera non ponis veſtigia, cogeris arcto
Limite, dum circa patulum verſaberis orbem;   70
Dumque ſtudes augere, tibi quæ tradita res eſt,
Quò minùs ingenium hìc ſudat, fæcundaque vena,
Tantò judicii magis exercetur acumen.

Exoſſare ſolum, cui ſemen credere tendis
Pierium, ſaxis primùm ſalebriſque decebit,   75
Vellere et urticas criticorum turpiter hirtas.
Avertit Phœbus, trepidat Parnaſſia rupes,

5.

For none have been with admiration read
But who befide their learning were well bred.   70
   The firft great work (a tafk perform'd by few)
Is, that yourfelf may to yourfelf be true :
No mafk, no tricks, no favour, no referve;
Diffect your mind, examine ev'ry nerve.
Whoever vainly on his ftrength depends   75
Begins like Virgil, but like Mævius ends.
That wretch, in fpite of his forgotten rhymes,
Condemn'd to live to all fucceeding times,
With pompous nonfenfe and a bellowing found
Sung lofty Ilium tumbling to the ground.   80

Cùm ftrepitu horrifono Baralipton vulnerat aures.
Dignus nemo legi, atque diu retinere legentes,
Ni bene moratas doctus qui poffidet artes.   80
   Difficilis labor, et paucis fuperabilis hic eft;
Fallere te ut nolis ipfum : procul abfit iniqua
Gratia, fperne dolos, probitas fpectetur, et imas
Pande animi latebras, atque omnes excute nervos. ·
Qui vanè propriis confidere viribus audet,   85
Prodeat ille Maro forfan, fed Mævius exit;
Infelix! cujus, poftquam data carmina fcombris,
Damnatur vitâ poft fcripta fuperftite nomen,
Pænam immortalem mortali ex carmine pendens :
Is tumidis ruptus buccis, vacuoque böatu   90
Torva Mimalloneis implevit cornua bombis.

And (if my Mufe can thro' paft ages fee)
That noify, naufeous, gaping, fool was he,
Exploded when with univerfal fcorn
The mountains labour'd and a moufe was born.

    " Learn, learn," Crotona's brawny wreftler cries,
" Audacious Mortals! and be timely wife;   86
" 'Tis I that call; remember Milo's end,
" Wedg'd in that timber which he ftrove to rend."
    Each poet with a diff'rent talent writes;
One praifes, one inftructs, another bites.   90
Horace did ne'er afpire to epic bays,
Nor lofty Maro ftoop to lyric lays.

Si bene lapfa memor repetat mihi fæcula Mufa,
Mævius ille fuit vano promiffor hiatu
Contemptûs meritò, cùm parturientibus altis   94
Montibus, (horrendum!)--mox prodîit exiguus mus.

    Difcite, jam magnâ conclamans voce per umbras
Ille lacertofus, clarus pugil ille Crotonis,
Milo jubet fua fata docens, temerarius olim
Viribus ipfe fuis nodofum in robur adactus,
Findere quod primò nimis eft feliciter aufus.   100
    Diverfi fcribunt diverfo nuniine vates,
Laudibus hic pollet, falibus tu, moribus alter.
Non epicas aufus Flaccus fibi pofcere lauros,
Ipfe nec ad lyricum celfus defcendere carmen   104
Dignatus Maro. Tu, quà mens iter ipfa frequentat,

Examine how your humour.is inclin'd,
And which the ruling paſſion of your mind;
Then ſeek a poet who your way does bend,   95
And chuſe an author as you chuſe a friend;
United by this ſympathetic bond,
You grow familiar, intimate, and fond;
Your thoughts, your words, your ſtyles, your ſouls,
No longer his interpreter, but he.   ·   :   [agree,

     With how much eaſe is a young Muſe betray'd!
How nice the reputation of the maid!   102
Your early, kind, paternal, care appears
By chaſte inſtruction of her tender years:
The firſt impreſſion in her infant breaſt   105
Will be the deepeſt, and ſhould be the beſt.

Quæ primùm, explores, rapit ultrò pectora flamma.
Tum tibi cognatum, qui tramite vergit eodem,
Autoremque legas, tanquam legeretur amicus.
Dumque pari ſtringunt vos vincula mutua nexu,
Mirus erit confenſus, amabis, amaberis idem;   110
Mens eadem, ſimilis ſententia, vox, et utrique,
Interpres jam tu non illius, alter at ille.

     Circumſtant cunas quàm prona pericula Muſæ
Virginis! intactæ quàm lubrica fama puellæ!
Commendat fefe patris indulgentia primùm,   115
Molle lutum caſto ſi fingas pollice : forma
Vultûs prima manet, fingàtur et optima prima.

                 D ij

Let not auſterity breed ſervile fear,

No wanton ſound offend her virgin ear :

Secure from fooliſh pride's affected ſtate,

And ſpecious flatt'ry's more pernicious bait,   113

Habitual innocence adorns her thoughts,

But your neglect muſt anſwer for her faults.

     Immodeſt words admit of no defence,

For want of decency is want of ſenſe.   114

What mod'rate fop would rake the Park or ſtews

Who among troops of faultleſs nymphs may chuſe ?

Ne premat ingenium, libertatemque decoram

Auſteri ſervus timor, imperiumque magiſtri ;

Nec verba intereà violent laſciva pudicam :   120

Non illa ætatis ventoſo turgida faſtu

Addicat pronas aſſentatoribus aures,

Nec nimis illa procis pateat laudantibus ultrò ;

Sic decor ingenuus mentem huic ſine fraudibus ornet,

Sed culpa arguitur tua ſiquid neſcia peccat.   125

     Fas nunquam obſcœnis veniam concedere dictis,

Communi ſenſu planè caret horridus ille,

Quid deceat, quid non, pravè, aut ſecurus ineptè.

Ecquis enim ſapiens mediocriter, uſque profuſus

Æris, et uſque adeò nugator ſplendidus, inter   130

Libera cui nymphas commercia dentur honeſtas,

Solicitare velit plebem et de fæce lupanar ?

Ergò tuum eligere eſt dignè, cùm ſuppetat ingens,

Variety of fuch is to be found;
Take then a fubject proper to expound,
But moral great, and worth a poet's voice;
For men of fenfe defpife a trivial choice;   120
And fuch applaufe it muft expect to meet
As would fome painter bufy in a ftreet
To copy bulls and bears, and ev'ry fign
That calls the ftaring fots to nafty wine.
    Yet 't is not all to have a fubject good;   125
It muft delight us when 't is underftood.
He that brings fulfome objects to my view,
(As many old have done, and many new)
With naufeous images my fancy fills,
And all goes down like oxymel of fquills.   130

Dignaque materies, et rerum copia prægnans,
Quàm vertas etiam dignè quæ viribus apta eft;   135
Sit grandis, magnùmque fonans, morataque rectè.
Materiem fapiens fectantes fpernit inanem;
Hi fperent plaufus, quales per compita pictor
Excipit ille, artis qui ftultæ prodigus urfos,
Exprimit, et tauros, et fiquod penfile fignum   140
Attonito ad vappæ fæces trahit ore popellum.
    Nec tamen hoc fatìs eft fic elegiffe potenter
Materiem, nifi et hæc demùm intellecta placebit.
Objicit ante oculos mihi qui deformia vifu,
(Quod multi e prifcis, multi fecêre recentes)   145
Averfandâ animum malè torquet imagine, qualis

Inftruct the lift'ning world how Maro fings
Of ufeful fubjects and of lofty things;
Thefe will fuch true, fuch bright, ideas raife
As merit gratitude as well as praife:
But foul defcriptions are offenfive ftill,   135
Either for being like, or being ill:
For who, without a qualm, hath ever look'd
On holy garbage tho' by Homer cook'd?
Whofe railing heroes and whofe wounded gods
Makes fome fufpect he fnores as well as nods.   140
But I offend——Virgil begins to frown,
And Horace looks with indignation down;

Pharmaca guftantùm gravis ofcula torquet amaror.
Te duce, Virgilium attonitus latè audiat orbis,
Ut cecinit fublime! ut mifcuit utile dulci!
Omnibus hinc verè formofa orietur imago,   150
Devinctofque habeas, non tantùm laudibus æquos:
Te laudàffe parum eft, meritis ni præmia donent.
At non arridet defcribens turpia, vitam
Si bene pingat, idem eft, fi pravè: nam quis iniquæ
Tam patiens cænæ, ut faftidia ferre culinæ   155
Mæöniæ immotus fibi temperet? hìc fua divi
Vulnera dum plorant, et dum rixatur Achilles,
Non modò dormitat, vereor, fed ftertit Homerus.
Parciùs ifta:——Maro cœlo indignatus ab alto
Avertit, Flaccufque oculos: mea Mufa recedit   160

My blufhing Mufe with confcious fear retires,
And whom they like implicitly admires.

On fure foundations let your fabric rife,   145
And with attractive majefty furprife,
Not by affected meretricious arts,
But ftrict harmonious fymmetry of parts,
Which thro' the whole infenfibly muft pafs,
With vital heat to animate the mafs :   150
A pure, an active, an aufpicious, flame,
And bright as heav'n, from whence the blefling came ;
But few, oh ! few fouls, preordain'd by Fate,
The race of gods, have reach'd that envy'd height.

Tincta rubore genas, et quem par nobile fratrum
Vindicat, obfequio probat, et miratur in illis.

Manfurâ fundata bafi fe fabrica tollat,
Ut videam plenum gratæ, ftupeamque videndo
Majeftatis opus : miferâ non fplendeat arte   165
Fucatum, fed fit fimplex duntaxat, et unum,
Corpore compacto robuftum, et partibus aptis.
Hinc pura, hinc velox, hinc feliciffima flamma
Lumine divino (donum eft divinitùs ortum)
Per varias tacitè partes labatur, et intùs   170
Totam animet molem, foveatque caloribus almis,
Heu tamen, heu ! pauci, (quos Jupiter æquus amavit)
Pulchra Deûm foboles, mirum tetigêre cacumen.
Non novus huc Titan accedere crimine poffit

No rebel, Titan's facrilegious crime,   155
By heaping hills on hills, can hither climb;
The grizly ferryman of hell deny'd
Æneas entrance till he knew his guide:
How juftly then will impious mortals fall,
Whofe pride would foar to heav'n without a call!

    Pride (of all others the moft dang'rous fault) 161
Proceeds from want of fenfe or want of thought.
The men who labour and digeft things moft
Will be much apter to defpond than boaft;
For if your author be profoundly good   165
'Twill coft you dear before he's underftood.

Sacrilego, montes iterum fi montibus addat.   175
Squallidus, haud visâ primùm duce, portitor orci
Dardanio Heröi cymbamque, aditumque negavit,
Nec nifi monftratâ potuit mitefcere virgâ.
Quo non jure ruent noftrorum crimina, faftu
Qui vetito cœlum arripiunt, et non fua captant? 180

    Faftus, quo vitium non perniciofius ullum,
Arguit aut celeres animos, curâque carentes,
Aut turpis parit hunc infcitia, craffus et error.
Nam fiqui fudant impenfiùs, atque laborant,
Defperare magis, quàm funt jaduare parati.   185
Sic fi contineat fenfus tuus ille profundos,
Sæpe ftylum vertis, limæque incumbere totus
Cogeris, exprimere ut valeas, et reddere purum.

How many ages fince has Virgil writ!
How few are they who underftand him yet!
Approach his altars with religious fear,
No vulgar deity inhabits there :   170
Heav'n fhakes not more at Jove's imperial nod
Than poets fhould before their Mantuan god.
Hail, mighty Maro! may that facred name
Kindle my breaft with thy celeftial flame,
Sublime ideas and apt words infufe,   175
The Mufe inftruct my voice, and thou infpire the
    What I have inftanc'd only in the beft   [Mufe!
Is, in proportion, true of all the reft.

Sæc'lorum en! retrò quàm fluxit plurimus ordo,
Ex quo Virgilius legitur! fed pars quota vatem   190
Lectorum affequitur vulgò! tu pronus ad aras
Relligione pavens procumbe, habitat Deus intùs,
Nec de plebe deus : nutu Jovis altus Olympus
Si quatitur, trepidare Andina ad numina turbam
Fas pariter vatum, atque fuum placare Tonantem. 195
Salve magno Maro! fanctum, et venerabile nomen,
Noftra tuâ accendas cœlefti pectora flammâ.
Hinc O! res liceat, vivas hinc ducere voces,
Mufa mihi infpiret cantus, fed tu rege Mufam.
    Jamque ego de fummo dixi quodcunque poetâ, 2co
Id quoque de reliquis poteras dixiffe gradatim.
Sit primò proprium tibi curæ exquirere fenfum,

'Take pains the genuine meaning to explore,
There sweat, there strain, tug the laborious oar; 180
Search ev'ry comment that your care can find,
Some here, some there, may hit the poet's mind;
Yet be not blindly guided by the throng;
The multitude is always in the wrong.
When things appear unnatural or hard,   185
Consult your author, with himself compar'd;
Who knows what blessing Phœbus may bestow,
And future ages to your labour owe?
Such secrets are not easily found out,
But once discover'd leave no room for doubt: 190
Truth stamps conviction in your ravish'd breast,
And peace and joy attend the glorious guest.

Fortiter hoc contende, et totas exere vires.
Omnes ne pigeat criticorum evolvere chartas,
Forsitan hic ille, et rectè alter judicet illic.   205
At cave, ne turbam malefuada libido sequendi
Te teneat; semper præceps it vulgus, et errat.
Si quædam dura, et nimiùm detorta putabis,
Autorem sibi componens modò consule; quis scit,
Felici annuerit dexter si Cynthius aufo,   210
Quantùm fera tui ditârint sæc'la labores?
Hæc arcana quidem non cuilibet obvia curæ,
Sed simul ut patuêre, error fugit antè, metusque:
Intima pertentat solidum tibi pectora verùm,
Et pace æterná cumulat te candidus hofpes.   215

Truth ſtill is one; Truth is divinely bright,
No cloudy doubts obſcure her native light;
While in your thoughts you find the leaſt debate,
You may confound but never can tranſlate :   196
Your ſtyle will this thro' all diſguiſes ſhow,
For none explain more clearly than they know.
He only proves he underſtands a text
Whoſe expoſition leaves it unperplex'd.   200
They who too faithfully on names inſiſt,
Rather create than diſſipate the miſt,
And grow unjuſt by being over-nice,
(For ſuperſtitious virtue turns to vice.)

Simplex eſt Verum, et divinâ luce coruſcum,
Nec premit ingenuos vultus dubitabilis error.
Hoc certum eſt, tibi in ambiguo dum ſenſus adhæret,
Perplexum turbare magìs, ſed vertere nunquam
Sincerum dabitur : falſos per mille colores   220
Te prodet ſtylus ipſe cavâ ſub imagine ludens.
Nemo etenim verbis rem clariùs explicat, antè
Pectore quàm concepit ; et is concepit acutè,
Qui nil obſcurum verborum in nube relinquit.
Interpres fidus, nimiùm qui nomina curat,   225
Inducit potiùs tenebras, quàm diſſipat ; et fit
Jure adeò ex ſummo ſummè idem injurius : odit
Cœca ſuperſtitio, ſtultè quem diligit : ipſa
Sponte ſuâ in vitium virtus delabitur, ultrà

Let Craffus' * ghoft and Labienus tell 205
How twice in Parthian plains their legions fell;
Since Rome hath been fo jealous of her fame,
That few know Pacorus' or Monæfes' name.

Words in one language elegantly us'd
Will hardly in another be excus'd: 210
And fome that Rome admir'd in Cæfar's time
May neither fuit our genius nor our clime.
The genuine fenfe, intelligibly told,
Shews a Tranflator both difcreet and bold.

Excurfions are inexpiably bad, 215
And 't is much fafer to leave out than add.

Quàm par eft textûfque tenax, et mordicùs hærens.
Ut bis Romanas Parthi fregêre phalanges, 231
Aut, Labiene, tua, aut Craffi hoc edifferat umbra;
Quando ita confuluit famæ pia Roma fuorum,
Ut Pacorum vix noftra, agnofcant vix fæc'la Monæfen.

Quæ verba alterius linguæ fplendore nitefcunt,
Fortè carent veniâ, fi vis transferre; nec olim, 236
Omnia, quæ fovêre Augufti tempora, noftro
Conveniunt genio, nec honore ferentur eodem
Reddita: fed propriè fenfus, quos continet autor,
Qui docet, hic interpres erit confultus, et audax. 240

Longè a propofito nullis luftranda piac'lis
Culpa recedendi: nihil addas, fiquid omittas
Tutius eft, verbis cultum patientibus ægrè.

* Hor. lib. iii. ode 5.

2

Abſtruſe and myſtic thoughts you muſt expreſs
With painful care, but ſeeming eaſineſs,
For truth ſhines brighteſt thro' the plaineſt dreſs.
Th' Ænean Muſe, when ſhe appears in ſtate,　220
Makes all Jove's thunder on her verſes wait,
Yet writes ſometimes as ſoft and moving things
As Venus ſpeaks or Philomela ſings.
Your author always will the beſt adviſe;
Fall when he falls, and when he riſes riſe.　225
Affected noiſe is the moſt wretched thing
That to contempt can empty ſcribblers bring.
Vowels and accents, regularly plac'd,
On even ſyllables (and ſtill the laſt)

Myſtica ſi vatum quandoque arcana reſolves,
Lima tibi facilem cura mentita laboret,　245
Nativa ut videatur; amat ſplendeſcere verum
Simplex munditiis: cùm ſeſe Æneïa Muſa
Inferat inceſſu magno, Jovis æmula cingit
Flamma latus, fulmenque: interdum mollia ſcribit,
Quæ, Philomela, canas, quæ tu, Cytherëa, loquaris.
Conſilium dabit ipſe autor, rectèque monebit,　251
Cumque cadente cadas, et cum ſurgente reſurgas.
Crede mihi, nugas miſerum affectare canoras:
Nil aliud premit inferiùs per inania raptos.
Syllabanam modò par cadat omnis, et ultima ſemper,
(Quæ levis eſt cura) et propriis accentibus aüres 256
Ordo petat numeroſus, habebunt verba ſonos, et

E

Tho' grofs innumerable faults abound, 230
In fpite of nonfenfe never fail of found.
But this is meant of even vérfe álone,
As being moft harmonious and moft known ;
For if you will unequal numbers try,
There accents on odd fyllables muft lie. 235
Whatever fifter of the learned Nine
Does to your fuit'a willing ear incline,
Urge your fuccefs, deferve a lafting name,
She 'll crown a grateful and a conftant flame;
But if a wild uncertainty prevail, 240
And turn your veering heart with ev'ry gale,
You lofe the fruit of all your former care
For the fad profpect of a juft defpair.

Juftum adeò modulamen inania plurima rerum.
Hæc modò vera pari de carmine dicere fas eft,
Notum aliis quoniam magìs, et quià dúlcius; at fi
Forfan inæquales numeros tentare libebit, 261
Quà cadit accentus, cave, fyllaba quæq; fit impar.
E doctâ Aonidum turbâ quæcunque fororum
Arridens precibus furdam non admovet aurem,
Utere forte tuâ, decus immortale mereri 265
Nunc aude ; flammæ Mufa immemor effe fidelis
Non ingrata folet : quòd fi tibi mobile pectus
Fluctuat, et facili quòvis impellitur aurà,
Præteritus fordefcet honos, mæftufque videbis
Spem meritò ereptam tibi cum mercede laborum. 270

A quack (too.fcandaloufly mean to name)
Had by man-midwifery got wealth and fame : 245
As if Lucina had forgot her trade; ... ...
The lab'ring wife invokes his furer aid. :
Well-feafon'd bowls the goffip's fpirits raife,
Who while fhe guzzles chats the doctor's praife;
And largely, what fhe wants in words fupplies 250
With maudlin-eloquence of trickling eyes.
But what a thoughtlefs animal is man !
(How very active in his own trepan!).
For, greedy of phyficians' frequent fees,
From female mellow praife he takes degrees; 255

Ille, ferunt,(prohibent fed multa opprobria nomen)
Obftetricis erat functus dum munere; Agyrta
Et famam, et nummos peperit : quafi non memor artis
Ilithyïa fuæ; fer opem tu certior, inquit: ...
Parturiens, vir docte, uxor recreantur aniles. 275
Multâ fæce animi, et media inter pocula, Agyrtæ
Facta falutiferi refonant : fi copia verbis
Defit, facundos oculis litat ebria rores. [corpus!
Aft homo quàm brutum eft (prô dii!) fine pectore
Quàm fibimet promptâ molitur fraude ruinam ! 280
Nam medicorum avidè dum mercenarius aurum
Appetit, en! pariter doctam fibi vendicat artem
Syrmate non licito mirantia compita verrens;
Judice quòd vetulâ medicus fæpe audiit, ultrò

E·ij

Struts in a new unlicens'd gown, and then
From faving women falls to killing men.
Another fuch had left the nation thin,
In fpite of all the children he brought in.
His pills as thick as hand-grenadoes flew,   260
And where they fell as certainly they flew;
His name ftruck every where as great a damp
As Archimedes thro' the Roman camp.
With this the doctor's pride began to cool,
For fmarting foundly may convince a fool.   265
But now repentance came too late for grace,
And meagre Famine ftar'd him in the face:

Prodiit et medicus, defertâque arte tuendi   285
Uxorum vitas, properat jugulare maritos.
Huic alter geminus (talis fi fortè fuiffet
In terris) fexum jam noftrum abolere nefandis
Artibus, artis inops valuiffet, tot licèt edens
In lucem natos: telorum haud ferreus imber   290
Denfior emitti folet, hinc quàm emiffa volabant
Pharmaca, quàque cadunt, fimilem traxêre ruinam,
Nec certam minùs, ac quondam fublimis ab arce
Ille Syracofius Romanis undique caftris
Spargebat geometra; novus vel nomine folo   295
Dat ftragem medicus: fic defervefcere faftus
Paulatim cæpit; ftultus fua damna remordent
Supplicio edoctos tandem: factum dolet; at quid
Serò dolere juvat, fi gratia victa ferendo eft,

Fain would he to the wives be reconcil'd,
But found no husband left to own a child.
The friends that got the brats were poison'd too;
In this sad case what could our vermine do?　271
Worry'd with debts, and past all hope of bail,
Th' unpity'd wretch lies rotting in a jail;
And there, with basket-alms scarce kept alive,
Shews how mistaken talents ought to thrive.　275
　　I pity, from my soul, unhappy men,
Compell'd by want to prostitute their pen;
Who must, like lawyers, either starve or plead,
And follow, right or wrong, where guineas lead!

Jamque óculos si macra Famîs turbavit imago?　300
Sæpiùs optavit sponsas placare relictas,
Sed non sponsus erat, proles quem agnoscere posset.
Ipse etiam cecidit medicinâ extinctus eâdem
Furtivus pater: en! quò nunc se proripit ille
Accisis pennis, multo et gravis ære, nec usquam　305
Spes vadis? ergò miser nulli miserabilis imo
Carcere putrescit, vitam vix asse rogato
Sustentans, tristisque monet, quæ fata meretur,
Qui ruit ingenium contra, et temerarius errat.
　　Illius ipse vicem sincero ex pectore acerbam　310
Ingemo, qui Laribus durè compressus iniquis
Prostituit calamos, ét conditione maligñâ
Scribendo quæstum meritorius urget, ut actor
Causarum, non, quid pulchrum, quid turpe, requirit,

But you, Pompilian, wealthy, pamper'd, heirs, 280
Who to your country owe your swords and cares,
Let no vain hope your easy mind seduce,
For rich ill poets are without excuse.
'Tis very dang'rous tamp'ring with a Muse;
The profit 's small, and you have much to lose; 285
For tho' true wit adorns your birth or place,
Degen'rate lines degrade th' attainted race;
No poet any passion can excite
But what they feel transport them when they write.

At, dictante gulâ, rapit imperiofior auri 315
Majeflas cum voce fidem : fed vos, quibus ingens
Luxuries rerum, patriæ quos cuncta faluti
Confecrare decet, vos, Pompiliana propago,
Ne vanæ illecebræ captent, et pectora fallant;
Namque malis fimul, et locupletibus effe poëtis 320
Non homines, non dii, non conceffêre columnæ.
Extremum difcrimen adis, illudere dives
Qui chartis audes; nimìs alea luditur impar
Hæc tibi : committis totum, dum quærere pauca
Vix tandem poteris fudans. Feliciter ortus 325
Quamvìs fortè tuos cognatæ carmina venæ
Illuftrent, clarum inficiunt tibi ftemma viciffim
Degeneres verfus, ultrò accerfitus et error.
Jam fruftrà ftimulis animum mihi tangis ineftem,
Scribentis nifi mens affectibus æftuat iifdem, 330
Ni rabie fera corda tument, et fanguinis undis.

Have you been led thro' the Cumæan cave, 290
And heard th' impatient maid divinely rave?
I hear her now; I fee her rolling eyes:
And panting, " Lo! the god, the god!" fhe cries;
With words not her's, and more than human found,
She makes th' obedient ghofls peep trembling thro'
     the ground. 295
But tho' we muft obey when Heav'n commands,
And man in vain the facred call withftands,
Beware what fpirit rages in your breaft;
For ten infpir'd ten thoufand are poffeft.
Thus make the proper ufe of each extreme, 300
And write with fury, but correct with phlegm.

Túne per Euböice deductus virginis antrum
Senfifti vatem violento numine ferri,
Cùm Phœbi impatiens bacchatur? Ego audio, circùm
Disjectos ego cerno oculos, et pectus anhelum, 335
" Et deus, ecce deus!" clamat: jam non fua verba,
Nec mortale fonans, pallentes undique manes
Elicit, éque imis trepidos jubet ire fepulcris.
His licèt imperiis parendum haud mollibus ultrò eft,
Atque homines magnum furiato corde laborant 340
Excuffiffe Deum fruftrà; at qui fæviat intùs
Spiritus; intererit multùm; fortè unus, et alter
Phœbo agitur, falfis dum mille furoribus acti.
Affectu fic, fi fapies, utroque fruaris
Pectoris, extremo licèt hinc, atque inde remoto, 345

As when the cheerful hours too freely pafs,
And fparkling wine fmiles in the tempting glafs,
Your pulfe advifes, and begins to beat·
Thro' ev'ry fwelling vein a loud retreat; · 305
So when a Mufe propitioufly invites;
Improve her favours, and indulge her flights;
But when you find that vig'rous heat abate,
Leave off, and for another fummons wait.
Before the radiant fun a glimm'ring lamp, 310
Adult'rate metals to the fterling ftamp,
Appear not meaner than mere human lines
Compar'd with thofe whofe infpiration fhines:

Bile canens calidâ, frigenti carmina limans.
Ut nimis illa volant celeri cùm tempora lapfu,
Plena coronato rident ubi fpumea Baccho ·
Pocula, dant monitus venæ, motuque frequenti
Subfultant, canit et toto tuba corde receffum. 350
Mufa ubi te aufpiciis, pronifque furoribus urget,
Utere muneribus, nec celfa fub aftra volatus
Compefce ardentes, fed cùm tibi deficit ardor
Pectoris, inceptos præfens in tempus iämbos
Deponas, meliora et te ad momenta referves. 355
Non magis ad Phœbi radiatum lumen hebefcit,
Fax tremulum fplendens, aut diftant ære lupini,
Quàm fonat humanâ carmen triviale monetâ
Percuffum, fi divinis componitur inde
Carminibus, vérum quæ fpirant enthea Phœbum. 360

These nervous, bold; those languid and remiss;
There cold salutes, but here a lover's kiss.   315
Thus have I seen a rapid headlong tide.
With foaming waves the passive Soane divide,
Whose lazy waters without motion lay,
While he, with eager force, urg'd his impetuous way.

    The privilege that ancient poets claim,   320
Now turn'd to licenfe by too just a name,
Belongs to none but an establish'd fame,
Which scorns to take it——
Absurd expressions, crude abortive thoughts,
All the lewd legion of exploded faults,   325

Hic vires, animique, ibi stagnat frigidus humor,
Aut natat in labris delumbis, ut ofcula libat
Casta parens puero : sed in his furor omnis amantùm.
Haud aliter quondam magno cum murmure vidi
Per medium ire Ararim, et tacitum distinguere flumen
Æstu præcipiti Rhodanum : stagnantibus undis   366
Miratur patiens Araris, dum fpumeus amnis
Urget iter, fervenfque fretis petit æquora torrens.
    Libertas, prisci sibi quam arripuêre poetæ,
(Nomine jam nimiùm quæ dicta licentia justo)   370
Famæ securo scriptori propria soli est,
Quam parcè veniam tamen is, fumetque pudenter.
Absurdi sensus, cruda, imperfectaque vocum
Progenies, malè nata cohors, et Apolline lævo
Affectare proterva diem, se hoc jure tuetur :   375

Bafe fugitives to that afylum fly,
And facred laws with infolence defy;
Not thus our heroes of the former days
Deferv'd and gain'd their never-fading bays;
For I miftake, or far the greateft part   330
Of what fome call neglect was ftudy'd art:
When Virgil feems to trifle in a line,
'Tis like a warning-piece, which gives the fign
To wake your fancy, and prepare your fight
To reach the noble height of fome unufual flight.
I lofe my patience when with faucy pride   336
By untun'd ears I hear his numbers try'd.

Defendit numerus quia fcilicet improbus; et plebs,
Jam Phœbum impunè, et rident Parnaffia jura.
Non fic heroes, quos fæc'la priora tulerunt,
Æternùm virides lauros fecêre merendo.
Fallor enim, vel quæ multis incuria vifa eft, 380
Artis opus fummum fuit; ut cùm fortè videtur
Ludere Virgilius vulgari in carmine, fignum hoc
Præmittit, jubet huc totas intendere curàs,
Huc geminas acies, oculo furgentis ut acri
Infolitos valeas nifus æquare fequendo.   385
Aft ego jam bili non impero, nam quis iniqui
Tam patiens faftûs, quis ferreus, ut teneat fe?
Omnia jam fiunt præpoftera! quippe ubi fanæ
Plebs rationis inops, imitatrix turba novorum,
Improba folicitat divini fcripta Maronis: 390

Reverfe of Nature! fhall fuch copies then
Arraign th'originals of Maro's pen!
And the rude notions of pedantic fchools   340
Blafpheme the facred founder of our rules!

   The delicacy of the niceft ear
Finds nothing harfh or out of order there.
Sublime or low, unbended or intenfe,
The found is ftill a comment to the fenfe.   345

   A fkilful ear in numbers fhould prefide,
And all difputes without appeal decide :
This ancient Rome and elder Athens found,
Before miftaken ftops debauch'd the found.

Cùm facrum exemplar, leges qui condidit ipfas,
Ad trutinam revocant tyrones lege foluti;
Et prædulce melos, ftatuit quod maximus autor,
Vocibus, et linguâ violat fchola ráuca profaná.

   Cunⅽta licèt judex digitis, et callidus aure   395
Sufpendat, nihil hìc durum reprehendere poffit,
Nil incompofitum; five is fublimia tentat,
Seu modò deduⅽtus, lenis, feu tenfus, et acer,
Ipfe aperit fenfum fonus, et commendat in aurem.

   De numeris litem dirimat folertior auris,   400
Judiciumque iftâ ferat irrevocabile causâ.
Illud Roma vetus, feniores illud Athenæ
Expertæ, cùm non titubarent carmina punⅽtis
Pravè difpofitis, quæ contiguos malè fenfus,
Nativofque fonos intempeftiva premebant.   405

When, by impulfe from Heav'n, Tyrtæus fung,
In drooping foldiers a new courage fprung,   351
Reviving Sparta now the fight maintain'd,
And what two gen'rals loft a poet gain'd.
By fecret influence of indulgent Skies
Empire and poefy together rife.   355
True poets are the guardians of a ftate,
And when they fail portend approaching fate;
For that which Rome to conqueft did infpire
Was not the Veftal but the Mufes' fire;
Heav'n joins the bleffings: no declining age   360
Ere felt the raptures of poetic rage.

Impellente *Deo* cecinit cum carmina quondam
Tyrtæus, fubiît nova victi pectora virtus
Militis, immotam in medio fe turbine belli
Sparta revivifcens tenuit, vatefque redemit
Unicus a gemino amiffos ductore triumphos.   410
Sic arcana jubet placidi indulgentia Fati,
Surgat ut imperium, furgit cùm dia poëfis.
Regnorum fervant facro fub pectore vates
Palladium, pariterque ruunt cum vatibus illa,
Aut nutant ruitura brevi: qui fubdidit olim   415
Romæ animi vires, tantoque accendit amore
Lauri, non Veftalis erat, fed Delius ignis.
Munera conjungunt Superi; vergentia fæc'la
Gaudia Pierii nunquam fenfêre furoris.

Of many faults rhyme is perhaps the caufe;
Too ftrict to rhyme, we flight more ufeful laws,
For that in Greece or Rome was never known,
'Till by barbarian deluges o'erflown;   365
Subdu'd, undone, they did at laft obey,
And change their own for their invader's way.
 I grant that from fome moffy idol oak,
In double rhymes, our Thor and Woden fpoke,
And by fucceffion of unlearned times,   370
As Bards began, fo Monks rung on the chimes.
 But now that Phœbus and the facred Nine,
With all their beams, on our blefs'd ifland fhine,

Forte mali caput eft dominans fub fine fonorum 420
Rhythmus; qui rhythmo paret, meliora relinquit
Turpe jugum fubiens; Latium hunc, necGræcia nôrat,
Diluvies prius in linguas quàm fluxerat ambas
Barbara, cùm victi tandem ceffêre, fuafque
Mutavêre vias victoris jura fequuti.   425
 Mufcosâ, fateor, Vodinus ab ilice nofter,
Et Thorus pede bis percuffo oracula fudit
Auribus ingeminans agreftibus: hinc mala porrò
Fluxit in ætatem obfcuram prurigo fonandi,
Pulfâruntque greges Monachorum, Helicone relicto,
Pulfârant primi quæ tintinnabula Bardi.   431
 At cùm Caftalides Divæ, et Thynibræus Apollo
Jam pleno Britonum redeuntes lumine terras

F

Why should not we their ancient rites restore,
And be what Rome or Athens were before?   375
    " Have we forgot how Raphael's num'rous profe *
" Led our exalted fouls thro' heav'nly camps,
" And mark'd the ground where proud apostate
" Defy'd Jehovah! Here'twixt host and host, [thrones
" (A narrow but a dreadful interval!)   380
" Portentous fight! before the cloudy van
" Satan with vast and haughty strides advanc'd,
" Came tow'ring arm'd in adamant and gold:
" There bellowing engines with their fiery tubes
" Difpers'd ethereal forms, and down they fell   385

Illuftrant, licent Phœbi, ritufque Sororum
Inftaurare, iterum hìc Roma, atque legantur Athenæ.
    " Ergòne Miltoni numerofa oratio lapfa eft   436
" Pectoribus, noftras cùm per cœleftia caftra
" Sublimes animas rapuit, campumque notavit,
" Quò demente tumens faftu, procerumque rebellis
" Explicuit fe multa cohors, ipfumque Tonantem
" Solicitare aufa eft armis! hìc inter utramque   441
" Ecce! aciem (horrendum vifu, brevè at intervallum)
" Arduus, arma tenens nimbosâ in fronte phalangum
" Lucifer exultat, faltuque ingente fuperbus
" Prorumpit rapidè, galeâ fpectabilis aureâ,   445
" Munitufque humeros latos folido adamante.
" Rauco illic fremitu tormenta vomentia flammam
" Ætherias fternunt formas, et turbine vafto

    * An effay on blank verfe out of Paradife Loft, Book VI.

" By thoufands, angels on archangels roll'd;
" Recover'd, to the hills they ran, they flew, [woods)
" Which (with their pond'rous load, rocks, waters,
" From their firm feats torn by the fhaggy tops 389
" They bore like fhields before them thro' the air,
" Till more incens'd they hurl'd them at their foes.
" All was confufion, heav'n's foundations fhook,
" Threat'ning no lefs than univerfal wreck,
" For Michael's arm main promontories flung,
" And over-prefs'd whole legions weak with fin: 395
" Yet they blafphem'd and ftruggled as they lay,

" Undique cernere erat magni per inania cœli
" Agmina mille fimul fuper agmina mille voluta. 450
" Ut rediêre animi, colles petiêre volatu
" Præcipiti, fubitò quos ex radicibus altis,
" Rupefque, fluviofque, immenfaque pondera, fylvas,
" Avellunt unà, latèque per aëra torquent
" Pro clypeis, vel cùm rabies magìs arfit, in hoftem
" Ipfas vi rapidâ ex alto mifêre ruinas. 456
" Jam chàos omnia erant; totus fundamine ab ipfo
" Æther contremuit, dirum promittere vifus
" Naturæ exitium: Michäel nam fedibus imis
" Tota vibrat folus jam promontoria dextrâ 460
" Extorquens, totas vitiis, et crimine fractas
" Obruit ille acies, fed nec fpirare fuperbi
" Ceffavêre minas, et adhuc fremuêre jacentes;

" Till the great enfign of Mefliah blaz'd,

" And, arm'd with vengeance, God's victorious Son

" (Effulgence of paternal Deity)

" Grafping ten thoufand thunders in his hand, 400

" Drove th' old orig'nal rebels headlong down,

" And fent them flaming to the vaft abyfs."

O may I live to hail the glorious day,

And fing loud Pæans thro' the crowded way,

When in triumphant ftate the Britifh Mufe, 405

True to herfelf, fhall barb'rous aid refufe,

And in the Roman majefty appear,

Which none know better, and none come fo near. 408

" Dum Chrifti effulgens vexillum apparuit altè,

" Ingens, terribilique incumbens hoftibus umbrâ,

" Ultricemque ferens Pænam invictiffima proles 466

" Numinis æterni (quantum Patris inftar in ipfo!)

" Mifcet agens telis, et vivo fulphure fixos

" Dextrâ præcipitans barathrum deturbat ad imum."

O! mihi tam longæ fuperet pars ultima vitæ, 470

Spiritus, et quantum fat erit plaudentibus inter-

Effe, triumphali cùm Mufa Britannica pompâ

Per denfas hominum læto Pæane catervas

Procedet verâ facie, non barbara cultu,

Ipfa fuis opibus pollens, atque æmula Romæ, 475

Majeftate pari, et nativo lumine fulgens,

Juncta duci, claudenfque latus, quam nulla recentûm

Callet Mufa magis, fequitur nec paffibus æquis. 478

THE DREAM.

To the pale tyrant who to horrid graves
Condemns so many thousand helpless slaves,
Ungrateful we do gentle sleep compare,
Who, tho' his victories as num'rous are,
Yet from his slaves no tribute does he take,   5
But woful cares that load men while they wake.
When his soft charms had eas'd my weary sight
Of all the baleful troubles of the light,
Dorinda came, divested of the scorn
Which the unequall'd maid so long had worn;   10
How oft', in vain, had Love's great god essay'd
To tame the stubborn heart of that bright maid!
Yet, spite of all the pride that swells her mind,
The humble god of Sleep can make her kind.
A rising blush increas'd the native store   15
Of charms that but too fatal were before.
Once more present the vision to my view,
The sweet illusion, gentle Fate! renew;
How kind, how lovely she, how ravish'd I!
Shew me, bless'd god of Sleep! and let me die.   20

THE GHOST

OF THE OLD HOUSE OF COMMONS TO THE NEW ONE,

Appointed to meet at Oxford.

From deepeft dungeons of eternal night,
The feats of Horror, Sorrow, Pains, and Spite,
I have been fent to tell you, tender youth!
A feafonable and important truth.
I feel (but, oh! too late) that no difeafe   5
Is like a furfeit of luxurious eafe;
And of all others the moft tempting things
Are too much wealth and too indulgent kings.
None ever was fuperlatively ill
But by degrees, with induftry and fkill;   10
And fome, whofe meaning hath at firft been fair,
Grow knaves by ufe, and rebels by defpair.
My time is paft, and yours will foon begin;
Keep the firft bloffoms from the blaft of fin,
And by the fate of my tumultuous ways   15
Preferve yourfelves, and bring ferener days.
The bufy, fubtle, ferpents of the law,
Did firft my mind from true obedience draw.
While I did limits to the king prefcribe,
And took for oracles that canting tribe,   20
I chang'd true freedom for the name of Free,
And grew feditious for variety:

All that oppos'd me were to be accus'd,
And by the laws illegally abus'd;
The robe was fummon'd, Maynard in the head,   25
In legal murder none fo deeply read;
I brought him to the bar, where once he ftood,
Stain'd with the (yet unexpiated) blood
Of the brave Strafford, when three kingdoms rung
With his accumulative hackney-tongue;   30
Pris'ners and witneffes were waiting by,
Thefe had been taught to fwear, and thofe to die,
And to expect their arbitrary fates,
Some for ill faces, fome for good eftates.
To fright the people, and alarm the Town,   35
Bedloe and Oates employ'd the rev'rend gown;
But while the triple mitre bore the blame,
The king's Three Crowns were their rebellious aim:
I feem'd (and did but feem) to fear the Guards,
And took for mine the Bethels and the Wards,   40
Anti-monarchic Heretics of ftate,
Immoral Atheifts, rich and reprobate:
But above all I got a little guide
Who ev'ry ford of villany had try'd;
None knew fo well the old pernicious way   45
To ruin fubjects, and make kings obey;
And my fmall Jehu, at a furious rate,
Was driving Eighty back to Forty-eight;
This the king knew, and was refolv'd to bear,
But I miftook his patience for his fear.   50

All that this happy ifland could afford
Was facrific'd to my voluptuous board.
In his whole paradife one only tree
He had excepted by a ftrict decree;
A facred tree! which royal fruit did bear,　55
Yet it in pieces I confpir'd to tear:
Beware, my Child! divinity is there.
This fo undid all I had done before,
I could attempt and he endure no more;
My unprepar'd and unrepenting breath　60
Was fnatch'd away by the fwift hand of Death,
And I, with all my fins about me, hurl'd
To th' utter darknefs of the lower world;
A dreadful place! which you too foon will fee,
If you believe feducers more than me.　65

ROSS'S GHOST.

Shame of my life, difturber of my tomb,
Bafe as thy mother's proftituted womb;
Huffing to cowards, fawning to the brave,
To knaves a fool, to cred'lous fools a knave,
The king's betrayer, and the people's flave!　5
Like Samuel, at thy necromantic call
I rife, to tell thee God has left thee, Saul.
I ftrove in vain th' infected blood to cure;
Streams will run muddy where the fpring's impure.

In all your meritorious life we fee   10
Old Taaf's invincible fobriety.
Places of Mafter of the Horfe, and Spy,
You (like Tom Howard) did at once fupply :
From Sidney's blood your loyalty did fpring ;
You fhow us all your parents but the king,   15
From whofe too tender and too bounteous arms
(Unhappy he who fuch a viper warms! .
As dutiful a fubject as a fon !)
To your true parent, the whole Town, you run.
Read, if you can, how th' old apoftate fell,   20
Outdo his pride, and merit more than hell :
Both he and you were glorious and bright,
The firft and faireft of the fons of light ;
But when, like him, you offer'd at the crown,
Like him, your angry father kick'd you down.   25

A PARAPHRASE ON PS. CXLVIII.

O AZURE vaults! O cryftal fky!
The world's tranfparent canopy,
Break your long filence, and let mortals know
With what contempt you look on things below.

Wing'd fquadrons of the god of War,   5
Who conquer wherefoe'er you are,
Let echoing anthems make his praifes known
On earth his footftool, as in heav'n his throne.

Great eye of all, whofe glorious ray
Rules the bright empire of the day,   10
O praife his name! without whofe purer light
Thou hadft been hid in an abyfs of night.

Ye Moon and Planets! who difpenfe
By God's command your influence,
Refign to him, as your Creator due,   15
That veneration which men pay to you.

Faireft, as well as firft, of things,
From whom all joy, all beauty, fprings,
O! praife th'Almighty Ruler of the globe,
Who ufeth thee for his empyreal robe.   20

Praife him ye loud harmonious Spheres!
Whofe facred ftamp all Nature bears;
Who did all forms from the rude chaos draw,
And whofe command is th' univerfal law.

Ye wat'ry Mountains of the fky,   25
And you fo far above our eye,
Vaft ever-moving Orbs! exalt his name,
Who gave its being to your glorious frame.

Ye Dragons! whofe contagious breath
Peoples the dark retreats of Death,   30

Change your fierce hiffing into joyful fong,
And praife your Maker with your forked tongue.

Praife him, ye Monfters of the deep!
That in the feas' vaft bofoms fleep,
At whofe command the foaming billows roar,   35
Yet know their limits, tremble and adore.

Ye Mifts and Vapours, Hail and Snow!
And you who thro' the concave blow,
Swift executors of his holy word,
Whirlwinds and Tempefts! praife th' Almighty Lord.

Mountains! who to your Maker's view   41
Seem lefs than molehills do to you,
Remember how, when firft Jehovah fpoke,
All heav'n was fire, and Sinai hid in fmoke.

Praife him, fweet Offspring of the ground,   45
With heav'nly nectar yearly crown'd!
And ye tall Cedars! celebrate his praife,
That in his temple facred altars raife.

Idle Muficians of the fpring,
Whofe only care 's to love and fing,   50
Fly thro' the world, and let your trembling throat
Praife your Creator with the fweeteft note.

Praife him each favage furious Beaft
That on his ftores do daily feaft!
And you tame Slaves of the laborious plow,   55
Your weary knees to your Creator bow.

Majeftic Monarchs, mortal gods!
Whofe pow'r hath here no periods,   .
May all attempts againft your crowns be vain!
But ftill remember by whofe pow'r you reign.   60

Let the wide world his praifes fing
Where Tagus and Euphrates fpring,
And from the Danube's frofty banks, to thofe
Where from an unknown head great Nilus flows.

                                                      .

You that difpofe of all our lives,   65
Praife him from whom your pow'r derives;
Be true and juft like him, and fear his word,
As much as malefactors do your fword.

Praife him old Monuments of time!
O praife him in your youthful prime!   70
Praife him, fair Idols of our greedy fenfe!
Exalt his name, fweet age of Innocence!

Jehovah's name fhall only laft
When heav'n, and earth, and all is paft:
        I

Nothing, great God! is to be found in thee   75
But unconceivable eternity.

Exalt, O Jacob's facred race!
The God of gods, the God of grace!
Who will above the ftars your empire raife,
And with his glory recompenfe your praife.   80

ODE UPON SOLITUDE.

I.

Hail, facred Solitude! from this calm bay
I view the world's tempeftuous fea,
And with wife pride defpife
All thofe fenfelefs vanities:
With pity mov'd for others, caft away   5
On rocks of hopes and fears, I fee them toft
On rocks of folly, and of vice I fee them loft:
Some the prevailing malice of the great,
Unhappy men or adverfe Fate,
Sunk deep into the gulfs of an afflicted ftate: 10
But more, far more, a numberlefs prodigious train,
Whilft Virtue courts them, but, alas! in vain,
Fly from her kind embracing arms,
Deaf to her fondeft call, blind to her greateft charms,
And, funk in pleafures and in brutifh eafe,   15
They in their fhipwreck'd ftate themfelves obdurate
     pleafe.

G

II.

Hail, facred Solitude! foul of my foul,
It is by thee I truly live;
Thou doft a better life and nobler vigour give;
Doft each unruly appetite control;   20
Thy conftant quiet fills my peaceful breaft
With unmix'd joy, uninterrupted reft.
Prefuming Love does ne'er invade
This private folitary fhade;
And, with fantaftic wounds by Beauty made,   25
The joy has no allay of jealoufy, hope, and fear,
The folid comforts of this happy fphere:
Yet I exalted love admire,
Friendfhip abhorring fordid gain,
And purify'd from luft's difhoneft ftain: 30
Nor is it for my Solitude unfit,
For I am with my friend alone,
As if we were but one;
'Tis the polluted love that multiplies,
But friendfhip does two fouls in one comprife.   35

III.

Here in a full and conftant tide doth flow
All bleffings man can hope to know;
Here in a deep recefs of thought we find
Pleafures which entertain and which exalt the mind;
Pleafures which do from friendfhip and from know-
          ledge rife,   40
Which make us happy, as they make us wife:

Here may I always on this downy grafs,
Unknown, unfeen, my eafy minutes pafs,
'Till with a gentle force victorious Death
My Solitude invade, 45
And, ftopping for a while my breath,
With eafe convey me to a better fhade. 47

ON THE

DEATH OF A LADY'S DOG.

Thou, happy Creature! art fecure
From all the torments we endure;
Defpair, ambition, jealoufy,
Loft friends, nor love, difquiet thee;
A fullen prudence drew thee hence 5
From noife, fraud, and impertinence.
Tho' life effay'd the fureft wile,
Gilding itfelf with Laura's fmile,
How didft thou fcorn life's meaner charms,
Thou who couldft break from Laura's arms! 10
Poor Cynic! ftill methinks I hear
Thy awful murmurs in my ear,
As when on Laura's lap you lay,
Chiding the worthlefs crowd away.
How fondly human paffions turn!
What we then envy'd now we mourn! 16

ON THE DAY OF JUDGMENT.

I.

The day of wrath, that dreadful day!
Shall the whole world in afhes lay,
As David and the Sibyls fay.

II.

What horror will invade the mind
When the ftrict Judge, who would be kind,　　5
Shall have few venial faults to find!

III.

The laft loud trumpet's wondrous found
Shall thro' the rending tombs rebound,
And wake the nations under ground.

IV.

Nature and Death fhall, with furprife,　　10
Behold the pale offender rife,
And view the Judge with confcious eyes.

V.

Then fhall, with univerfal dread,
The facred myftic book be read,
To try the living and the dead.　　15

VI.

The Judge afcends his awful throne;
He makes each fecret fin be known;
And all with fhame confefs their own.

VII.

O then! what int'reft fhall I make
To fave my laft important ftake,   20
When the moft juft have caufe to quake?

VIII.

Thou mighty formidable King!
Thou mercy's unexhaufted fpring!
Some comfortable pity bring.

IX.

Forget not what my ranfom coft,   25
Nor let my dear-bought foul be loft,
In ftorms of guilty terror toft.

X.

Thou who for me didft feel fuch pain,
Whofe precious blood the crofs did ftain,
Let not thofe agonies be vain.   30

XI.

Thou whom avenging pow'rs obey,
Cancel my debt (too great to pay)
Before the fad accounting-day.

XII.

Surrounded with amazing fears,
Whofe load my foul with anguifh bears,   35
I figh, I weep : accept my tears.

XIII.

Thou who wert mov'd with Mary's grief,
And, by abfolving of the thief,
Haft given me hope, now give relief.

XIV.

Reject not my unworthy pray'r;   40
Preserve me from that dang'rous snare
Which Death and gaping Hell prepare.

XV.

Give my exalted soul a place
Among thy chosen right-hand race,
The sons of God, and heirs of grace.   45

XVI.

From that insatiable abyss,
Where flames devour and serpents hiss,
Promote me to thy seat of bliss.

XVII.

Prostrate my contrite heart I rend,
My God! my Father! and my Friend!   50
Do not forsake me in my end.

XVIII.

Well may they curse their second breath
Who rise to a reviving death;
Thou! great Creator of mankind!
Let guilty man compassion find.   55

A PROSPECT OF DEATH.

I.

Since we can die but once, and after death
Our ftate no alteration knows,
But when we have refign'd our breath
Th' immortal fpirit goes
To endlefs joys or everlafting woes;⁣   5
Wife is that man who labours to fecure
That mighty and important ftake,
And by all methods ftrives to make
His paffage fafe, and his reception fure.
Merely to die no man of reafon fears,   10
For certainly we muft,
As we are born, return to duft;
'Tis the laft point of many ling'ring years:
But whither then we go,
Whither we fain would know,   15
But human underftanding cannot fhow:
This makes us tremble, and creates
Strange apprehenfions in the mind,
Fills it with reftlefs doubts and wild debates,
Concerning what we, living, cannot find.   20
None know what death is but the dead,
Therefore we all by nature dying dread,
As a ftrange doubtful way we know not how to tread.

II.

When to the margin of the grave we come,
And scarce have one black painful hour to live,   25
No hopes, no prospect, of a kind reprieve
To stop our speedy passage to the tomb,
How moving and how mournful is the sight!
How wondrous pitiful, how wondrous sad!
Where then is refuge, where is comfort, to be had 30
In the dark minutes of the dreadful night
To cheer our drooping souls for their amazing flight?
Feeble and languishing in bed we lie,
Despairing to recover, void of rest,
Wishing for death, and yet afraid to die;   35
Terrors and doubts distract our breast,
With mighty agonies and mighty pains opprest.

III.

Our face is moisten'd with a clammy sweat;
Faint and irregular the pulses beat;
The blood unactive grows,   40
And thickens as it flows,
Depriv'd of all its vigour, all its vital heat.
Our dying eyes roll heavily about,
Their lights just going out,
And for some kind assistance call;   45
But pity, useless pity, is all
Our weeping friends can give
Or we receive;
Tho' their desires are great their pow'rs are small.

The tongue 's unable to declare 50
The pains, the griefs, the miferies, we bear.
How infupportable our torments are!
Mufic no more delights our deaf'ning ears,
Reftores our joys, or diffipates our fears,
But all is melancholy, all is fad, 55
In robes of deepeft mourning clad;
For ev'ry faculty and ev'ry fenfe
Partakes the woe of this dire exigence.

IV.

Then we are fenfible too late
'Tis no advantage to be rich or great; 60
For all the fulfome pride and pageantry of ftate
No confolation brings;
Riches and honours then are ufelefs things,
Taftelefs or bitter all,
And like the book which the Apoftle ate, 65
To their ill-judging palate fweet,
But turn at laft to naufeoufnefs and gall!
Nothing will then our drooping fpirits cheer
But the remembrance of good actions paft:
Virtue 's a joy that will for ever laft, 70
And make pale Death lefs terrible appear;
Takes out his baneful fting, and palliates our fear.
In the dark antichamber of the grave
What would we give, even all we have,
All that our care and induftry had gain'd, 75
All that our fraud, our policy, or art, obtain'd,

Could we recall thofe fatal hours again
Which we confum'd in fenfelefs vanities,
Ambitious follies and luxurious eafe;   79
For then they urge our terrors, and increafe our pain.

V.

Our friends and relatives ftand weeping by,
Diffolv'd in tears to fee us die,
And plunge into the deep abyfs of wide eternity.
In vain they mourn, in vain they grieve,
Their forrows cannot ours relieve.   85
They pity our deplorable eftate,
But what, alas! can pity do
To foften the decrees of Fate?
Befides the fentence is irrevocable too.
All their endeavours to preferve our breath,   90
Tho' they do unfuccefsful prove,
Shew us how much, how tenderly, they love,
But cannot cut off the entail of Death.
Mournful they look, and crowd about our bed;
One, with officious hafte,   95
Brings us a cordial we want fenfe to tafte;
Another foftly raifes up our head,
This wipes away the fweat, that, fighing, cries,
" See what convulfions, what ftrong agonies,
" Both foul and body undergo !   100
" His pains no intermiffion know;
" For ev'ry gafp of air he draws returns in fighs."

Each would his kind affiftance lend
To ferve his dear relation or his dearer friend;
But ftill in vain with Deftiny they all contend.　105
VI.
Our father, pale with grief and watching grown,
Takes our cold hand in his and cries, " Adieu!
" Adieu, my Child! now I muft follow you;"
Then weeps, and gently lays it down.
Our fons, who in their tender years　　　　110
Were objects of our cares and of our fears,
Come trembling to our bed, and, kneeling, cry,
" Blefs us, O Father! now before you die;
" Blefs us, and be you blefs'd to all eternity!"
Our friend, whom equal to ourfelves we love,　115
Compaffionate and kind,
Cries, " Will you leave me here behind?
" Without me fly to the blefs'd feats above?
" Without me did I fay? Ah! no;
" Without thy friend thou can'ft not go:　　　120
" For tho' thou leav'ft me grov'lling here below,
" My foul with thee fhall upward fly,
" And bear thy fpirit company
" Thro' the bright paffage of the yielding fky.
" Ev'n Death, that parts thee from thyfelf, fhall be
" Incapable to feparate　　　　　　　　126
" (For 't is not in the pow'r of Fate)
" My friend, my beft, my deareft, friend and me.

" But since it must be so, farewell!
" For ever? No; for we shall meet again,   130
" And live like gods, tho' now we die like men,
" In the eternal regions where just spirits dwell."

VII.

The soul, unable longer to maintain
The fruitless and unequal strife,
Finding her weak endeavours vain   135
To keep the commerce up of life,
By slow degrees retires more near the heart,
And fortifies that little fort
With all the kind artillerom of art,
Because it grows guarding on by part :   140
But Death, whose arms no mortal can repel,
A cruel siege disdains to lay,
Summons his force his allies to the fray,
And in a mioore storms the feeble citadel.
Sometimes we may capitulate, and he   145
Proceeds to make a solid peace;
But 't is all sham, all artifice,
That we may negligent and careless be;
For if his armies are withdrawn to-day,
And we believe no danger near,   150
But all is peaceable and all is clear,
His troops return some unsuspected way :
While in the soft embrace of sleep we lie
The secret murd'rers stab us, and we die.

Since our firft parents' fall   155
Inevitable Death defcends on all,
A portion none of human race can mifs;
But that which makes it fweet or bitter is
The fears of mifery or certain hope of blifs:
For when th' impenitent and wicked die,   160
Loaded with crimes and infamy,
If any fenfe at that fad time remains,
They feel amazing terrors, mighty pains,
The earneft of that vaft ftupendous woe
Which they to all eternity muft undergo,   165
Confin'd in hell with everlafting chains.
Infernal fpirits hover in the air
Like rav'nous wolves to feize upon their prey,
And hurry the departed fouls away
To the dark receptacles of Defpair,   170
Where they muft dwell till that tremendous day
When the loud trumpet calls them to appear
Before a Judge moft terrible and moft fevere,
By whofe juft fentence they muft go
To everlafting pains and endlefs woe,   175
Which always are extreme, and always will be fo.

VIII.

But the good man, whofe foul is pure,
Unfpotted, regular, and free
From all the ugly ftains of luft and villany,
Of mercy and of pardon fure,   180

H

Looks thro' the darknefs of the gloomy night,
And fees the dawning of a glorious day;
Sees crowds of angels ready to convey
His foul, whenc'er fhe takes her flight,
'To the furprifing manfions of immortal light :   185
'Then the celeftial guards around him ftand,
Nor fuffer the black demons of the air
'T" oppofe his paffage to the Promis'd Land,
Or terrify his thoughts with wild defpair,
But all is calm within, and all without is fair.   190
His pray'rs, his charity, his virtues prefs
To plead for mercy when he wants it moft,
Not one of all the happy number 's loft;
And thofe bright advocates ne'er want fuccefs.
But when the foul 's releas'd from dull mortality, 195
She paffes up in triumph thro' the fky,
Where fhe 's united to a glorious throng
Of angels, who, with a celeftial fong,
Congratulate her conqueft as fhe flies along.

IX.

If therefore all muft quit the ftage,   2co
When, or how foon, we cannot know,
But, late or early, we are fure to go
In the frefh blood of youth or wither'd age,
We cannot take too fedulous a care
In this important grand affair;   ·   205
For as we die we muft remain;

Hereafter all our hopes are vain
To make our peace with Heav'n, or to return again.
The Heathen, who no better understood
Than what the light of Nature taught, declar'd 210.
No future miseries could be prepar'd
For the sincere, the merciful, the good;
But if there was a state of rest,
They should with the same happiness be bless'd
As the immortal gods, if gods there were, possess'd.
We have the promise of eternal Truth   216
Those who live well, and pious paths pursue,
To man and to their Maker true,
Let them expire in age or youth
Can never miss   220
Their way to everlasting bliss;
But from a world of misery and care
To mansions of eternal ease repair,
Where joy in full perfection flows,
No interruption, no cessation, knows,
But in a mighty circle round for ever goes.   226

ON

MR. DRYDEN'S RELIGIO LAICI.

Begone, you slaves! you idle vermine! go,
Fly from the scourges, and your master know;
Let free impartial men from Dryden learn
Mysterious secrets of a high concern,

And weighty truths, folid convincing fenfe,   5
Explain'd by unaffected Eloquence.
What can you (Rev'rend Levi !) here take ill ?
Men ftill had faults, and men will have them ftill;
He that hath none, and lives as angels do,
Muft be an angel; but what 's that to you ?   10

 While mighty Lewis finds the Pope too great,
And dreads the yoke of his impofing feat,
Our fects a more tyrannic pow'r affume,
And would for fcorpions change the rods of **Rome**;
That church detain'd the legacy divine;   15
Fanatics caft the pearls of Heav'n to fwine :
What then have honeft thinking men to do
But chufe a mean between th' ufurping two?

 Nor can th' Egyptian Patriarch blame my Mufe,
Which for his firmnefs does his heat excufe;   20
Whatever councils have approv'd his creed,
The preface, fure, was his own act and deed.
Our church will have that preface read, you 'll fay;
'Tis true, but fo fhe will th'Apocrypha,
And fuch as can believe them freely may.   25

 But did that God, (fo little underftood)
Whofe darling attribute is being good,
From the dark womb of the rude chaos bring
Such various creatures, and make man their king,
Yet leave his fav'rite man, his chiefeft care,   30
More wretched than the vileft infects are ?

O! how much happier and more safe are they?
If helpless millions must be doom'd a prey
To yelling Furies, and for ever burn
In that sad place from whence is no return,　　　35
For unbelief in one they never knew,
Or for not doing what they could not do!
The very fiends know for what crime they fell,
(And so do all their foll'wers that rebel);
If then a blind well-meaning Indian stray,　　　40
Shall the great gulf be show'd him for the way?
　　For better ends our kind Redeemer dy'd,
Or the fall'n angels' rooms will be but ill supply'd.
　　That Christ, who at the great deciding day
(For he declares what he resolves to say)　　　45
Will damn the goats for their ill-natur'd faults,
And save the sheep for actions, not for thoughts,
Hath too much mercy to send men to hell
For humble charity and hoping well.
　　To what stupidity are zealots grown,　　　50
Whose inhumanity profusely shown,
In damning crowds of souls may damn their own.
I'll err at least on the securer side,
A convert free from malice and from pride.　　　54

H iij

THE PRAYER OF JEREMIAH

PARAPHRASED.

*Prophetically reprefenting the paffionate grief of the Jewifh
people for the lofs of their town and fanctuary.*

I.

STAND, fun of Juftice! fov'reign God Moft High!
In Libra fix thy bench of equity,
And weigh our cafe——
Look down on earth, nay look as low again
As we 're inferior to the reft of men;   5
We wretched, once like thy archangels bright,
Are caft down headlong with diminifh'd light:
So meteors fall, and as they downwards fly
Leave a long train of lefs'ning light and die.

II.

Then let that other fmoother face of thine,   10
The fun of Juftice, take its turn and fhine;
If not alone, at leaft to mix allays,
And ftreak thy juftice with alternate rays,
To fee and pity our diftrefs; for, oh!
As thou 'rt exalted our condition 's low.   15

III.

Houfes, eftates, our temple, and our town,
Which God and birthright long had made our own,
To barb'rous nations now are fall'n a prey,
And we from all we love are torn away.
Thus, early orphans whilft our fathers live,   20
We know no comfort, they no comfort give:

Our mothers are but widows under chains
Of wedlock, and of all their nuptial gains
None of the mother but the pangs remains.
Famish'd with want, we wilds and deserts tread,   25
And, fainting, wander for our needful bread
Where wolves and tigers round in ambush lie,
And hosts with naked swords stand threat'ning by;
But keener hunger, more a beast of prey,
More sharp than these, more ravenous than they,
Thro' swords, and wolves, and tigers, breaks our

IV.   [bitter way.

The fowls, and beasts, and ev'ry sylvan kind,   32
Down to the meanest insects, Heav'n design'd
To be the slaves of man, were always free
Of waters, woods, and common air; but we,   35
We slaves, and beasts, and more than insects vile,
That half-born wanton on the banks of Nile,
Are glad to buy the leavings they can spare
Of waters, woods, and the more common air.

V.

With loads of chains our foes pursue their stroke, 40
And lug our aking necks beneath their yoke:
No intermission gives the weary breath,
But endless drudging drags us on to death.
Our cries ascend, and like a trumpet blow,
All Egypt and Assyria hear our woe: 45
Here nights we labour, there whole days we sweat,
And barely earn the heartless bread we eat.

VI.

Our old forefathers finn'd, and are no more;
They pawn'd their children to defray their fcore.
O happy they! by death from fuff'ring freed,   50
But all our fathers' fcourges lafh their feed.
Vengeance, at which great Sion's entrails fhakes,
Shoots thro' the inmoft of the foul, and rakes
Where pride lurks deepeft, there we feel our pain,
Our flaves are mafters, and our menials reign;   55
Whilft we, unrefcu'd, fend our cries around
To feek relief, but no relief is found.

VII.

Look on our cheeks, and in each furrow trace
A ftorm of famine driving on our face;
The fcorching tempeft lets its fury go,   60
And pours upon us in a burft of woe:
The figns of confcious guilt our brows impart,
Black as our fin, and harden'd as our heart.

VIII.

From Sion's Mount the humble matrons cry,
With mournful echoes Judah's maids reply;   65
Our great ones fall beneath their fweeping hand,
Ev'n venerable Age cannot withftand
Their impious fcoffs; our youth, in bloomy prime ⎫
Compell'd, fubmit to their indecent crime,   ⎬
And children, 'whelm'd with labour, fail before ⎭
      their time.   70
Thus prince and people, infancy and age,
Promifc'ous objects of an impious rage,

But ferve to haunt us wherefoe'er we go
With horrid fcenes of univerfal woe.

IX.

Old men no more in Sion's council fit, 75
Nor young in conforts of her mufic meet;
Such foolifh change fond profligates devife,
The old turn fingers, and the young advife;
Perverted order to confufion runs,
And all our dwindling mufic ends in groans. 80
Sion! thy ancient glories are decay'd,
Thy laurels wither, and thy garlands fade;
Oh, Sin! 't is thou haft this deftruction made.

X.

'Tis Sion then, 't is Sion we deplore,
For her we grieve, for Sion is no more! 85
Our eyes condole in tears, and jointly fmart
With all the anguifh of an akeing heart;
For who can hold to fee the woful fight,
All nations envy and the world's delight!
Now grown a defert where the foxes range, 90
And howling wolves lament the difmal change?

XI.

But thou, unfhaken God! fhalt ever be;
Thy throne ftands faft upon eternity;
Then muft we thus by thee forfaken lie,
Or, loft for ever, in oblivion die? 95
Turn but to us, O Lord! we 'll mend our ways;
Oh! once reftore the joys of ancient days:

Ev'n tho' we seem the outcasts of thy care,
Refuse of death,.and gleanings of the war,
Resume the Father, and let sinners know
'Thy mercy 's greater than thy people's woe.　　101

SONG.

On a young lady who sung finely, and was afraid of a cold.

Winter! thy cruelty extend
Till fatal tempests swell the sea :
In vain let sinking pilots pray ;
Beneath thy yoke let Nature bend,
Let piercing frost and lasting snow　　5
Thro' woods and fields destruction sow!

Yet we unmov'd will sit and smile,
While you these lesser ills create,
These we can bear ; but, gentle Fate!
And thou, bless'd Genius of our isle!　　10
From Winter's rage defend her voice,
At which the list'ning gods rejoice.

May that celestial sound each day
With ecstasy transport our souls,
Whilst all our passions it controls,　　15
And kindly drives our cares away !
Let no ungentle cold destroy
All taste we have of heav'nly joy!　　18

PROLOGUE

TO POMPEY. A TRAGEDY.

TRANSLATED BY MRS. CATH. PHILIPS,

From the French of Monsieur Corneille, and acted at the theatre in Dublin.

THE mighty rivals, whose destructive rage
Did the whole world in civil arms engage,
Are now agreed, and make it both their choice
To have their fates determin'd by your voice.
Cæsar from none but you will have his doom;   5
He hates th' obsequious flatteries of Rome:
He scorns where once he rul'd now to be try'd,
And he hath rul'd in all the world beside.
When he the Thames, the Danube, and the Nile,
Had stain'd with blood, Peace flourish'd in this isle;
And you alone may boast you never saw
Cæsar till now, and now can give him law.

   Great Pompey, too, comes as a suppliant here,
But says he cannot now begin to fear:
He knows your equal justice, and (to tell   15
A Roman truth) he knows himself too well.

Succefs, 't is true, waited on Cæfar's fide,
But Pompey thinks he conquer'd when he dy'd.
His fortune, when fhe prov'd the moft unkind,
Chang'd his condition but not Cato's mind.   20
Then of what doubt can Pompey's caufe admit,
Since here fo many Catos judging fit?

But you, bright Nymphs! give Cæfar leave to woo
The greateft wonder of the world but you,
And hear a Mufe who has that hero taught   25
To fpeak as gen'roufly as e'er he fought,
Whofe eloquence from fuch a theme deters
All tongues but Englifh, and all pens but her's.
By the juft Fates your fex is doubly bleft!
You conquer'd Cæfar, and you praife him beft.   30

And you (illuftrious Sir * !) receive as due
A prefent Deftiny referv'd for you :
Rome, France, and England, join their forces here
To make a poem worthy of your ear.
Accept it then, and on that Pompey's brow
Who gave fo many crowns beftow one now.   36

* To the Lord Lieutenant.

A PROLOGUE

SPOKEN TO HIS ROYAL HIGHNESS

THE DUKE OF YORK, AT EDINBURGH.

FOLLY and vice are eafy to defcribe,
The common fubjects of our fcribbling tribe;
But when true virtues, with unclouded light,
All great, all royal, fhine divinely bright,
Our eyes are dazzled, and our voice is weak; 5
Let England, Flanders, let all Europe, fpeak;
Let France acknowledge that her fhaken throne
Was once fupported, Sir! by you alone;
Banifh'd from thence for an ufurper's fake,
Yet trufted then with her laft defp'rate ftake: 10
When wealthy neighbours ftrove with us for pow'r,
Let the fea tell how in their fatal hour,
Swift as an eagle, our victorious prince,
Great Britain's genius, flew to her defence;
His name ftruck fear, his conduct won the day, 15
He came, he faw, he feiz'd, the ftruggling prey,
And while the heav'ns were fire and th'ocean blood,
Confirm'd our empire o'er the conquer'd flood.
 Oh, happy Iflands! if you knew your blifs,
Strong by the fea's protection, fafe by his; 20

I

Exprefs your gratitude the only way,
And humbly own a debt too vaft to pay :
Let Fame aloud to future ages tell
None e'er commanded, none obey'd, fo well;
While this high courage, this undaunted mind, 25
So loyal, fo fubmiffively refign'd,
Proclaim that fuch a hero never fprings
But from the uncorrupted blood of kings. 28

EPILOGUE

When acted in the theatre in Dublin.

You 'ave feen to-night the glory of the Eaſt,
The man who all the then known world poſſeſt,
That kings in chains did Son of Ammon call, ·
And kingdoms thought divine, by treaſon fall.
Him Fortune only favour'd for her ſport,   5
And when his conduct wanted her ſupport   ·
His empire, courage, and his boaſted line,
Were all prov'd mortal by a ſlave's deſign.
Great Charles! whoſe birth has promis'd milder ſway,
Whoſe awful nod all nations muſt obey,   10
Secur'd by higher pow'rs, exalted ſtands
Above the reach of ſacrilegious hands;
Thoſe miracles that guard his crowns declare
That Heav'n has form'd a monarch worth their care,
Born to advance the loyal, and depoſe   15
His own, his brother's, and his father's, foes.
Faction, that once made diadems her prey,   ⎫
And ſtopp'd our prince in his triumphant way, ⎬
Fled like a miſt before this radiant day.   ⎭
So when, in heav'n, the mighty rebels roſe,   20
Proud, and reſolv'd that empire to depoſe,
Angels fought firſt, but unſucceſsful prov'd,
God kept the conqueſt for his beſt Belov'd;

At fight of fuch omnipotence they fly
Like leaves before autumnal winds, and die.   25
All who before him did afcend the throne
Labour'd to draw three reftiff nations on;
He boldly drives them forward without pain;
They hear his voice and ftraight obey the rein.
Such terror fpeaks him deftin'd to command;   30
We worfhip Jove with thunder in his hand,
But when his mercy without pow'r appears
We flight his altars, and neglect our pray'rs.
How weak in arms did Civil Difcord fhew!
Like Saul, fhe ftruck with fury at her foe,   35
When an immortal hand did ward the blow.
Her offspring, made the royal hero's fcorn,
Like fons of Earth, all fell as foon as born.
Yet let us boaft, for fure it is our pride,   39
When with their blood our neighbour lands were dy'd,
Ireland's untainted loyalty remain'd,
Her people guiltlefs, and her fields unftain'd.   42

TRANSLATIONS.

HORACE'S ART OF POETRY *.

Scribendi recte, fapere eft et principium et fons.

PREFACE.

I HAVE feldom known a trick fuccced, and will put none upon the reader, but tell him plainly that I think it could never be more feafonable than now to lay down fuch rules as, if they be obferved, will make men write more correctly, and judge more difcrectly. But Horace muft be read ferioufly or not at all, for elfe the reader will not be the better for him, and I fhall have loft my labour. I have kept as clofe as I could both to the meaning and the words of the author, and done nothing but what I believe he would forgive if he were alive; and I have often afked myfelf that queftion. I know this is a field,

Per quem magnus equos Au unce flexit Alumnus.

But with all the refpect due to the name of Ben. Johnfon, to which no man pays more veneration than I, it cannot be denied that the conftraint of rhyme, and a

---

* Printed from Dr. Rawlinfon's copy, corrected by the Earl of Rofcommon's own hand.

literal tranflation, (to which Horace in this book declares himfelf an enemy) has made him want a comment in many places.

My chief care has been to write intelligibly, and
where the Latin was obfcure I have added a line or
two to explain it.

I am below the envy of the critics ; but if I durfl I
would beg them to remember that Horace owed his
favour and his fortune to the charadler given of him
by Virgil and Varius, that Fundanius and Pollio are
ftill valued by what Horace fays of them, and that,
in their golden age, there was a good underftanding
among the ingenious, and thofe who were the moft
efteemed were the beft-natured.

HORACE

IF in a picture, Pifo, you fhould fee
A handfome woman with a fifh's tail,
Or a man's head upon a horfe's neck,
Or limbs of beafts of the moft diff'rent kinds
Cover'd with feathers of all forts of birds,   5
Would you not laugh, and think the painter mad?
Truft me that book is as ridiculous
Whofe incoherent ftyle (like fick men's dreams)
Varies all fhapes, and mixes all extremes.
Painters and poets have been ftill allow'd   10

DE ARTE POETICA LIBER,

HUMANO capiti cervicem pictor equinum
Jungere fi velit, et varias inducere plumas,
Undique collatis membris: ut turpiter atrum
Definat in pifcem mulier formofa fuperne :
Spectatum admiffi rifum teneatis amici ?   5
Credite, Pifones, ifti tabulæ fore librum
Perfimilem, cujus, velut ægri fomnia, vanæ
Fingentur fpecies: ut nec pes nec caput uni
Reddatur formæ. Pictoribus atque poëtis

Their pencils and their fancies unconfin'd:
This privilege we freely give and take;
But Nature and the common laws of sense
Forbid to reconcile antipathies,
Or make a snake engender with a dove,   15
And hung'ry tigers court the tender lambs.
    Some, that at first have promis'd mighty things,
Applaud themselves when a few florid lines
Shine thro' th' insipid dulness of the rest;
Here they describe a temple or a wood,   20
Or streams that thro' delightful meadows run,
And there the rainbow or the rapid Rhine;
But they misplace them all, and crowd them in,
And are as much to seek in other things
As he that only can design a tree   25

Quidlibet audendi semper fuit æqua potestas.   10
Scimus,et hanc veniam petimusque damusque viciſſim.
Sed non ut placidis coëant immitia, non ut
Serpentes avibus geminentur, tigribus agni.
    Inceptis gravibus plerumque et magna profeſſis
Purpureus, latè qui splendeat, unus et alter   15
Aſſuitur pannus: quum lucus, et ara Dianæ
Et properantis aquæ per amœnos ambitus agros,
Aut flumen Rhenum, aut pluvius describitur arcus.
Sed nunc non erat his locus: et fortaſſe cupreſſum
Scis simulare. Quid hoc? si fractis enatat exspes   20

Would be to draw a shipwreck or a storm.
When you begin with so much pomp and show,
Why is the end so little and so low?
Be what you will, so you be still the same.

    Most poets fall into the grossest faults,   30
Deluded by a seeming excellence:
By striving to be short they grow obscure,
And when they would write smoothly they want
Their spirits sink; while others, that affect [strength;
A lofty style, swell to a tympany.   35
Some tim'rous wretches start at ev'ry blast,
And, fearing tempests, dare not leave the shore;
Others, in love with wild variety,
Draw boars in waves and dolphins in a wood.
Thus fear of erring, join'd with want of skill,   40
Is a most certain way of erring still.

Navibus, ære dato qui pingitur? amphora cœpit
Inſtitui; currente rota cur urceus exit?
Denique fit quod vis simplex duntaxat et unum.

    Maxima pars vatum, pater, et juvenes patre digni,
Decipimur specie recti. brevis esse laboro,   25
Obscurus fio: sectantem levia, nervi
Deficiunt animique: professus grandia, turget:
Serpit humi tutus nimium, timidusque procellæ:
Qui variare cupit rem prodigialiter unam,
Delphinum sylvis appingit, fluctibus aprum.   30
In vitium ducit culpæ fuga, si caret arte.

The meaneſt workman in th' Æmilian ſquare
May grave the nails, or imitate the hair,
But cannot finiſh what he hath begun:
What can be more ridiculous than he?   45
For one or two good features in a face,
Where all the reſt are ſcandalouſly ill,
Make it but more remarkably deform'd.

Let poets match their ſubject to their ſtrength,
And often try what weight they can ſupport,   50
And what their ſhoulders are too weak to bear.
After a ſerious and judicious choice,
Method and eloquence will never fail.

As well the force as ornament of verſe
Conſiſt in chuſing a fit time for things,   55

Æmilium circa ludum ſaber imus et ungues
Exprimet, et molles imitabitur ære capillos:
Infelix operis ſummâ, quia ponere totum
Neſciet. hunc ego me, ſi quid componere curem,   35
Non magis eſſe velim, quam pravo vivere naſo,
Spectandum nigris oculis, nigroque capillo.

Sumite materiam veſtris, qui ſcribitis, æquam
Viribus, et verſate diu, quid ferre recuſent,
Quid valeant humeri, cui lecta potenter erit res,   40
Nec facundia deſeret hunc, nec lucidus ordo.

Ordinis hæc virtus erit et venus, aut ego fallor,
Ut jam nunc dicat, jam nunc debentia dici

And knowing when a Mufe may be indulg'd
In her full flight, and when fhe fhould be curb'd.
    Words muft be chofen and be plac'd with fkill:
You gain your point when by the noble art
Of good connexion an unufual word   60
Is made at firft familiar to our ear;
But if you write of things abftrufe or new,
Some of your own inventing may be us'd,
So it be feldom and difcreetly done:
But he that hopes to have new words allow'd,   65
Muft fo derive them from the Grecian fpring,
As they may feem to flow without conftraint.
Can an impartial reader difcommend
In Varius or in Virgil what he likes
In Plautus or Cæcilius? Why fhould I   70

Pleraque differat, et præfens in tempus omittat.
Hoc amet, hoc fpernat promiffi carminis auctor. 45
    In verbis etiam tenuis cautufque ferendis:
Dixeris egregiè, notum fi callida verbum
Reddiderit junctura novum. fi fortè neceffe eft
Indiciis monftrare recentibus abdita rerum,   ·
Fingere cinctutis non exaudita Cethegis   ·   50
Continget: dabiturque licentia fumta pudenter.
Et nova fictaque nuper habebunt verba fidem, fi
Græco fonte cadant, parce detorta. quid autem
Cæcilio Plautoque dabit Romanus ademtum
Virgilio Varioque? ego, cur acquirere pauca   55

Be envy'd for the little I invent,
When Ennius and Cato's copious style
Have so enrich'd and so adorn'd our tongue?
Men ever had, and ever will have, leave
To coin new words well suited to the age.　　75
Words are like leaves, some wither ev'ry year,
And ev'ry year a younger race succeeds.
Death is a tribute all things owe to Fate;
The Lucrine mole (Cæsar's stupendous work)
Protects our navies from the raging north;　　80
And (since Cethegus drain'd the Pontine lake)
We plough and reap where former ages row'd.
See how the Tiber (whose licentious waves
So often overflow'd the neighb'ring fields)
Now runs a smooth and inoffensive course,　　85

Si possum, invideor? quum lingua Catonis et Enni
Sermonem patrium ditaverit, et nova rerum
Nomina protulerit? licuit, semperque licebit,
Signatum præsente nota procudere nomen.
Ut sylvæ foliis pronos mutantur in annos,　　60
Prima cadunt: ita verborum vetus interit ætas,
Et juvenum ritu florent modò nata, vigentque.
Debemur morti nos, nostraque; sive receptus
Terra Neptunus classes aquilonibus arcet,
Regis opus; sterilisve diu palus, aptaque remis,　　65
Vicinas urbes alit, et grave sentit aratrum:
Seu cursum mutavit iniquum frugibus amnis,

3

Confin'd by our great Emperor's command :
Yet this, and they, and all, will be forgot ;
Why then fhould words challenge eternity',
When greateft men and greateft actions die ?
Ufe may revive the obfoleteft words,   90
And banifh thofe that now are moft in vogue.
Ufe is the judge, the law, and rule of fpeech.

    Homer firft taught the world in epic verfe
To write of great commanders and of kings.

    Elegies were at firft defign'd for grief,   95.
Tho' now we ufe them to exprefs our joy ;
But to whofe Mufe we owe that fort of verfe
Is undecided by the men of fkill.

    Rage with Iambics arm'd Archilochus,
Numbers for dialogue and action fit,   100

Doctus iter melius. mortalia facta peribunt,
Nedum fermonum ftet honos, et gratia vivax.
Multa renafcentur quæ jam cecidêre, cadentque, 70
Quæ nunc funt in honore vocabula, fi volet ufus,
Quem penes arbitrium eft et jus et norma loquendi.

    Res geftæ regumque ducumque, et triftia bella,
Quo fcribi poffent numero, monftravit Homerus.

    Verfibus impariter junctis querimonia primùm,
Poft etiam inclufa eft voti fententia compos.   76
Quis tamen exiguos elegos emiferit auctor,
Grammatici certant, et adhuc fub judice lis eft.

    Archilochum proprio rabies armavit Iambo.
                K

And favourites of the dramatic Muse;
Fierce, lofty, rapid, whose commanding sound
Awes the tumultuous noises of the pit,
And whose peculiar province is the stage.

Gods, heroes, conquerors, Olympic crowns,   105
Love's pleasing cares, and the free joys of wine,
Are proper subjects for the lyric song.

Why is he honour'd with a Poet's name
Who neither knows nor would observe a rule,
And chuses to be ignorant and proud,   110
Rather than own his ignorance and learn?
Let ev'ry thing have its due place and time.

A comic subject loves an humble verse;
Thyestes scorns a low and comic style;

Hunc focci cepere pedem grandesque cothurni,   80
Alternis aptum sermonibus, et populares
Vincentem strepitus, et natum rebus agendis.

Musa dedit fidibus divos, puerosque deorum,
Et pugilem victorem, et equum certamine primum,
Et juvenum curas, et libera vina referre.   85

Descriptas servare vices, opesumque colores
Cur ego, si nequeo ignoroque, Poëta falutor?
Cur nescire, pudens prave, quam discere, malo?

Versibus exponi tragicis res comica non vult;
Indignatur item privatis ac prope focco   90
Dignis carminibus narrari coena Thyestae.
Singula quaeque locum teneant fortita decenter.

Yet Comedy fometimes may raife her voice,   115
And Chremes be allow'd to foam and rail.
Tragedians, too, lay by their ftate to grieve;
Peleus and Telephus, exil'd and poor,
Forget their fwelling and gigantic words.
He that would have fpectators fhare his grief   120
Muft write not only well but movingly,
And raife men's paffions to what height he will.
We weep and laugh as we fee others do:
He only makes me fad who fhews the way,
And firft is fad himfelf: then, Telephus!   125
I feel the weight of your calamities,
And fancy all your miferies my own,
But if you act them ill I fleep or laugh;

Interdum tamen et vocem Comœdia tollit,
Iratufque Chremes tumido delitigat ore:
Et tragicus plerumque dolet fermone pedeftri.   95
Telephus et Peleus, quum pauper et exul uterque,
Projicit ampullas, et fefquipedalia verba,
Si curat cor fpectantis tetigiffe querelâ.
Non fatis eft pulcra effe poëmata: dulcia funto,
Et quocunque volent, animum auditoris agunto.
Ut ridentibus arrident, ita flentibus adflent   101
Humani vultus. fi vis me flere, dolendum eft
Primùm ipfi tibi: tunc tua me infortunia lædent,
Telephe, vel Peleu: malè fi mandata loquèris,
Aut dormitabo, aut ridebo. triftia mæftum   105

Your looks muſt alter as your ſubject does,
From kind to fierce, from wanton to ſevere;   130
For Nature forms and ſoftens us within,
And writes our fortune's changes in our face.
Pleaſure enchants, impetuous rage tranſports,
And grief dejects, and wrings the tortur'd ſoul,
And theſe are all interpreted by ſpeech;   135
But he whoſe words and fortunes diſagree,
Abſurd, unpity'd, grows a public jeſt.
Obſerve the characters of thoſe that ſpeak,
Whether an honeſt ſervant or a cheat,
Or one whoſe blood boils in his youthful veins, 140
Or a grave matron, or a buſy nurſe,
Extorting merchants, careful huſbandmen,
Argives or Thebans, Aſians or Greeks.

Vultum verba decent: iratum, plena minarum:
Ludentem, laſciva: ſeverum, ſeria dictu.
Format enim Natura prius nos intus ad omnem
Fortunarum habitum: juvat, aut impellit ad iram
Aut ad humum mœrore gravi deducit, et angit: 110
Poſt effert animi motus interprete linguâ.
Si dicentis erunt fortunis abſona dicta,
Romani tollent equites pediteſque cachinnum.
Intererit multum divuſne loquatur an heros:
Maturuſne ſenex, an adhuc florente juventâ 115
Fervidus: an matrona potens, an ſedula nutrix:
Mercatorne vagus, cultorve virentis agelli:
Colchus, an Aſſyrius: Thebis nutritus, an Argis.

Follow report, or feign coherent things;
Defcribe Achilles as Achilles was,   145
Impatient, rafh, inexorable, proud,
Scorning all judges, and all law but arms:
Medea muft be all revenge and blood,
Ino all tears, Ixion all deceit,
Io muft wander, and Oreftes mourn.   150

   If your bold Mufe dare tread unbeaten paths,
And bring new characters upon the ftage,
Be fure you keep them up to their firft height.
New fubjects are not eafily explain'd,
And you had better chufe a well-known theme 155
Than truft to an invention of your own;
For what originally others writ
May be fo well difguis'd and fo improv'd,

Aut famum fequere, aut fibi convenientia finge
Scriptor. honoratum fi fortè reponis Achillem : 120
Impiger, iracundus, inexorabilis, acer,
Jura neget fibi nata, nihil non arroget arnïis.
Sit Medea ferox, invictaqne : flebilis Ino,
Perfidus Ixion, Io vaga, triftis Oreftes.

   Si quid inexpertum fcenæ committis, et audes 125
Perfonam formare novam, fervetur ad imum
Qualis ab incepto procefferit, et fibi conftet.
Difficile eft propriè communia dicere : tuque
Rectiùs Iliacum carmen dediicïs in actus,
Quàm fi proferres ignota indictaque primus.   130

K iij

That with some justice it may pass for your's;
But then you must not copy trivial things,   ·160
Nor word for word too faithfully translate,
Nor (as some servile imitators do)
Prescribe at first such strict uneasy rules
As you must ever slavishly observe,
Or all the laws of decency renounce.   -   165
    Begin not as th' old poetaster did,
" Troy's famous war, and Priam's fate, I sing."
In what will all this ostentation end ?
The lab'ring mountain scarce brings forth a mouse :
How far is this from the Mæonian style ?   170
" Muse! speak the man who, since the siege of Troy,
" So many towns, such change of manners, saw."
One with a flash begins, and ends in smoke,

Publica materies privati juris erit, si
Nec circa vilem patulumque moraberis orbem : .
Nec verbum verbo curabis reddere, fidus
Interpres : nec desilies imitator in arctum,
Unde pedem proferre pudor vetet, aut operis lex.
    Nec si incipies, ut scriptor Cyclicus olim :   136
"Fortunam Priami cantabo et nobile bellum."
Quid dignum tanto feret hic promissor hiatu ?   ..
Parturient montes, nascetur ridiculus mus.
Quanto rectius hic, qui nil molitur inepte :   140
(Dic mihi, Musa, virum, captæ post tempora Trojæ,
Qui mores hominum multorum vidit et urbes.)   ,

The other out of fmoke brings glorious light,
And (without raifing expectation high)   175
Surprifes us with daring miracles,
The bloody Leftrygons, Charybdis' gulf,
And frighted Greeks, who near the Ætna fhore
Hear Scylla bark and Polyphemus roar.
He doth not trouble us with Leda's eggs   180
When he begins to write the Trojan war;
Nor, writing the return of Diomed,
Go back as far as Meleager's death:
Nothing is idle; each judicious line
Infenfibly acquaints us with the plot;   185
He chufes only what he can improve,
And truth and fiction are fo aptly mix'd
That all feems uniform and of a piece.
    Now hear what ev'ry auditor expects,

Non fumum ex fulgore, fed ex fumo dare lucem
Cogitat : ut fpeciofa dehinc miracula promat :
Antiphaten, Scyllamque, et cum Cyclope Charybdin.
Nec riditum Diomedis ab interitu Meleagri,   146
Nec gemino bellum Trojanum orditur ab ovo:
Semper ad eventum feftinat : et in medias res,
Non fecus ac notas, auditorem rapit : et quæ
Defperat tractata nitefcere poffe, relinquit :   150
Atque ita mentitur, fic veris falfa remifcet,
Primo ne medium, medeo ne difcrepet imum.
    Tu, quid ego, et populus mecum defideret, audi,

If you intend that he fhould ftay to hear   190
The epilogue, and fee the curtain fall:
Mind how our tempers alter in our years,
And by that rule form all your characters.
One that hath newly learn'd to fpeak and go
Loves childifh plays, is foon provok'd and pleas'd, 195
And changes ev'ry hour his wav'ring mind.
A youth that firft cafts off his tutor's yoke
Loves horfes, hounds, and fport, and exercife,
Prone to all vice, impatient of reproof,
Proud, carelefs, fond, inconftant, and profufe.   200
Gain and ambition rule our riper years,
And make us flaves to intereft and pow'r.

Si plauforis eges aulæa manentis, et ufque
Seffuri, donec cantor, vos plaudite, dicat :   155
Ætatis cujufque notandi funt tibi mores?
Mobilibufque decor naturis dandus et annis.
Reddere qui voces jam fcit puer, et pede certo
Signat humum, geftit paribus colludere, et iram
Colligit ac ponit temerè et mutatur in horas.   160
Imberbis juvenis, tandem cuftode remoto,
Gaudet equis canibufque et aprici gramine campi :
Cereus in vitium flecti, monitoribus afper :
Utilium tardus provifor, prodigus æris :
Sublimis, cupidufque et amata relinquere pernix.165
Converfis ftudiis ætas animufque virilis
Quærit opes et amicitias, infervit honori :

Old men are only walking hofpitals,
Where all defects and all difeafes crowd
With reftlefs pain, and more tormenting fear, 205
Lazy, morofe, full of delays and hopes,
Opprefs'd with riches which they dare not ufe;
Ill-natur'd cenfors of the prefent age,
And fond of all the follies of the paft : ·
Thus all the treafure of our flowing years 210
Our ebb of life for ever takes away. ·
Boys muft not have th' ambitious care of men,
Nor men the weak anxieties of age.

Some things are acted, others only told;
But what we hear moves lefs than what we fee. 215

Commififfe cavet quod mox mutare laboret.
Multa fenem circumveniunt incommoda : vel quod
Quærit, et inventis mifer abftinet, ac timet uti : 170
Vel quod res omnes timidè gelidèque miniftrat,
Dilator, fpe longus, iners, avidufque futuri,
Difficilis, querulus : laudator temporis acti
Se puero, cenfor caftigatorque minorum.
Multa ferunt anni venientes commoda fecum, 175
Multa recendentes adimunt. ne fortè feniles
Mandentur juveni partes, pueroque viriles,
Semper in adjunctis ævoque morabimur aptis. ·
   Aut agitur res in fcenis, aut acta refertur.
Segnius irritant animos demiffa per aurem, 180

Spectators only have their eyes to trust,
But auditors must trust their ears and you;
Yet there are things improper for a scene,
Which men of judgment only will relate.
Medea must not draw her murd'ring knife,   220
And spill her children's blood, upon the stage,
Nor Atreus there his horrid feast prepare.
Cadmus and Progné's metamorphosis,
(She to a swallow turn'd, he to a snake)
And whatsoever contradicts my sense   225
I hate to see, and never can believe.

    Five acts are the just measure of a play.
Never presume to make a god appear
But for a bus'ness worthy of a god;
And in one scene no more than three should speak.

Quam quæ sunt oculis subjecta fidelibus, et quæ
Ipse sibi tradit spectator. Non tamen intus
Digna geri, promes in scenam : multaque tolles
Ex oculis, quæ mox narret facundia præsens.
Nec pueros coram populo Medea trucidet;   185
Aut humana palam coquat exta nefarius Atreus :
Aut in avem Progne vertatur, Cadmus in anguem.
Quodcumque ostendis mihi sic, incredulus odi.

    Neve minor, neu sit quinto productior actu
Fabula, quæ posci vult, et spectata reponi.   190
Nec deus intersit, nisi dignus vindici nodus
Inciderit : nec quarta loqui persona laboret.

A chorus fhould fupply what action wants,   231
And hath a generous and manly part,
Bridles wild rage, loves rigid honefty,
And ftrict obfervance of impartial laws,
Sobriety, fecurity, and peace,   235
And begs the gods, who guide blind Fortune's wheel,
To raife the wretched and pull down the proud :
But nothing muft be fung between the acts
But what fome way conduces to the plot.

First the fhrill found of a fmall rural pipe   240
(Not loud like trumpets, nor adorn'd as now)
Was entertainment for the infant ftage,
And pleas'd the thin and bafhful audience
Of our well-meaning frugal anceftors;

Actoris partes chorus officiumque virile
Defendat : neu quid medios intercinat actus,
Quod non propofito conducat et hæreat apte.   195
Ille bonis faveatque, et concilietur amicis :
Et regat iratos, et amet peccare timentes :
Ille dapes laudet menfæ brevis, ille falubrem
Juftitiam, legefque, et apertis otia portis :
Ille tegat commiffa : deofque precetur et oret   200
Ut redeat miferis, abeat Fortuna fuperbis.
Tibia non, ut nunc, orichalco vincta, tubæque
Æmula, fed tenuis fimplexque, foramine pauco
Afpirare, et adeffe choris erat utilis, atque
Nondum fpiffa nimis complere fedilia flatu,   205

But when our walls and limits were enlarg'd,   245
And men (grown wanton by profperity)
Study'd new arts of luxury and eafe,
The verfe, the mufic, and the fcene, is improv'd;
For how fhould ignorance be judge of wit,
Or men of fenfe applaud the jefts of fools?   250
Then came rich clothes and graceful action in,
Then inftruments were taught more moving notes,
And Eloquence with all her pomp and charms
Foretold us ufeful and fententious truths,
As thofe deliver'd by the Delphic god.   255
　　The firft tragedians found that ferious ftyle

Quò fanè populus numerabilis, utpote parvus,
Et frugi, caftufque verecundufque coibat.
Poftquam cœpit agros extendere victor, et urbem
Latior amplecti murus: vinoque diurno
Placari genius feftis impunè diebus,   210
Acceffit numerifque modifque licentia major.
Indoctus quid enim faperet, liberque laborum
Rufticus urbano confufus, turpis honefto?
Sic prifcæ motumque et luxuriam addidit arti
Tibicen: traxitque vagus per pulpita veftem.   215
Sic etiam fidibus voces crevere feveris,
Et tulit eloquium infolitum facundia præceps:
Utiliumque fagax rerum, et divina futuri
Sortilegis non difcrepuit fententia Delphis.
　　Carmine qui tragico vilem certavit ob hircum,

2

Too grave for their uncultivated age,
And so brought wild and naked Satyrs in,
Whose motion, words, and shape, were all a farce,
(As oft' as decency would give them leave)   260
Because the mad ungovernable rout,
Full of confusion, and the fumes of wine,
Lov'd such variety and antic tricks:
But then they did not wrong themselves so much
To make a god, a hero, or a king,   265
(Stript of his golden crown and purple robe)
Descend to a mechanic dialect,
Nor (to avoid such meanness) soaring high
With empty sound and airy notions fly;
For Tragedy should blush as much to stoop   270
To the low mimic follies of a farce,

Mox etiam agrestes Satyros nudavit, et asper   221
Incolumi gravitate jocumtentavit: eo quod
Illecebris erat et grata novitate morandus
Spectator, functusque sacris, et potus, et exlex.
Verum ita risores, ita commendare dicaces   225
Conveniet Satyros, ita vertere seria ludo:
Ne, quicumque deus, quicumque adhibebitur heros,
Regali conspectus in auro nuper et ostro,
Migret in obscuras humili sermone tabernas:
Aut, dum vitat humum, nubes et inania captet. 230
Effutire leves indigna Tragoedia versus:
Ut festis matrona moveri jussa diebus,

                                              L

As a grave matron would to dance with girls.
You muſt not think that a ſatiric ſtyle
Allows of ſcandalous and brutiſh words,
Or the confounding of your characters.   275
Begin with truth, then give invention ſcope,
And if your ſtyle be natural and ſmooth,
All men will try and hope to write as well,
And (not without much pains) be undeceiv'd.
So much good method and connexion may   280
Improve the common and the plaineſt things.
A Satyr that comes ſtaring from the woods
Muſt not at firſt ſpeak like an orator;
But tho' his language ſhould not be refin'd,

Intererit Satyris paulum pudibunda protervis.
Non ego inornata et dominantia nomina ſolùm,
Verbaque, Piſones, ſatyrarum ſcriptor amabo :   235
Nec ſic enitar tragico differre colori,
Ut nihil interſit Davuſne loquatur, et audax
Pythias, emuncto lucrata Simone talentum :
An cuſtos famuluſque dei Silenus alumni.
Ex noto fictum carmen ſequar : ut ſibi quivis   240
Speret idem : ſudet multum, fruſtraque laboret
Auſus idem. tantum ſeries juncturaque pollet,
Tantum de medio ſumtis accedit honoris.
Sylvis deducti caveant, me judice, Fauni,
Ne, velut innati triviis, ac penè forenſes,   245
Aut nimiùm teneris juvenentur verſibus unquam,

It muſt not be obſcene and impudent;   285
The better ſort abhors ſcurrility,
And often cenſures what the rabble likes.
Unpoliſh'd verſes paſs with many men,
And Rome is too indulgent in that point;
But then to write at a looſe rambling rate,   290
In hope the world will wink at all our faults,

Aut immunda crepent ignominioſaque dicta.
Offenduntur enim quibus eſt equus et pater et res:
Nec, ſi quid fricti ciceris probat et nucis emtor,
Æquis accipiunt animis, donantve corona.   250
Syllaba longa breva ſubjecta, vocatur ïambus,
Pes citus: unde etiam trimetris accreſcere juſſit
Nomen ïambis: quum ſenos redderet ictus, - - - -
Primus ad extremum ſimilis ſibi. non ita pridem,
Tardior ut paulo graviorque veniret ad aures,   255
Spondeos ſtabiles in jura paterna recepit
Commodus et patiens: non ut de ſede ſecunda
Cederet aut quarta ſocialiter. hic et in Accî
Nobilibus trimetris apparet rarus, et Ennî.
In ſcenam miſſos magno cum pondere verſus,   260
Aut operæ celeris nimium, curaque carentis,
Aut ignoratæ premit artis crimine turpi.
Non quivis videt immodulata poëmata judex:
Et data Romanis venia eſt indigna poëtis.
Idcircone vager, ſcribamque licenter? an omnes 265
Viſuros peccata putem mea, tutus et intra
                        L ij

Is such a rash ill-grounded confidence
As men may pardon, but will never praise.
Be perfect in the Greek originals;
Read them by day, and think of them by night. 295
But Plautus was admir'd in former time
With too much patience, (not to call it worse)
His harsh unequal verse was music then,
And rudeness had the privilege of wit.

When Thespis first expos'd the Tragic Muse, 300
Rude were the actors, and a cart the scene,
Where ghastly faces, stain'd with lees of wine,
Frighted the children and amus'd the crowd;
This Æschylus (with indignation) saw,
And built a stage, found out a decent dress, 305

Spem veniæ cautus ? vitavi denique culpam,
Non laudem merui. vos exemplaria Græca
Nocturna versate manu, versate diurna.
At nostri proavi Plautinos et numeros et 270
Laudavere sales : nimium patienter utrumque,
Ne dicam stulte, mirati : si modo ego et vos
Scimus inurbanum lepido seponere dicto,
Legitimumque sonum digitis callemus et aure.

Ignotum Tragicæ genus invenisse Camœnæ 275
Dicitur, et plaustris vexisse poëmata Thespis :
Quæ canerent agerentque peruncti fæcibus ora.
Post hunc personæ pal;læque repertor honestæ
Æschylus, et modicis instravit pulpita tignis,

Brought vizards in, (a civiler difguife)
And taught men how to fpeak and how to act.
Next Comedy appear'd with great applaufe,
Till her licentious and abufive tongue
Waken'd the magiftrate's coercive pow'r,   310
And forc'd it to fupprefs her infolence.

  Our writers have attempted ev'ry way;
And they deferve our praife whofe daring Mufe
Difdain'd to be beholden to the Greeks,
And found fit fubjects for her verfe at home.   315
Nor fhould we be lefs famous for our wit
Than for the force of our victorious arms;
But that the time and care that are requir'd

Et docuit magnumque loqui, nitique cothurno. 280
Succeffit vetus his comœdia, non fine multa
Laude: fed in vitium libertas excidit, et vim
Dignam lege regi. lex eft accepta: chorufque
Turpiter obticuit, fublato jure nocendi.

  Nil intentatum noftri liquere poëtæ: 285
Nec minimum meruêre decus, veftigia Græca
Aufi deferere, et celebrare domeftica facta:
Vel qui prætextas, vel qui docuêre togatas.
Nec virtute foret clarifve potentius armis,
Quam lingua, Latium: fi non offenderet unum- 290
Quemque poëtarum limæ labor et mora. Vos ô
Pompilius fanguis, carmen reprehendite quod non
Multa dies et multa litura coërcuit, atque

To overlook, and file, and polish well,
Fright poets from that neceſſary toil.   320
   Democritus was ſo in love with wit,
And ſome men's natural impulſe to write,
That he deſpis'd the help of art and rules,
And thought none poets till their brains were crackt;
And this hath ſo intoxicated ſome,   325
That (to appear incorrigibly mad)
They cleanlineſs and company renounce
For lunacy beyond the cure of art;
With a long beard, and ten long dirty nails,
Paſs current for Apollo's livery.   330
O! my unhappy ſtars! if in the ſpring
Some phyſic had not cur'd me of the ſpleen,
None would have writ with more ſucceſs than I;
But I muſt reſt contented as I am,

Perfectum decies non caſtigavit ad unguem.
   Ingenium miſera quia fortunatius arte   295
Credit, et excludit ſanos Helicone poëtas
Democritus: bona pars non ungues ponere curat,
Non barbam: ſecreta petit loca, balnea vitat.
Nanciſcetur enim pretium nomenque poëtæ,
Si tribus Anticyris caput inſanabile nunquam   300
Tonſori Licino commiſerit. ô ego lævus,
Qui purgor bilem ſub verni temporis horam!
Non alius faceret meliora poëmata. verum
Nil tanti eſt. ergo fungar vice cotis, acutum

And only ferve to whet that wit in you 335
To which I willingly refign my claim.
Yet without writing I may teach to write,
Tell what the duty of a poet is,
Wherein his wealth and ornaments confift,
And how he may be form'd, and how improv'd, 340
What fit, what not, what excellent or ill.

 Sound judgment is the ground of writing well;
And when Philofophy directs your choice
To proper fubjects rightly underftood,
Words from your pen will naturally flow; 345
He only gives the proper characters
Who knows the duty of all ranks of men,
And what we owe our country, parents, friends,
How judges and how fenators fhould act,
And what becomes a general to do: 350

Reddere que ferrum valet, exors ipfa fecandi: 305
Munus et officium, nil fcribens ipfe, docebo:
Unde parentur opes: quid alat formetque poëtam:
Quid deceat, quid non: quo virtus, quo ferrat error.

 Scribendi rectè, fapere eft et principium et fons.
Rem tibi Socraticæ poterunt oftendere chartæ: 310
Verbaque provifam rem non invita fequentur.
Qui didicit, patriæ quid debeat, et quid amicis:
Quo fit amore parens, quo frater amandus et hofpes:
Quod fit confcripti, quod judicis officium: quæ
Partes in bellum miffi ducis: ille profecto 315

Thofe are the likeft copies which are drawn
By the original of human life.
Sometimes in rough and undigefted plays
We meet with fuch a lucky character
As, being humour'd right, and well purfu'd,   355
Succeeds much better than the fhallow verfe
And chiming trifles of more ftudious pens.

Greece had a genius, Greece had eloquence,
For her ambition and her end was fame.
Our Roman youth is diligently taught   360
The deep myfterious art of growing rich,
And the firft words that children learn to fpeak
Are of the value of the names of coin.
Can a penurious wretch, that with his milk
Hath fuck'd the bafeft dregs of ufury,   365

Reddere perfonæ fcit convenientia-cuique.
Refpicere exemplar vitæ morumque jubebo
Doctum imitatorem, et veras hinc ducere voces.
Interdum fpeciofa locis morataque recte
Fabula, nullius veneris, fine pondere et arte,   320
Valdius oblectat populum, meliufque moratur,
Quam verfus inopes rerum, nugæque canoræ.

Graiis ingenium, Graiis dedit ore rotundo
Mufa loqui, præter laudem nullius avaris.
Romani pueri longis rationibus affem   325
Difcunt in partes centum diducere. dicat
Filius Albini; fi de quincunce remota eft

Pretend to gen'rous and heroic thoughts?
Can ruft and avarice write lafting lines?
But you, brave youth! wife Numa's worthy heir,
Remember of what weight your judgment is,
And never venture to commend a book   370
That has not paf'd all judges and all tefts.
    A poet fhould inftruct, or pleafe, or both:
Let all your precepts be fuccinct and clear,
That ready wits may comprehend them foon,
And faithful memories retain them long;   375
All fuperfluities are foon forgot.
Never be fo conceited of your parts
To think you may perfuade us what you pleafe,
Or venture to bring in a child alive

Uncia, quid fuperat? Poteras dixiffe, triens. eu,
Rem poteris fervare tuam. redit uncia: quid fit?
Semis. At hæc animos ærugo et cura peculi'   330
Quum femel imbuerit, fperamus carmina fingi
Poffe linenda cedro, et levi fervanda cupreffo?
    Aut prodeffe volunt, aut delectare poëtæ,
Aut fimul et jucunda et idonea dicere vitæ.
Quicquid præcipies, efto brevis: ut cito dicta   335
Percipiant animi dociles, tencantque fideles.
Omne fupervacuum pleno de pectore manat.
Ficta voluptatis causâ fint proxima veris.
Nec, quodcumque volet, pofcat fibi fabula credi:

That Canibals have murder'd and devour'd.   380
Old age explodes all but morality;
Aufterity offends afpiring youths;
But he that joins inftruction with delight,
Profit with pleafure, carries all the votes:
Thefe are the volumes that enrich the fhops,   385
'Thefe pafs with admiration thro' the world,
And bring their author to eternal fame.

    Be not too rigidly cenforious;
A ftring may jar in the beft mafter's hand,
And the moft fkilful archer mifs his aim: 390
But in a poem elegantly writ
I would not quarrel with a flight miftake,

Neu pranfæ Lamiæ vivum puerum extrahat alvo. 340
Centuriæ feniorum agitant expertia frugis,
Celfi prætereunt auftera poëmata Rhamnes.
Omne tulit punctum qui mifcuit utile dulci,
Lectorem delectando, pariterque monendo.
Hic meret æra liber Sofiis: hic et mare tranfit,   345
Et longum noto fcriptori prorogat ævum.
    Sunt delicta tamen quibus ignoviffe velimus.
Nam neque chorda fonum reddit quem vult manus
        et mens,
Pofcentique gravem perfæpe remittit acutum:
Nec femper feriet quodcumque minabitur arcus. 350
Verùm ubi plura nitent in carmine, non ego paucis

Such as our nature's frailty may excufe;
But he that hath been often told his fault,
And ftill perfifts, is as impertinent   395
As a mufician that will always play,
And yet is always out at the fame note :
When fuch a pofitive abandon'd fop
(Among his numerous abfurdities)
Stumbles upon fome tolerable line,   400
I fret to fee them in fuch company;
And wonder by what magic they came there.
But in long works fleep will fometimes furprife :
Homer himfelf hath been obferv'd to nod.

    Poems, like pictures, are of different forts,   405
Some better at a diftance, others near ;
Some love the dark, fome chufe the cleareft light,

Offendar maculis, quas aut incuria fudit,
Aut humana parum cavit Natura. quid ergo ?
Ut fcriptor fi peccat idem librarius-ufque,
Quamvis eft monitus, veniâ caret : et citharœdus
Ridetur, chordâ qui femper oberrat eâdem :   356
Sic mihi, qui multum ceffat, fit Chœrilus ille,
Quem bis terque-bonum, cum rifu miror : et idem
Indignor, quandoque bonus dormitat Homerus.
Verùm opere in longo fas eft obrepere fomnum. 360
    Ut pictura, poëfis erit, quæ, fi propiùs ftes,
Te capiet magis : et quædam, fi longiùs abftes.
Hæc amat obfcurum, volet hæc fub luce videri,

And boldly challenge the moſt piercing eye;
Some pleaſe for once, ſome will for ever pleaſe.

   But, Piſo! (tho' your knowledge of the world, 410
Join'd with your father's precepts, make you wiſe)
Remember this as an important truth:
Some things admit of mediocrity;
A counſellor or pleader at the bar
May want Meſſala's pow'rful eloquence,   415
Or be leſs read than deep Caſſellius; ·
Yet this indiff'rent lawyer is eſteem'd;
But no authority of gods nor men
Allow of any mean in poeſy.
As an ill concert and a coarſe perfume   420
Diſgrace the delicacy of a feaſt,
And might with more diſcretion have been ſpar'd;

Judicis argutum quæ non formidat acumen:
Hæc placuit ſemel, hæc decies repetita placebit. 365
   O major juvenum, quamvis et voce paterná
Fingeris ad rectum, et per te ſapis, hoc tibi dictum
Tolle memor: certis medium et tolerabile rebus
Rectè concedi. conſultus juris, et actor
Cauſarum mediocris, abeſt virtute diſerti   370
Meſſalæ, nec ſcit quantum Caſſelius Aulus:
Sed tamen in pretio eſt: mediocribus eſſe poëtis
Non homines, non dî, non conceſſere columnæ.
Ut gratas inter menſas ſymphonia diſcors,   374
Et craſſum unguentum et Sardo cum melle papaver,

So poefy, whofe end is to delight,
Admits of no degrees, but muft be ftill
Sublimely good or defpicably ill.   425
    In other things men have fome reafon left,
And one that cannot dance, or fence, or run,
Defpairing of fuccefs, forbears to try;
But all (without confideration) write,
Some thinking that th' omnipotence of wealth   430
Can turn them into poets when they pleafe.
But, Pifo! you are of too quick a fight
Not to difcern which way your talent lies,
Or vainly with your genius to contend;
Yet if it ever be your fate to write,   435
Let your productions pafs the ftricteft hands

Offendunt, poterat duci quia cœna fine iftis:
Sic animis natum inventumque poëma juvandis,
Si paulùm à fummo difceffit, vergit ad imum.
    Ludere qui nefcit, campeftribus abftinet armis:
Indoctufque pilæ difcive trochive quiefcit,   380
Ne fpiffæ rifum tollant impunè coronæ:
Qui nefcit, verfus tamen audet fingere. quidni?
Liber et ingenuus, præfertim cenfus equeftrem
Summam nummorum, vitioque remotus ab omni.
Tu nihil invita dices faciefve Minerva: 385
Id tibi judicium eft, ea mens: fi quid tamen olim
Scripferis, in Metii defcendat judicis aures,

M

Mine and your father's, and not fee the light
Till time and care have ripen'd ev'ry line.
What you keep by you you may change and mend,
But words once fpoke can never be recall'd.   440
   Orpheus, infpir'd by more than human pow'r,
Did not, as poets feign, tame favage beafts,
But men as lawlefs and as wild as they,
And firft diffuaded them from rage and blood.
Thus when Amphion built the Theban wall   445
They feign'd the ftones obey'd his magic lute.
Poets, the firft inftructers of mankind,
Brought all things to their proper native ufe;
Some they appropriated to the gods,
And fome to public fome to private ends: 450
Promifcuous love by marriage was reftrain'd,

Et patris, et noftras: nonumque prematur in annum
Membranis intus pofitis, delere licebit
Quod non edideris: nefcit vox miffa reverti.   390
   Sylveftres homines facer interprefque deorum
Cædibus et victu fœdo deterruit Orpheus:
Dictus ob hoc lenire tigres rapidofque leones :   .
Dictus et Amphion, Thebanæ conditor arcis
Saxa movere fono teftudinis, et prece blanda   395
Ducere quò vellet. fuit hæc fapientia quondam,
Publica privatis fecernere, facra profanis:
Concubitu prohibere vago, dare jura maritis,   .

Cities were built and useful laws were made:
So great was the divinity of verse,
And such observance to a poet paid.
Then Homer's and Tyrtæus' martial Muse 455
Waken'd the world, and founded loud alarms.
To verse we owe the sacred oracles
And our best precepts of morality:
Some have by verse obtain'd the love of kings,
(Who with the Muses ease their weary'd minds) 460
Then blush not, noble Piso! to protect
What gods inspire, and kings delight to hear.

 Some think that poets may be form'd by art,
Others maintain that Nature makes them so;
I neither see what art without a vein 465
Nor wit without the help of art can do,

Oppida moliri; leges incidere ligno.
Sic honor et nomen divinis vatibus atque 400
Carminibus venit. post hos insignis Homerus
Tyrtæusque mares animos in Martia bella
Versibus exacuit. dictæ per carmina fortes:
Et vitæ monstrata via est: et gratia regum
Pieriis tentata modis: ludusque repertus, 405
Et longorum operum finis: ne forte pudori
Sit tibi Musa lyræ solers, et cantor Apollo.
 Natura fieret laudabile carmen, an arte,
Quæsitum est: ego nec studium sine divite vena,
Nec rude quid profit video ingenium. alterius sic 410

But mutually they crave each other's aid.
He that intends to gain th' Olympic prize
Must use himself to hunger, heat, and cold,
Take leave of wine, and the soft joys of love ;   470
And no musician dares pretend to skill
Without a great expense of time and pains;
But ev'ry little busy scribbler now
Swells with the praises which he gives himself,
And, taking sanctuary in the crowd,   475
Brags of his impudence, and scorns to mend.

    A wealthy poet takes more pains to hire
A flatt'ring audience than poor tradesmen do
To persuade customers to buy their goods.
'Tis hard to find a man of great estate   480

Altera poscit opem res, et conjurat amice.
Qui studet optatam cursu contingere metam,
Multa tulit fecitque puer : sudavit, et alsit:
Abstinuit venere et vino. qui Pythia cantat
Tibicen, didicit prius, extimuitque magistrum.   415
Nunc satis est dixisse, ego mira poëmata pango.
Occupet extremum scabies : mihi turpe relinqui est,
Et, quod non didici, sane nescire fateri.

    Ut præco ad merces turbam qui cogit emendas,
Assentatores jubet ad lucrum ire poëta   420
Dives agris, dives positis in fœnore nummis.
Si verò est unctum qui recte ponere possit,
Et spondere levi pro paupere, et eripere atris

That can diftinguifh flatterers from friends.
Never delude yourfelf, nor read your book
Before a brib'd and fawning auditor,
For he 'll commend and feign an ecftafy,
Grow pale or weep, do any thing to pleafe :   485
True friends appear lefs mov'd than counterfeit;
As men that truly grieve at funerals
Are not fo loud as thofe that cry for hire.
Wife were the kings who never chofe a friend
Till with full cups they had unmafk'd his foul,   490
And feen the bottom of his deepeft thoughts.
You cannot arm yourfelf with too much care
Againft the fmiles of a defigning knave.

Litibus implicitam : mirabor fi fciet inter-
Nofcere mendacem verumque beatus amicum. -425
Tu feu donâris, feu quid donare voles cui,
Nolito ad verfus tibi factos ducere plenum
Lætitiæ, clamabit enim, Pulchrè, bene, Recte,
Pallefcet fuper his : etiam ftillabit amicis
Ex oculis rorem : faliet, tundet pede terram.   430
Ut qui conducti plorant in funere, dicunt
Et faciunt propè plura dolentibus ex animo : fic
Derifor verò plus laudatore movetur :
Reges dicuntur multis urgere culullis,
Et torquere mero, quem perfpexiffe laborent   435
An fit amicitia dignus. Si carmina condes,
Nunquam te fallant animi fub vulpe latentes.

Quintilius, if his advice were ask'd,
Would freely tell you what you should correct,   495
Or, if you could not, bid you blot it out,
And with more care supply the vacancy;
But if he found you fond and obstinate,
(And apter to defend than mend your faults)
With silence leave you to admire yourself,   500
And without rival hug your darling book.
The prudent care of an impartial friend
Will give you notice of each idle line,
Shew what sounds harsh, and what wants ornament,
Or where it is too lavishly bestow'd;   505
Make you explain all that he finds obscure,
And with a strict inquiry mark your faults,
Nor for these trifles fear to lose your love.

Quintilio si quid recitares, Corrige, sodes,
Hoc, aiebat, et hoc. melius te posse negares,
Bis terque expertum frustrà? delere jubebat,   440
Et malè tornatos incudi reddere versus.
Si defendere delictum quàm vertere malles,
Nullam ultra verbum aut operam sumebat inanem,
Quin sine rivali teque et tua solus amares.
Vir bonus et prudens versus reprehendet inertes: 445
Culpabit duros: incomtis allinet atrum
Transverso calamo signum: ambitiosa recîdet
Ornamenta: parum claris lucem dare coget:
Arguet ambiguè dictum: mutanda notabit:

Those things which now seem frivolous and slight
Will be of a most serious consequence   510
When they have made you once ridiculous.
    A poetaster, in his raging fit,
(Follow'd and pointed at by fools and boys)
Is dreaded and proscrib'd by men of sense;
They make a lane for the polluted thing,   515
And fly as from th' infection of the plague,
Or from a man whom, for a just revenge,
Fanatic Frenzy sent by Heav'n pursues.
If (in the raving of a frantic Muse)
And minding more his verses than his way,   520
Any of these should drop into a well,
Tho' he might burst his lungs to call for help
No creature would assist or pity him,

Fiet Aristarchus. nec dicet, Cur ego amicum   450
Offendam in nugis? Hæ nugæ seria ducent
In mala, derisum semel, exceptumque siniftre.
    Ut, mala quem scabies aut morbus regius urget,
Aut fanaticus error, et iracunda Diana,
Vesanum tetigisse timent fugiuntque poëtam,   455
Qui sapiunt; agitant pueri, incautique sequuntur.
Hic, dum sublimes versus ructatur, et errat,
Si veluti merulis intentus decidit auceps
In puteum, foveamve : licet, Succurrite, longum
Clamet, io, cives; non sit qui tollere curet.   460
Si quis curet opem ferre, et demittere funem,

But seem to think he fell on purpose in.
Hear how an old Sicilian poet dy'd;   525
Empedocles, mad to be thought a god,
In a cold fit leap'd into Ætna's flames.
Give poets leave to make themselves away,
Why should it be a greater sin to kill
Than to keep men alive against their will?   530
Nor was this chance, but a deliberate choice;
For if Empedocles were now reviv'd
He would be at his frolic once again
And his pretensions to divinity.
'Tis hard to say whether for sacrilege   535
Or incest, or some more unheard-of crime,
The rhyming fiend is sent into these men;
But they are all most visibly possess'd,
And, like a baited bear when he breaks loose,

Quî scis, an prudens huc se dejecerit? atque
Servari nolit? dicam, Siculique poëtæ
Narrabo interitum: deus immortalis haberi
Dum cupit Empedocles, ardentem frigidus Ætnam
Infiluit. sit jus, liceatque perire poëtis.   466
Invitum qui servat, idem facit occidenti,
Nec semel hoc fecit: nec, si retractus erit, jam
Fiet homo, et ponet famosæ mortis amorem.
Nec satis apparet cur versus factitet; utrum   470
Minxerit in patrios cineres, an tristi bidental
Moverit incestus. certè furit, ac velut ursus,

Without diſtinction ſeize on all they meet: 540
None ever 'ſcap'd that came within their reach,
Sticking like leeches, till they burſt with blood;
Without remorſe inſatiably they read,
And never leave till they have read men dead. 544

Objectos caveæ valuit ſi frangere clathros,
Indoctum doctumque fugat recitator acerbus. 474
Quem verò arripuit, tenet, occiditque legendo,
Non miſſura cutem niſi plena cruoris hirudo. 476

THE TWENTY-SECOND ODE

OF THE FIRST BOOK OF HORACE.

VIRTUE, dear Friend! needs no defence;
The fureft guard is innocence:
None knew till guilt created fear
What darts or poifon'd arrows were:

Integrity undaunted goes   5
Thro' Libyan fands or Scythian fnows,
Or where Hydafpes' wealthy fide
Pays tribute to the Perfian pride.

AD ARISTIUM.

ODE XXII.

Vitæ integritatem et innocentiam ubique eft tutam.

INTEGER vitæ, fcelerifque purus
Non eget Mauri jaculis, neque arcu,
Nec venenatis gravidâ fagittis,
Fufce, pharetrâ:

Sive per Syrtes iter æftuofas,   5
Sive facturus per inhofpitalem
Caucafum, vel quæ loca fabulofus
Lambit Hydafpes.

For as (by am'rous thoughts betray'd)
Carelefs in Sabine woods I ftray'd,   10
A grifly foaming wolf unfed,
Met me unarm'd, yet trembling fled.

No beaft of more portentous fize
In the Hercynian foreft lies;
None fiercer, in Numidia bred,   15
With Carthage were in triumph led.

Set me in the remoteft place
That Neptune's frozen arms embrace,
Where angry Jove did never fpare
One breath of kind and temp'rate air;   20

Namque me fylvâ lupus in Sabinâ
Dum meam canto Lalagen, et ultra   10
Terminum curis vagor expeditus,
Fugit inermem.

Quale portentum neque militaris
Daunia in latis alit efculetis:
Nec Jubæ tellus generat, leonum   15
Arida nutrix.

Pone me, pigris ubi nulla campis
Arbor æftivâ recreatur aurâ:
Quod latus mundi nebulæ, malúfque
Jupiter urget: 20

Set me where on some pathless plain
The swarthy Africans complain,
To see the chariot of the Sun
So near their scorching country run;

The burning zone, the frozen isles,   25
Shall hear me sing of Cælia's smiles:
All cold but in her breast I will despise,
And dare all heat but that in Cælia's eyes.   28

Pone sub curru nimiùm propinqui
Solis, in terrâ domibus negatâ:
Dulcè ridentem Lalagen amabo,
Dulcè loquentem.   24

THE SAME IMITATED.

I.

Virtue, dear Friend! needs no defence,
No arms but its own innocence:
Quivers and bows, and poison'd darts,
Are only us'd by guilty hearts.

II.

An honest mind safely alone   5
May travel thro' the burning zone,
Or thro' the deepest Scythian snows,
Or where the fam'd Hydaspes flows.

III.

While rul'd by a refiftlefs fire,
Our great Orinda * I admire,   10
The hungry wolves, that fee me ftray
Unarm'd and fingle, run away.

IV.

Set me in the remoteft place
That ever Neptune did embrace;
When there her image fills my breaft,   15
Helicon is not half fo bleft.

V.

Leave me upon fome Libyan plain,
So fhe my fancy entertain,
And when the thirfty monfters meet,
They 'll all pay homage to my feet.   20

VI.

The magic of Orinda's name
Not only can their fiercenefs tame,
But, if that mighty word I once rehearfe,
They feem fubmiffively to roar in verfe.   24

* Mrs. Catharine Philips.

N

THE SIXTH ODE

Of the corruption of the times.

Those ills your anceftors have done,
Romans! are now become your own,
And they will coft you dear,
Unlefs you foon repair
The falling temples, which the gods provoke,   5
And ftatues fully'd yet with facrilegious fmoke.

Propitious Heav'n, that rais'd your fathers high,
For humble grateful piety,

AD ROMANOS.

HOR. LIB. III. ODE VI.

Corruptos fuæ ætatis mores infeÉtatur.

Delicta majorum immeritus lues,
Romane : donec templa refeceris,
Ædéfque labentes deorum, et
Fœda nigro fimulacra fumo.

Dîs te minorem quòd geris, imperas.   5
Hinc omne principium, huc refer exitum.

{ As it rewarded their respect)
Hath sharply punish'd your neglect.   10
All empires on the gods depend;
Begun by their command, at their command they end.

Let Crassus' ghost and Labienus' tell
How twice by Jove's revenge our legions fell,
And, with insulting pride,   15
Shining in Roman spoils, the Parthian victors ride.

The Scythian and Egyptian scum
Had almost ruin'd Rome,
While our seditions took their part,   [dart.
Fill'd each Egyptian sail, and wing'd each Scythian

Dî multa neglecti dederunt
Hesperiæ mala luctuosæ.

Jam bis Monæses, et Pacori manus
Non auspicatos contudit impetus   10
Nostros, et adjecisse prædam
Torquibus exiguis renidet.

Penè occupatam seditionibus
Delevit urbem Dacus, et Æthiops:
Hic classe formidatus, ille   15
Missilibus melior sagittis.

First, thofe flagitious times   21
(Pregnant with unknown crimes)
Confpire to violate the nuptial bed,
From which polluted head
Infectious ftreams of crowding fins began,   25
And thro' the fpurious breed and guilty nation ran.

Behold a ripe and melting maid
Bound prentice to the wanton trade;
Ionian artifts, at a mighty price,
Inftruct her in the myfteries of vice;   30
What nets to fpread, where fubtle baits to lay,
And with an early hand they form the temper'd clay.

Marry'd, their leffons fhe improves
By practice of adult'rous loves,

Fœcunda culpæ fæcula, nuptias
Primùm inquinavere, et genus, et domos.
Hòc fonte derivata clades
In patriam, populùmque fluxit.   20

Motus doceri gaudet Ionicos
Matura virgo, et fingitur artubus
Jam nunc, et inceftos amores
De tenero meditatur ungui.

Mox juniores quærit adulteros   25
Inter mariti vina; neque eligit

And fcorns the common mean defign   35
To take advantage of her hufband's wine,
Or fnatch, in fome dark place,
A hafty illegitimate embrace.

No! the brib'd hufoand knows of all,
And bids her rife when lovers call.   40
Hither a merchant from the Straights,
Grown wealthy by forbidden freights,
Or city cannibal, repairs,
Who feeds upon the flefh of heirs;
Convenient brutes! whofe tributary flame   45
Pays the full price of luft, and gilds the flighted fhame.

'Twas not the fpawn of fuch as thefe
That dy'd with Punic blood the conquer'd feas,
And quafh'd the ftern Æacides;

Cui donet impermiffa raptim
Gaudia, luminibus remotis:

Sed juffa coràm non finè confcio
Surgit marito: feu vocat inftitor,   30
Seu navis Hifpanæ magifter,
Dedecorum pretiofus emptor.

Non his juventus orta parentibus
Infecit æquor fanguine Punico,

Made the proud Afian monarch feel   50
How weak his gold was againft Europe's fteel,
Forc'd ev'n dire Hannibal to yield,
And won the long-difputed world at Zama's fatal
                                         [field :
But foldiers of a ruftic mould,
Rough, hardy, feafon'd, manly, bold,   55
Either they dug the ftubborn ground,
Or thro' hewn woods their weighty ftrokes did found;
And after the declining fun
Had chang'd the fhadows, and their tafk was done,
Home with their weary team they took their way,
And drown'd in friendly bowls the labour of the day.

Pyrrhúmque, et ingentem cecidit   35
Antiochum, Annibalémque dirum :

Sed rufticorum mafcula militum
Proles, Sabellis docta ligonibus
Verfare glebas, et feveræ
Matris ad arbitrium recifos   40

Portare fuftes, fol ubi montium
Mutaret umbras, et juga demeret
Bobus fatigatis, amicum
Tempus agens abeunte curru.

Time fenfibly all things impairs;   62
Our fathers have been worfe than theirs,
And we than ours; next age will fee
A race more profligate than we
(With all the pains we take) have fkill enough to be.

Damnofa quid non imminuit dies?   45
Ætas parentum pejor avis tulit
Nos nequiores, mox daturos
Progeniem vitiofiorem.   48

SILENUS.

The Argument.

TWO young shepherds, Chromis and Mnasylus, having been often promised a song by Silenus, chance to catch him asleep in this eclogue; where they bind him hand and foot, and then claim his promise. Silenus, finding they would be put off no longer, begins his song, in which he describes the formation of the universe, and the original of animals, according to the Epicurean philosophy; and then runs through the most surprising transformations which have happened in Nature since her birth. This eclogue was designed as a compliment to Syro the Epicurean, who instructed Virgil and Varus in the principles of that philosophy. Silenus acts as tutor, Chromis and Mnasylus as the two pupils.

I FIRST of Romans stoop'd to rural strains,
Nor blush'd to dwell among Sicilian swains.
When my Thalia rais'd her bolder voice,
And kings and battles were her lofty choice,
Phœbus did kindly humbler thoughts infuse,   5
And with this whisper check th'aspiring Muse.

SILENUS.

ECLOGA VI.

Faunorum et Satyrorum et Sylvanorum dilectatio.

PRIMA Syracosio dignata est ludere versu,
Nostra nec erubuit sylvas habitare Thalia.
Cùm canerem reges, et prælia, Cynthius aurem
Vellit, et admonuit: Pastorem, Tityre, pingues

A shepherd, Tityrus! his flocks should feed,
And chuse a subject suited to his reed.
Thus I (while each ambitious pen prepares
To write thy praises, Varus! and thy wars)   10
My past'ral tribute in low numbers pay,
And tho' I once presum'd, I only now obey.
   But yet (if any with indulgent eyes
Can look on this, and such a trifle prize)
Thee only Varus! our glad swains shall sing,   15
And ev'ry grove and ev'ry echo ring.
Phœbus delights in Varus' fav'rite name,
And none who under that protection came
Was ever ill receiv'd, or unsecure of fame.·
   Proceed, my Muse!   20
Young Chromis and Mnasylus chanc'd to stray
Where (sleeping in a cave) Silenus lay,

Pascere oportet oves, deductum dicere carmen.   5
Nunc ego (namque super tibi erunt, qui dicere laudes,
Vare, tuas cupiant, et tristia condere bella)
Agrestem tenui meditabor arundine Musam.
Non injussa cano. si quis tamen hæc quoque, si quis ·
Captus amore leget; te nostræ, Vare, myricæ,   10
Te nemus omne canet. nec Phœbo gratior ulla est,
Quam sibi que Vari præscripsit pagina nomen.
Pergite, Pierides. Chromis et Mnasylus in antro
Silenum pueri somno videre jacentem,

Whofe conftant cups fly fuming to his brain,
And always boil in each extended vein:
His trufty flagon, full of potent juice,   25
Was hanging by, worn thin with age and ufe;
Dropp'd from his head, a wreath lay on the ground;
In hafte they feiz'd him, and in hafte they bound;
Eager, for both had been deluded long
With fruitlefs hope of his inftructive fong: 30
But while with confcious fear they doubtful ftood,
Ægle, the faireft Naïs of the flood,
With a vermilion dye his temples ftain'd.
Waking, he fmil'd, " And muft I then be chain'd?
" Loofe me," he cry'd; " 't was boldly done to find
" And view a god, but 't is too bold to bind.   36
" 'The promis'd verfe no longer I 'll delay,
" (She fhall be fatisfy'd another way)."

Inflatum hefterno venas, ut femper, Iaccho,   15
Serta procul tantùm capiti delapfa jacebant:
Et gravis attritâ pendebat cantharus ansâ.
Aggreffi (nam fæpe fenex fpe carminis ambo
Luferat) injiciunt ipfis ex vincula fertis.
Addit fe fociam, timidifque fupervenit Ægle;   20
Ægle Naïadum pulcherrima. jamque videnti
Sanguineis frontem moris, et tempora pingit.
    Ille dolum ridens, Quò vincula nectitis? inquit.
Solvite me, pueri. fatis eft potuiffe videri,

With that he rais'd his tuneful voice aloud,
The knotty oaks their lift'ning branches bow'd, 40
And favage beafts and fylvan gods did crowd:

For, lo! he fung the world's ftupendous birth,
How fcatter'd feeds of fea, and air, and earth,
And purer fire, thro' univerfal night
And empty fpace did fruitfully unite ;   45
From whence th' innumerable race of things
By circular fucceffive order fprings.

By what degrees this earth's compacted fphere
Was harden'd, woods, and rocks, and towns, to bear;
How finking waters (the firm land to drain)   50
Fill'd the capacious deep, and form'd the main,
While from above, adorn'd with radiant light,
A new-born fun furpris'd the dazzled fight;

Carmina quæ vultis, cognofcite : carmina vobis; 25
Huic aliud mercedis erit. fimul incipit ipfe.
Tum verò in numerum Faunófque feráfque videres
Ludere, tum rigidas motare cacumina quercus.
Nec tantùm Phœbo gaudet Parnaffia rupes :
Nec tantùm Rhodope mirantur et Ifmarus Orphea.
Namque canebat, utì magnum par inane coacta   31
Semina terrarúmque, animæque, marífve fuiffent,
Et liquidi fimul ignis : ut his exordia primis
Omnia, et ipfe tener mundi concreverit orbis.
Tum durare folum, et difcludere Nerea ponto   35
Cœperit, et rerum paulatim fumere formas.

How vapours turn'd to clouds obscure the sky,
And clouds dissolv'd the thirsty ground supply; 55
How the first forest rais'd its shady head, [tains fed.
Till when few wand'ring beasts on unknown moun-
    Then Pyrrha's stony race rose from the ground,
Old Saturn reign'd with golden plenty crown'd,
And bold Prometheus (whose untam'd desire 60
Rivall'd the Sun with his own heav'nly fire)
Now doom'd the Scythian vulture's endless prey,
Severely pays for animating clay.
He nam'd the nymph (for who but gods could tell?)
Into whose arms the lovely Hylas fell. 65
Alcides wept in vain for Hylas lost;
Hylas in vain resounds thro' all the coast.
    He with compassion told Pasiphae's fault,
Ah! wretched Queen! whence came that guilty
        thought?

Jamque novum ut terræ stupeant lucescere solem,
Altiùs atque cadant submotis nubibus imbres:
Incipiant sylvæ cùm primùm surgere, cúmque
Rara per ignotos errent animalia montes. 40
    Hinc lapides Pyrrhæ jactos, Saturnia regna,
Caucasiásque refert volucres, furtúmque Promethei.
His adjungit, Hylan nautæ quo fonte relictum
Clamâssent: ut litus, Hyla, Hyla, omne sonaret.
    Et fortunatam, si numquam armenta fuissent, 45
Pasiphaën nivei solatur amore juvenci.

6

The maids of Argos, who with frantic cries, 70
And imitated lowings fill'd the fkies,
(Tho' metamorphos'd in their wild conceit)
Did never burn with fuch unnat'ral heat.
Ah! wretched Queen! while you on mountains ftray,
He on foft flow'rs his fnowy fide does lay, 75
Or feeks in herds a more proportion'd love :
" Surround, my nymphs," fhe cries, " furround the
" Perhaps fome footfteps printed in the clay [grove ;
" Will to my love direct your wand'ring way ;
" Perhaps, while thus in fearch of him I roam, 80
" My happier rivals have entic'd him home."

Ah! Virgo infelix! quæ te dementia cepit ?
Prœtides implêrunt falfis mugitibus agros :
At non tam turpes pecudum tamen ulla fecuta eft
Concubitus, quamvis collo timuiffet aratrum, 50
Et fæpe in lævi quæfiffet cornua fronte.
Ah! Virgo infelix! tu nunc in montibus erras!
Ille, latus niveum molli fultus hyacintho,
Ilice fub nigrâ pallentes ruminat herbas, [phæ
Aut aliquam in magno fequitur grege. claudite nym-
Dictææ nymphæ, nemorum jam claudite faltus : 56
Si quà fortè ferant oculis fefe obvia noftris
Errabunda bovis veftigia. forfitan illum
Aut herbâ captum viridi, aut armenta fecutum,
Perducant aliquæ ftabula ad Gortynia vaccæ. 60

O

He fung how Atalanta was betray'd
By thofe Hefperian baits her lover laid,
And the fad fifters who to trees were turn'd,
While with the world th' ambitious brother burn'd.
All he defcrib'd was prefent to their eyes,   86
And as he rais'd his verfe the poplars feem'd to rife.

He taught which Mufe did by Apollo's will
Guide wand'ring Gallus to th' Aonian hill:
(Which place the god for folemn meetings chofe) 90
With deep refpect the learned fenate rofe,
And Linus thus (deputed by the reft)
The hero's welcome and their thanks expreft:
" This harp of old to Hefiod did belong,
" To this, the Mufes' gift, join thy harmoniousfong;
" Charm'd by thefe ftrings, trees ftarting from the
          ground   96
" Have follow'd with delight the pow'rful found.

Tum canit Hefperidum miratam mala puellam:
Tum Phaëthontiadas mufco circumdat amaræ
Corticis, atque folo.proceras erigit alnos.

Tum canit, errantem permefii ad flumina Gallum
Aonas in montes ut duxerit una fororum;   65
Utque viro Phœbi chorus adfurrexerit omnis;
Ut Linus hæc illi divino carmine paftor,
Floribus atque apio crines ornatus amaro,
Dixerit, Hos tibi dant calamos (en accipe) Mufæ;
Afcræo quos antè feni: quibus ille folebat   70

" Thus confecrated, thy Grynæan grove
" Shall have no equal in Apollo's love."
   Why fhould I fpeak of the Megarian maid,   ICO
For love perfidious, and by love betray'd?
And her who round with barking monfters arm'd,
The wand'ring Greeks (ah! frighted men!) alarm'd,
Whofe only hope on fhatter'd fhips depends,
While fierce fea-dogs devour the mangled friends? 105
   Or tell the Thracian tyrant's alter'd fhape,
And dire revenge of Philomela's rape,
Who to thofe woods directs her mournful courfe,
Where fhe had fuffer'd by inceftuous force,
While, loath to leave the palace too well known, 110
Progné flies hov'ring round, and thinks it ftill her
     own?

Cantando rigidas deducere montibus ornos.
His tibi Grynæi nemoris dicatur origo :
Nequis fit lucus, quo fe plùs jactet Apollo.
   Quid loquar aut Scyllam Nifi, quam fama fecuta eft,
Candida fuccinctam latrantibus inguina monftris 75
Dulichias vexâffe rates, et gurgite in alto
Ah timidos nautas canibus laceráffe marinis :
Aut ut mutatos Terei narraverit artus?
   Quas illi Philomela dapes, quæ dona parârit?
Quo curfu deferta petiverit, et quibus antè   8ᴏ
Infelix fua tecta fupervolitaverit alis?
        O ij

Whatever near Eurota's happy ſtream,
With laurels crown'd, had been Apollo's theme
Silenus ſings; the neighb'ring rocks reply,
And ſend his myſtic numbers thro' the ſky;   115
Till Night began to ſpread her gloomy veil,
And call'd the counted ſheep from ev'ry dale;
The weaker light unwillingly declin'd,
And to prevailing ſhades the murm'ring world re-
        ſign'd.   119

Omnia quæ, Phœbo quondam meditante, beatus
Audiit Eurotas, juſſitque ediſcere lauros,
Ille canit. pulſæ referunt ad ſidera valles.
Cogere donec oves ſtabulis, numerúmque referre
Juſſit, et invito proceſſit veſper Olympo.   86

GUARINI'S PASTOR FIDO,

TRANSLATED.

Ah! happy grove! dark and secure retreat
Of sacred Silence, Rest's eternal seat,
How well your cool and unfrequented shade
Suits with the chaste retirements of a maid!
Oh! if kind Heav'n had been so much my friend   5
To make my fate upon my choice depend,
All my ambition I would here confine,
And only this Elysium should be mine.

Part of the fifth Scene of the Second Act in

GUARINI'S PASTOR FIDO.

AMARILLI.

Care selue beate,
E voi solinghi, e taciturni horrori
Di riposo, e di pace alberghi veri.
O quanto volentieri
A riuederui i torno, e se le stelle   5
M' hauesser dato insorte
Di viuer à me stessa, e di far vita
Conforme à le mie voglie ;
Io già co campi Elisi

Fond men, by paſſion wilfully betray'd,
Adore thoſe idols which their fancy made;   10
Purchaſing riches with our time and care,
We loſe our freedom in a gilded ſnare;
And having all, all to ourſelves refuſe,
Oppreſs'd with bleſſings which we fear to uſe.
Fame is at beſt but an inconſtant good,   15
Vain are the boaſted titles of our blood;
We ſooneſt loſe what we moſt highly prize,
And with our youth our ſhort-liv'd beauty dies.

Fortunato giardin de ſemidei   10
La voſtr'ombra gentil non cangerei.
" Che ſe ben dritto miro
" Queſti beni mortali
" Altro non ſon che mali:
" Men' hà, chi più n' abbonda,   15
" E poſſeduto è più, che non poſſede,
" Ricchezze nò, ma lacci
" De l' altrui libertate.
" Che val ne più verdi anni
" Titolo di bellezza,   20
" O fama d'honeſtate,
" E'n mortal ſangue nobiltà celeſte:
" Tante grazie del cielo, e de la terra.
" Qui larghi, e lieti campi
" E là felici piagge,   25

In vain our fields and flocks increase our store,
If our abundance makes us wish for more :   20
How happy is the harmless country-maid
Who, rich by nature, scorns superfluous aid!
Whose modest clothes no wanton eyes invite,
But like her soul preserves the native white ;   24
Whose little store her well-taught mind does please,
Nor pinch'd with want, nor cloy'd with wanton ease ;
Who, free from storms, which on the great ones fall,
Makes but few wishes, and enjoys them all ;

" Fecondi pafchi, e più fecondo armento,
" Se'n tanti benì il cor non è contento ?"
Felice pastorella,
Cui cinge à pena il fiance
Pouera sì, ma schietta,   30
E candida gonnella.
Ricca sol di se stessa,
E de le grazie di Natura adorna,
Che'n dolce pouertate
Nè pouertà conosce, nè i disagi   35
De le ricchezze sente,
Ma tutto quel possiede
Per cui desio d'hauer non la tormenta ;
Nuda sì, ma contenta.
Co doni di natura   40
I doni di natura anco nudrica ;

No care but love can difcompofe her breaft,
Love! of all cares the fweeteft and the beft;   30
While on fweet grafs her bleating charge does lie,
Our happy lover feeds upon her eye;
Not one on whom or gods or men impofe,
But one whom Love has for this lover chofe,
Under fome fav'rite myrtle's fhady boughs,   35
They fpeak their paffions in repeated vows,

Col latte, il latte auuiua,
E col dolce de l' api
Condifce il mel de le natie dolcezze.
Quel fonte ond'ella beue,   45
Quel folo anco la bagna, e la configlia;
Paga lei, pago il mondo:
Per lei di nembi il ciel s'ofcura indarno,
E di grandine s' arma,
Che la fua pouertà nulla pauenta: 50
Nuda sì, ma contenta.
Sola una dolce, e d'ogn' affanno fgombra
Cura le fta nel core.
Pafce le verdi herbette
La greggia à lei commeffa, ed ella pafce   55
De fuo'begli occhi il paftorello amante,
Non qual le deftinaro
O gli huomini, o le ftelle,
Ma qual le diede Amore. ‘
E tra l' ombrofe piante   60

And whilſt a bluſh confeſſes how ſhe burns,
His faithful heart makes as ſincere returns;
Thus in the arms of Love and Peace they lie,
And while they live their flames can never die. 40

D'vn fauorito lor Mirteto adorno
Vagheggiata il vagheggia, nè per lui
Sente foco d' amor, che non gli ſcopra,
Ned' ella ſcopre ardor, ch'egli non ſenta,
Nuda sì, ma contenta.   65
O vera vita, che non fà che ſia
Morire innanzi morte.   67

CONTENTS.

PROLOGUES, &c.

TRANSLATIONS.

From the APOLLO PRESS,
    by the MARTINS,
    March 11. 1780.

THE END.

www.ingramcontent.com/pod-product-compliance
Lightning Source LLC
Chambersburg PA
CBHW020939030726
47496CB00005B/1259